THE CANDLESTICK MAKER

NATHAN BURROWS

1

It was fair to say that Jessica was a big girl. Some people would use the term bubbly, perhaps cuddly, or even plus size if they were trying to be particularly polite. Her mother told anyone who would listen that Jessica had big bones or that her size was in her genes. The fact that both her parents were stick thin seemed to pass everyone by.

Other less kind people would just use the term fat. Like her ex-boyfriend, which was the primary reason he was an ex-boyfriend. He couldn't, according to Jessica and her friends from Flab Fighters, appreciate the unique pleasure that only a woman of Jessica's size could offer. The anonymous people on the other end of the computer that Jessica was staring at now were a different breed altogether. They not only appreciated women of Jessica's size, they positively worshipped them.

Jessica hadn't turned her webcam on just yet. She had a set routine that she had to go through before she hit that magic switch. First, she had to make sure she was dressed appropriately for her digital visitors. She was. At least, from the front it looked as if she was. The webcam couldn't see the extra band of elastic she had fitted to the strap of her bra. The problem was that a bra that accentuated her not inconsequential bosom in the way that she wanted wouldn't do up at the back. Hence the elastic. Jessica used a small compact mirror to check her make-up and to ensure that she had just the right sheen of perspiration on her face. She knew that her customers liked that touch. The final check was to ensure that she had enough French Fancy Cakes in front of her, which she did. There was a further supply in her kitchen cupboard, just in case she had a successful evening on the webcam. Or got peckish later. Either way, the cupboard would probably be empty by the end of the evening come what may. With a trembling finger, she reached out to the touch screen to turn the webcam on, and was rewarded with the reassuring red glow of the light. She was live.

It was only a couple of minutes before her first potential customer arrived. Jessica could see from the admin screen of the website that she worked for how many people were watching. Waiting. Considering. Jessica didn't want to think about what else they might be doing in their private digital darkness. She didn't need to know, didn't want to know, and didn't care as long as they paid.

Jessica managed not to jump as a loud electronic 'ding' told her that wherever was watching her had just made a purchase. She glanced up at the screen, even though she knew that the customer had bought a French Fancy. After all, that was the only thing on her menu this evening. The only thing she was interested in was how much he had paid to watch her eat it.

'A tenner? Fuck me sideways,' Jessica whispered to herself. The normal going rate for a single French Fancy was only a quid. As she stared at the screen, an instant message popped up.

'A yellow one, please.'

Jessica grinned at the webcam and slowly waved her podgy fingers at the red light. In her head, she started to add up how many French Fancies she had, and how much they would earn her if her mysterious customer was willing to pay to watch her eat them all. Even if it was only the yellow ones, she was fairly sure that by the end of the evening she would be at least fifty quid up. And that was if no-one came in for any of the other colours. Sensing a very profitable evening ahead of her, Jessica reached forward and picked up one of the small square yellow cakes.

Looking at a French Fancy in a sensual manner wasn't a skill that Jessica had yet mastered. She'd watched a fair few videos on YouTube about how to look at food as if you wanted to fuck it, but none of them involved small square pieces of confectionary. One of the weirdest YouTube channels she had come across was called 'Crouching Woman Hidden Cucumber', but that hadn't really helped her much. It was interesting, if only in an anatomical sense, but not helpful for her area of expertise.

She narrowed her heavily made-up eyes at the yellow cake and licked her lips before taking a tentative nibble at the corner of the icing. There was a ding on the screen.

'Slow down,' the message said. For a tenner a cake, Jessica would happily take half an hour eating the bloody thing, but she was hungry. She made a valiant effort to caress the cake with her lips and tongue, but a moment later she crammed it into her mouth.

'Sorry,' she mouthed at the webcam through a mouthful of sponge and icing. 'I couldn't wait.' Jessica stared at the screen for what seemed like ages before it dinged again.

'Dirty girl.'

Jessica wiped her lips with a pre-moistened napkin that she'd prepared earlier.

'I can be dirtier,' she typed carefully while pouting at the screen. 'If you want?' There was another long wait before whoever was on the other end of the computer replied. The ding signalled another purchase. Twenty quid this time.

'A pink one, please,' the message popped up on the screen. 'And if you don't take your time eating it...'

Jessica waited for at least twenty seconds before replying. She had thought about turning the camera off and maybe cramming a couple of cakes into her mouth — the blue ones seemed particularly unpopular in her experience — but thought better of it if the price per cake was going up.

'What will happen?' she typed, taking her time to make sure that each finger only hit one key. There was another long wait for the reply.

'I will kill you.'

2

Emily Underwood pulled up in the pub car park, turned the engine off, and sighed. She looked through the windscreen at the pub that she had come to inspect. This would be her third food safety inspection that day, and hopefully, the final one. The previous two had gone okay, or at least in comparison to some of her other visits. She'd not been threatened, chased off the premises, or sexually assaulted in any way. In Emily's book, that made it a good day. Her first inspection was of a food stall selling fudge in Norwich's Castle Mall shopping centre. The Food Standards Agency was unreliable at the best of times, but sending her to inspect a fudge stall when the fudge itself was made in a completely different location was a new one. Although at some point someone would have to go and inspect the proprietor's kitchen — which was in a converted garage on a local council estate — the inspection of the stall itself had taken about ten seconds. Is it clean? Yes. Job done. Emily was planning on doing the inspection of his kitchen herself if she could swing it at the Food Standards Agency. The fudge was absolutely amazing, and the stall owner had given her several "samples" to sweeten her up. Emily's mouth started watering at the memory, and she thought with longing about the paper bag in the boot of her car. No matter how many calories were in it, she couldn't wait to get home.

The other inspection was a proper one, but dull as ditchwater. It was of a Burger Queen restaurant in Norwich's other shopping centre. Emily had never found so much as a napkin out of place in any Burger Queen restaurant she'd inspected, and this one was no different. No free samples, but she'd already been told off for docking a hygiene star or two off for that one by her boss.

The pub in front of her was potentially a completely different story. It was called "The Heartsease" after some bizarre pansy that only grew every other year in a small part of the Norfolk Broads, so Emily had heard. It was also the name of a large council estate nearby, which was a much more likely reason for the name. Targeted marketing. Looking at the shabby locals wandering aimlessly up and down what passed for a high street, Emily felt very over-dressed in her smart business suit. She would have looked posh in a shell suit.

The Heartsease was a fairly large building located right next to one of the most terrifying roundabouts in the whole of East Anglia — at least if you were a learner driver. There was nothing unusual about the roundabout, but for some reason, it was feared by anyone learning to drive and instructors alike. The generally accepted wisdom was that the best way to get over it was to shut your eyes and put your foot down. Every few months, a learner driver would end up accidentally parked in the middle of the roundabout itself but it didn't stop those bastards at the test facility down the road making everyone who took their test there going round it at least three times. Emily's flat mate had gone out with an invigilator for a while and apparently there was a sweepstake in their crew room for the most number of nervous breakdowns caused by the roundabout. If Emily remembered correctly, there was a scoring system with tears at the bottom and accidental soiling of the driver's seat at the top.

Emily got out of the car and walked as slowly as she could towards the door of the pub, shivering in the cold November air. According to her boss, the landlord had a soft spot for petite blondes. That being the reason why Emily had landed the job had been denied back at the Food Standards Agency, but if it was true, Emily planned on making the most of the fact that she was a petite blonde. Maybe not as petite as she would like to be — too much food after the need to fit into her summer clothes had disappeared — but those few extra pounds would soon disappear if she could ever be arsed to get to the gym. Besides, her boyfriend Andy claimed to like the extra bouncy bits. Emily wasn't sure whether that was a compliment or not but seeing as he was hardly male model material himself, it didn't really matter.

To Emily's surprise, the pub looked open even though it wasn't supposed to be at that time in the morning. The door swung open as she knocked on it, so Emily walked inside, waiting on the doormat for a moment to let her eyes adjust to the gloom. When she stepped into the pub itself, her shoes almost got abandoned at the door. If the doormat was that sticky, Emily thought, God only knew what the rest of the pub would be like.

Emily glanced around the interior of the pub, taking in the yellowed walls that hadn't seen a lick of paint since well before the smoking ban, the rickety looking tables with an assortment of chairs balanced on top, and the small child perched behind the bar. She walked towards him, plastering a smile on her face, and stopped a few feet away. He wasn't who she'd been expecting to be behind the bar when she walked in. The boy was maybe nine or ten, floppy blonde hair, with an innocent face and dressed in Star Wars pyjamas. He wouldn't have looked out of place in the cathedral choir, apart from the pyjamas of course, and Emily could well imagine him in a cassock with a ruff doing a solo with a crowd of elderly ladies simpering over him.

The boy was concentrating on a peanut that was on the bar in front of him. When Emily realised that he hadn't noticed her come in, she cleared her throat softly to avoid startling the young lad.

'Fuck off,' the boy said, not even looking up at her. 'We're closed.'

'Oh,' Emily replied, momentarily thrown. 'Er, I'm from the Food Standards Agency. Is your dad about?' She had no idea if this was the landlord's son or not, but it seemed like a fair call. He glanced at her for a second before staring back down at the peanut on the bar.

'Ssshh,' the boy replied, his index finger to his mouth. 'If you're not going to fuck off, at least shut your cake hole.' Emily bristled for a moment before replying.

'Is there a grown up here?' she asked. He didn't reply but just shushed her again.

'You need to be quiet, or he won't come out.'

'Who?' Emily's question was ignored. 'Your dad?'

'No. Mr Crisp.' The boy returned his attention to the peanut.

Emily took a deep breath and opened her briefcase. She pulled out the inspection paperwork and examined it to see what the landlord's last name was. A few seconds later, she found it — it wasn't Crisp.

'Who's Mr Crisp?' she asked. The boy raised his finger

to his lips. 'Who's Mr Crisp?' she repeated, this time in a whisper.

'Here he is.'

Emily followed the boy's gaze towards a small hole in the woodwork between the bar and the wall. The first thing she saw was a very small whiskered nose, followed by a mouse scampering across the bar. It dodged a suspicious looking stain on the bar before running over, grabbing the peanut in its mouth, and hurrying back through the hole. The boy looked at Emily and grinned, showing a mouth that must have cost the Tooth Fairy a fortune.

'That's Mr Crisp,' he said, triumphantly. 'He's a cheeky little bastard, isn't he?'

3

J ack Kennedy hated banks. He always had done, ever since he was a small boy. There wasn't any particular reason as far as he could remember. One of his earliest memories was sitting on his Dad's vestry floor helping him count up the coins in the collection from the old people at church. He and his father would sit there in a companionable silence while Jack counted up all the pennies and two pence pieces, and his Dad would count all the silver coins. By the time Jack was nine or ten, they had to swap over. There weren't anywhere near as many silver coins in the collection by then.

So, it wasn't money that was the problem. It was just banks. It hadn't been his father who'd taken the money to the bank though. It had been his mother, and she always took Jack with her. If any of the carefully labelled bags didn't have exactly the right amount of money in them — and the bank had a special machine that counted the coins — then Jack knew he'd be in for a beating later. No matter what colour the coins inside the bag were. If they were wrong, then he was in for the slipper when they got back to the vicarage.

'Mr Kennedy?' A woman's voice interrupted his unpleasant memories. 'Mr Kennedy? The bank manager's ready for you now.' The receptionist smiled at Jack, and he ran his finger around the collar of his shirt as he got to his feet.

'Thanks,' he mumbled at the receptionist, whose smile broadened. He could feel her staring at him as he walked through the door and into the manager's office.

The interior of the office was pretty much how he expected it would look. It was a corner office, with large windows looking out over the market square in the middle of Norwich. Prime real estate, if it wasn't owned by a bank.

'Mr Kennedy,' the bald-headed man behind the large mahogany desk said. 'I'm Mr Parsons, the manager of Norwich Mutual.' He got to his feet, his ill-fitting suit hanging off him, and shook Jack's hand.

'Hi,' Jack replied, ignoring the temptation to crush the other man's hand in his own. Mr Parsons's grip was so weak Jack didn't know whether to shake his hand or kiss it. The bank manager obviously didn't get to the gym much.

'Please, have a seat.' Mr Parsons gestured towards the chair on the other side of the desk. Jack sat, and the chair creaked under his bulk. He put his hands in his lap, and flexed his shoulder muscles to try to relieve the tension in his neck. When he heard the material complaining, he relaxed his shoulders. It wouldn't do to burst out of his shirt like a pink version of the Incredible Hulk. 'We've reviewed your business loan application, and I've just got a few follow up questions for you.'

'Okay,' Jack said.

'Right then.' Mr Parsons wriggled in his own much more comfortable chair and leafed through the paper-work in front of him. 'So, you're a fitness instructor, right?'

'Yep.'

'Good. Now, according to your application, you've been doing that here in Norfolk for a year. But, you're what, twenty-seven. Can I ask where you were living before moving here?'

'Up north,' Jack said. He wasn't going to be anymore specific than that with this odd looking man.

'Ah, I see.' Mr Parsons looked back at the paperwork. 'And what were you doing up there?'

'I was a medical student,' Jack replied with a sigh. He knew what the next question would be.

'You didn't finish your medical degree?' Mr Parsons asked.

'Obviously not,' he said, trying to keep the irritation out of his voice. 'Or I wouldn't be a fitness instructor, would I?'

'Er, no.' Mr Parsons found something very interesting to stare at on the piece of paper in his hands. 'Right, now where was I. Oh, yes. Your financial history.' Mr Parsons smiled, revealing some expensive dentistry. 'Quite healthy, really. No mortgage, sole ownership of Hill Top Farm.' His smile slipped for a second. 'You do know about the history of that place, don't you?'

'You've seen the price I paid for it?' Jack nodded at the paperwork. 'It wouldn't have been that cheap without some sort of strings attached.'

'Yes, very true. Bizarre business. First that mad butcher, then the weird vegetarian lot.' Mr Parsons looked at Jack. 'Very strange place indeed.'

Jack sat for a second, wondering whether that was some sort of question.

'Well, it's mine now and I've got plans for it.'

'Yes, your plans.' Mr Parsons' attention returned to the paperwork. 'It's a very comprehensive business plan, Mr Kennedy.'

'Thank you.'

'You're welcome. May I ask, do you have anyone who could put forward some additional capital to support your venture? Your parents, perhaps?'

'No.'

'Oh,' Mr Parsons face fell. 'I see.'

'My father passed away a year ago,' Jack explained, even though it was none of Mr Parson's business. 'I used the inheritance to buy the farm, do up the farmhouse and one of the outbuildings. But I can't convert the original pig shed into a fitness suite without a loan.' He took a breath, aware that was the longest sentence he'd said since he walked into the manager's office. 'It's all in there,' he continued with a nod at the papers.

'Yes, so it is,' Mr Parsons replied. 'It's just that the bank isn't sure of the long-term economic viability of a fitness suite in that particular location.'

'Because of the farm's history?'

'No, more the location. It's not exactly central, is it?'

Jack sighed. He thought he'd explained all this in the business plan.

'It's a very niche customer base,' he said, 'who will be more than happy to travel to a rural location.'

'Rural? It's in the middle of bloody nowhere!' Mr Parsons started laughing, but cut it short when Jack gave him a fierce look.

'Look, Mr Parsnip or whatever your name is. Can I have the money or not?'

Mr Parsons put Jack's business plan down on his desk.

'Mr Kennedy, it's not a no,' the bank manager said, a slight tremble creeping into his voice. 'It's just a "not now". We can assign you a business mentor to help you develop your plans and then re-evaluate in, say, six months?' Jack glared at the bank manager, imagining for a second what would happen if he just leapt across the desk and started throttling him. 'If you speak to Lynne, my receptionist, she'll assign you a mentor,' Mr Parsons continued, almost in a warble. Jack looked at him, shook his head, and got to his feet without another word.

Outside Mr Parsons' office, the receptionist was nothing but sympathetic.

'The thing is, Jack,' she said, 'Mr Parsons hardly ever gives anyone any money first time round, so you shouldn't be too upset.' He looked at her, noticing for the first time that she was quite pretty. A bit on the mousy side perhaps, and she wouldn't look out of place working in a library, but Jack thought she was pretty enough. If she got herself a decent haircut to replace her pony tail, and put a bit of make-up on, she wouldn't be half bad at all.

'Thanks, er, Lynne was it?'

'Yes,' she smiled, a touch of colour rising to her cheeks. Jack stared at her for a few seconds, watching her cheeks getting redder as he did so. 'Short for Lynnette.'

'Really?' Jack said, managing not to laugh. 'That's a lovely name.'

'Aw, thank you,' Lynne replied, almost in a whisper. She touched her hand to her ear and fixed a stray couple of hairs. 'I read in your business plan that you're a fitness instructor? That must be fun.'

They chatted for a few moments about nothing in

particular. Jack noticed that she managed to drop into the conversation that she was single, but stopped short of asking him if he was. It turned out that Lynne was a very keen painter, and Jack almost asked her if she would like him to pose for her sometime, but he wasn't sure if he'd be able to ask and keep a straight face.

'So what sort of things do you do, when you're not making people all fit and buff?' Lynne asked, running her eyes over his upper body. She was, Jack thought, definitely interested.

'I like doing things with my hands,' he replied, flexing his fingers.

'What sort of things?'

'All sorts. I like making things.'

'Stop teasing,' Lynne said with a giggle. 'What sort of things do you make?' Jack looked at her. He arched one eyebrow, a trick his father had taught him to do years before, and replied.

'I make candlesticks.'

4

'So, what is it exactly that you want the phone for?' Andy asked the elderly man in front of him. The customer had been in the shop for ages, smelt faintly of wee, and was beginning to annoy him. If it weren't for the targets that the manager had set, Andy would have tried to close the deal a long time ago. But, despite the odour, this customer looked like he might have a fair bit of money and a sale was a sale.

'I need it for the SnapChat,' the man replied, his voice warbling.

'Right,' Andy replied with a sigh. 'The SnapChat.'

Andy had been working at the phone shop in Chapelfield Shopping Centre for almost three months, ever since his position as an intern at a local supermarket firm had disappeared. To be fair, it wasn't just his position that had gone south, it was the entire supermarket chain. Andy knew that he was lucky to have this gig, even if the pay was shite and his boss was an utter wanker. Andy wasn't the only one who thought his boss was a wanker — the graffiti on the toilet wall backed him up on that. But if Andy was ever going to leave home and hopefully move in somewhere with his girlfriend, Emily, he needed the job.

'So, if you don't mind me asking, what are you looking to do with the SnapChat? That'll help me choose the best phone for you?' The old man paused for a few seconds before replying.

'Well, I've been on this interweb forum see,' he said, 'and there's a chap on there who's interested in my chickens.' Andy looked at him with amusement. 'I breed them.'

'Oh, wow,' he replied, as enthusiastically as he could manage. 'So do you want it for pictures, videos, or what?'

'No idea,' the man replied with a frown. 'I was hoping you might be able to explain it to me. You youngsters seem to know all about that sort of thing.'

'Well, it's not about how old you are, it's about how old you feel,' Andy replied, pleased with himself for slipping that line in. He'd read it on the internet.

'Well, I'm almost eighty and I feel every bloody year of it,' the customer replied. 'Hey, are you one of them gays?'

'I'm sorry?' Andy asked, not sure he'd heard him correctly.

'Jesus, and people say I'm deaf.' The man raised his voice. 'I said, are you one of them gays?' he asked, shouting.

Andy winced as every other customer in the shop turned to look at him.

'No, I'm not,' he replied just as loudly, pulling his phone out of his pocket. 'Look, here's a picture of my girlfriend.' As he showed the customer a photo of Emily, Andy realised that he didn't have to prove anything to the man, but he showed him anyway.

'Well, she's a mucky looking little thing, isn't she,' the

elderly man replied with a rictus grin. 'I'd have a go on that, for certain.'

Andy hurriedly put his phone away before reaching behind the counter and selecting the most expensive phone in the shop, just in case. As he placed the phone in front of the man, he felt his own phone vibrating in his pocket.

'Why don't you have a little look at this bad boy,' he said. 'I just need to take this call.' He had no idea who was on the phone, but a bit of fresh air would do him no harm at all. When he realised it was Emily, he grinned. Stepping away from the counter and leaving the elderly man holding the phone up in front of her eyes and squinting at it, he answered the call.

'Hey you,' he said. 'How's tricks?'

'Meh,' Emily's disjointed voice came down the line. 'Had better days. I'm in the Heartsease.'

'Oh,' Andy replied. 'Have you closed it down?'

'Not yet. But I think it's likely based on the first five minutes. I'll fill you in later.'

'Maybe I can fill you in later,' Andy replied with what he hoped was a seductive laugh.

'Calm down, tiger. I don't know if Catherine's in or out tonight.'

'She won't mind either way. You know what she's like. Anyhow, I can't be on for long. I've got a punter on the vinegar strokes. He's quite keen to meet you, in fact. Thinks you're mucky looking.'

'Er, no thanks,' Emily said. 'Just thought I'd call to avoid having to talk to the staff in the Heartsease.'

'If Catherine is out tonight,' Andy replied, lowering his voice, 'how about the utility room?'

'What?'

'Well, we've only got that and the downstairs toilet to go.'

'I am not having sex with you in the utility room, Andy,' Emily whispered, but Andy could tell from the sound of her voice that she was smiling. 'Or the downstairs toilet.'

'Oh, Emily. Come on,' Andy pleaded. 'I'll put the washing machine on spin?'

'I've got to go,' Emily said with a giggle. 'The landlord's here.' Andy looked over at the customer who was waving the phone at him.

'Me too. I'll see you later, yeah? When I come round to fix your washing machine.' He heard Emily laughing before he disconnected the call.

'I want this one,' the customer said. Andy tried to put the thought of Emily, the utility room, and the spin cycle to the back of his mind.

'Excellent choice, sir,' he said as he took the phone back off him and started preparing the paperwork for the sale. 'So, this forum, is it just for chicken fanciers?'

'Not really,' he replied. 'It's a social networking thing. To be honest, I might have lied about my age just a bit so he doesn't think I'm some old fart from Norfolk. He seems very interested, though. I've told him all about my chickens, and about how I'd like to breed them.'

'That's nice.' Andy wrapped up the phone in the shop's most expensive tissue paper. It was reserved for their top end customers, and God help anyone who used it to wrap up anything that cost under a hundred quid.

'It was him who suggested that I get the SnapChat.'

'Cool. Do you know why?' Andy asked.

'So he can send me pictures of his cock.'

5

E mily sat on a chair near the door of the pub, tapping her foot on the floor while she waited for the land-lord to come back. According to the foul-mouthed young-ster, the old tosser had just gone to Lidl to get some stuff. Emily wasn't sure what the rules were for kids, but she was fairly sure that one as young as Mr Crisps' friend seemed to be shouldn't be unattended at all, let alone unattended and in charge of a pub.

A few moments later, the door to the pub opened and a large man eased his way through it, a bulging carrier bag in each hand. Emily got to her feet, assuming that this must be the landlord. He noticed her standing there and fixed her with a hard stare through small red-rimmed eyes. The broken veins on his nose marked him out as a land-lord who took the quality control of his stock very seriously.

'Who the fuck are you?' he barked. Emily could see where the youngster got his manners from. She flashed him her identification card.

'Emily Underwood,' she said with a sweet smile,

hoping to capitalise on his preference for blondes. 'Food Standards Agency.'

'Oh, sweet Jesus,' he replied with a snarl. 'That's all I need.' He clenched his fists around the handles of the carrier bags, causing the various tattoos on his arms to flex underneath his yellowed singlet.

'I did try to make her go away, Uncle Pete,' the boy called out from his perch behind the bar. 'But she wasn't having it. At least she's easy on the eye.'

The landlord made his way over to the bar and hefted the carrier bags onto the counter. He wasn't small by a long stretch, but he still struggled to lift them up. When Emily glanced at the back of his head, she saw a tattooed England flag clearly visible through a very short buzz cut.

'Put these away, would you Jimmy?' he asked the young lad. As he let go of the bags, one of them split, emptying several Lidl 'Saver Sausage Rolls' onto the counter.

'Usual place, Uncle Pete? Or do you want them in the fridge seeing as there's a woman from the Food place here?'

'Why don't you put them in the fridge as usual?' The lad was about to say something else, but he looked at the landlord and obviously thought better of it.

The landlord walked back over to where Emily was still standing by the door. As he approached her, he held out a hand for her to shake. Uncertain at first, Emily shook his hand and tried to ignore the word HATE tattooed across the back of his fingers.

'Sorry, that was a bit rude of me just now. Bit uncalled for,' he said with an approximation of a smile. 'I've had a shit day.'

'Yeah, I know that feeling,' Emily replied with a wry smile.

'I'm Pete anyway. The landlord, just in case you didn't guess. Did Jimmy look after you?'

'Kind of. He's got a way with words, hasn't he? Is he your son?'

Pete laughed, a wheezing cacophony that shook his jowls.

'Christ no,' he said, still grinning. 'I'm his uncle. His Dad's in nick, and Jimmy's suspended from school at the moment, so I'm looking after him.'

'What for?'

'Armed robbery.'

'No, sorry. What's Jimmy suspended for?' Emily asked. Pete's smile disappeared.

'I just said. Armed robbery. He held up a bunch of posh kids from the independent school down the road and did them over for their lunch money.'

'What, armed?'

'Kind of. He lifted a potato peeler from the school kitchen and went at them with it. The posh kids hadn't seen one before. Shat themselves, apparently,' Pete explained. Emily could feel a smile start to twitch at the corners of her mouth. The landlord was starting to grow on her. 'Do you want a brew?'

'Do you know what, I'd love one. Bloody parched, I am.'

Twenty minutes later, the two of them were sitting around a table. Emily had established that since the last inspection, Pete's pub hadn't actually been serving food apart from some bar snacks. According to the menu that Emily had sneaked a look at while Pete was refilling their mugs of tea, the only bar snacks that they served were sausage rolls. Pete had confirmed that they weren't made on the premises, but were "locally sourced". Emily knew that she had more than enough to serve an immediate notice on the place, but how would that help? Pete, despite his tattoos and hard man appearance, was trying his best to make an honest living while he was bringing up his wayward nephew. Emily doubted that any of his customers were going to be poisoned by a luke-warm sausage roll from Lidl reheated in Pete's kitchen. The biggest problem at the last inspection of the pub – a Chinese chef with a very uncertain source of meat – was no longer employed there. The number of missing cats in the neighbourhood had apparently gone right down after he'd left.

'Pete, the thing is this.' She leaned forward and whispered in a conspiratorial tone. 'What I'm supposed to do is inspect the kitchen, confirm the cleanliness and standards, and also the food sources. But I can only do that if I can actually get into the establishment. If you were closed when I visited, then I wouldn't be able to do that, would I?' She fished in her briefcase and pulled out a couple of sheets of paper. 'I've got a checklist that I have to do. If every box is ticked, then it's a pass. But the checklist itself isn't available to facilities in advance.' Emily put the papers down on the seat next her and gave Pete a knowing look. 'Are you with me?'

'I think so,' Pete replied with a sideways glance at the papers.

'So, if a place is closed when I try to inspect it, I have to come back in about twenty-four hours.'

'Right.'

'But if I find a mouse running around the bar, then it's a fail.'

'Right,' Pete repeated, his lips thinning. 'That won't happen.'

'But do it nicely. Maybe the mouse, if it indeed existed, could be relocated,' Emily said. 'Not killed.'

'Oh,' Pete's face fell. 'Okay.'

'That's the deal, Pete,' Emily said. 'Take it or leave it.'

Pete grinned, showing off his smoker's teeth.

'Twenty-four hours?'

'Give or take.'

Emily stepped back out into the car park of the pub, knowing full well that if the Food Standards Agency knew what she had just done, she would be an ex-food inspector in a matter of minutes. But they didn't know, and Pete didn't strike her as a grass, so where was the harm?

She took a few steps toward her little red Mini, and then jumped as a car horn sounded from the road next to the pub. It was followed by a series of horns. Emily turned to see a learner driver stuck at the roundabout, a long queue of cars behind it. The driver was a young woman, probably not far off Emily's age, with white knuckles on the steering wheel and tears streaming down her face. As Emily watched, the learner driver closed her eyes tightly and accelerated, narrowly missing a Number 24 double decker bus that was hammering its way over the roundabout. Missing the bus by inches, the learner made it safely to the other side. Emily let out a deep breath, not realising that she'd been holding it in, as the car with L plates disappeared down the road.

6

———

Although he was parked, Jack left the engine of his van on so that he could keep it warm. It was pretty cold out and according to the weather forecast he'd heard earlier, might or might not snow. Jack was parked at the far end of a lay-by on the outskirts of Thetford, but even though it was night-time, there were quite a few other cars parked there. That was one of the reasons he had chosen this spot to meet her. It wasn't the type of lay-by where cars coming and going would be noticed, and the occupants of them were very unlikely to own up to having been there.

He assembled his burner phone and turned it on. A few seconds later, Jack grinned as it buzzed.

Are you there? I'll be there at seven thirty exactly. He looked at his watch. He was a little bit early as it was only just gone seven, but he didn't mind waiting. It would help build the excitement. Jack tilted his head from side to side. He'd overdone it on the trapezoid machine earlier at the gym and was beginning to pay for it now.

I'm here.

As he waited, he watched cars drifting in and out of the lay-by. Some of them didn't stop at all, some stopped and parked. There was one car at the far end of the lay-by that he'd noticed as he'd driven in. The windows were completely steamed up, and it was rocking gently from side to side. Not particularly subtle, he thought as he watched.

Right on the nose of half-past seven, Jack saw a small blue car pull into the far end of the lay-by. It stopped in front of the car with steamy windows, and a few seconds later, his phone buzzed.

I'm here.

So am I. White van right at the end.

The small car moved forward and parked in front of him. Jack could feel his heart thumping in his chest. He wasn't sure if it was anticipation, excitement, or fear, but thought it was probably a combination of all three. He had been planning this evening for a long time, before he even moved to Norfolk from up north, and it was all finally coming together.

The lights on the car flicked off, and Jack noticed it was slightly on the wonk, with the driver's side a fair few inches lower than the passenger side. When the driver's door opened and the occupant stepped out, Jack took a sharp intake of breath as the car settled back on its suspension. She was perfect. The pictures he'd seen on the internet hadn't been lying.

The woman glanced around her and then turned to look at Jack's van. Despite the cold, she was wearing a dress with short sleeves and clutching a small handbag. She raised a podgy arm and waved, and Jack saw the flesh under her arm wobble in the faint light.

'Oh, you are absolutely perfect,' Jack whispered as the woman made her way towards the van's passenger door. A second later, it opened and she peered in.

'I'm hoping you're Aaron?' Jack was about to correct her when he realised that was the name he'd given her. *Bloody hell*, he thought. *That was close.*

'I'm hoping you're Beth?' he replied with a disarming smile. The woman didn't need any disarming though. She put a hand out to grab the side of the van and heaved herself up into the passenger seat. As she did so, the van lurched, and the suspension creaked as if it was in pain.

'I wasn't sure if you'd be here,' she said, out of breath from the exertion of climbing into the van. 'Whether it was all a wind-up or not.'

'I wouldn't have missed this evening for the world,' Jack replied. He wasn't lying either — he was looking forward to this. 'Would you like a drink?'

'Ooh, yes please,' Beth said. 'I'm parched, I am.' She looked across at him with a hopeful smile, and Jack noticed a thin sheen of perspiration on her forehead.

Jack reached behind the driver's seat ignoring the twinge in his neck that the movement caused and grabbed a bottle of wine and a glass he'd stashed there earlier.

'I'd better not have any until we get back to the farm,' he said. 'Not if I'm driving.'

'Okay, no problem,' Beth replied, licking her lips with an unusually small tongue for such a large lady. Jack poured her a glass which she took with a smile. 'Thanks. So, this is all a bit cloak and dagger, isn't it?'

'It is, but like I explained, it's a very exclusive programme. I only want people who are serious about their weight.'

'Oh, I'm serious about it alright,' Beth said. 'Even though if I lose too much, I'll probably lose my job on the website.' She laughed and took a sip from her glass. 'This is lovely, this is.'

'So you followed all my instructions then?'

'To the letter.'

'You've not told anyone about the programme?'

'Not a soul. All I left was a note for my Mum saying I've gone on holiday for a couple of weeks.'

'No phone?'

'Nope. I left it in the car. Are we going soon?'

'Yeah, in a bit. I just need to be one hundred per cent sure that you're serious,' Jack replied. 'I can't let anything jeopardise the programme.'

'Oh, okay,' Beth replied. 'In that case, we can stay here as long as you want. Do you want to check my bag to make sure I've not hidden a phone in it?' Jack looked at her and smiled. There were a number of places that she could have hidden a phone. Several in fact. For all he knew, she had an entire shop full hidden under the rolls of her abdomen.

'No, that's fine. I'll trust you. You're here, aren't you?

'Yes, I am,' Beth said, draining her glass. 'Could I have some more wine?'

'Of course you can,' Jack replied.

About ten or fifteen minutes later, Jack realised that she'd almost finished the entire bottle. It was a good job he'd got some more tucked behind the seat. He was just about to reach back for another bottle when there was a knock on the window. Before he could say anything to Beth, she'd wound the window down. Jack put his hands over his face and peered through a gap in his fingers. This had not been in the plan. Outside the van, there was a man wearing a pig mask that covered most of his face, leaving just his mouth and jaw visible.

'Ooh, hello,' Beth giggled like a schoolgirl, and Jack realised that the wine was finally starting to take effect. 'Look at you all dressed up.'

'Are you starting soon?' the man in the mask said, his voice muffled. 'Only it's chuffing freezing out here.'

'Private party, mate,' Jack said. 'Sorry.' He saw the visitor stare at Beth through the mask.

'You're in the wrong place for a private party, fella,' the man said. As he walked away, Beth wound the window back up and started laughing hard.

'Aaron, you'll never guess what?' she said when she had got her breath. 'That bloke had his winky out. I saw it, so I did.'

'Bloody pervert,' Jack said, fetching the bottle from behind his seat. 'Here, have some more wine.'

By the time Beth had finished the second bottle of wine, she was almost where Jack wanted her to be.

'I can't believe,' she said, slurring, 'that we met on the internet and now here we are in real life. It's amazing, the internet. You can get anything on it.' Beth sat back, rested her head on the seat rest, and closed her eyes. 'What's the weirdest thing you've ever bought on the internet, Aaron?' Jack waited for a moment or two before replying.

'Horse anaesthetic,' he whispered, looking at the empty bottle of wine. But Beth didn't hear him. She was snoring gently in the passenger seat. Jack prodded her, grimacing as his finger disappeared almost up to the knuckle in her abdomen, but she didn't respond. If anything, her breathing got deeper.

'It's showtime,' he said, a broad smile creeping across his face.

7

C atherine sat back in the uncomfortable office chair and crossed her arms over her chest. She was, as her flat mate would put it, deep in the shit, and given her rocky start to her job as a Food Inspector, Emily was uniquely qualified to know. Catherine had been working at the Norfolk Broads Recruitment Agency — a boutique recruiter who only employed women — for over a year. Technically, she was a recruitment consultant, but in reality, she was the office bitch. Or office bike if the graffiti on the walls of the Gents toilet was to be believed. Catherine only knew what was written on the toilet walls of the Gents as she'd been in there several times for various reasons. The irony was that most of the graffiti was true. Apart from the bit about glory holes. She'd never done that. Not in the Gents toilet at work, anyway.

'So, Catherine,' Mrs Cave, her boss, said as she breezed back into the office. 'Have you had a moment to reflect on the allegations about the incident in the boardroom?'

Catherine regarded her boss who was staring at a spot

on the wall, avoiding any eye contact at all. It wasn't that long ago that Mrs Cave had revealed that she wasn't as exclusively heterosexual as she pretended to be. Catherine only knew this as she had been the other person in the very confined environment of the stationery cupboard at a leaving party when this revelation occurred.

'Mrs Cave?' Catherine asked. 'Or can I call you Margaret?'

'Mrs Cave is fine,' she replied. Catherine sighed. The other woman had been all about 'call me Margaret' and 'say my name' when she'd been quivering on top of the photocopier.

'I deny them all,' she said. 'Especially the one with the dwarf.'

'Really?' Mrs Cave replied. 'I've not heard that one.'

'It's not true,' Catherine said. 'But how come I'm the only one in the shit? I wasn't the only one in the board-room, was I?'

'Oh, you want to play that game, do you?'

'No, I don't want to play any games at all. I just want to do the job, and go home.'

'Well, I'm sorry Catherine,' Mrs Cave replied. 'But given the serious nature of the allegations, I have no choice but to suspend you for the good of the agency.' Catherine's breath caught in the back of her throat. She knew that being suspended was a possibility, but she didn't think Mrs Cave would have the bottle to actually do it.

'Right, okay, whatever,' Catherine said, trying for nonchalance but from the almost sympathetic look on her boss's face, failing. 'Do I still get paid?'

'Initially, yes. Until the investigation is completed. Then we'll see where we are then.'

Catherine walked out of the building, holding her head high. The whole mess hadn't been her fault in her opinion, and the fact that the christening of the new boardroom table with a couple of the non-executive directors was accidentally streamed live over the company's intranet was totally beyond her control. Being a woman wasn't a prerequisite for being a non-executive director, and the younger of the two was particularly masculine. She took a deep breath and looked up at the sky which was unusually blue for November. This was, she thought, an unusual opportunity. A free afternoon, leading to several free days, and all on full pay.

'I think a pint at the Murderers is called for,' she said to herself. 'And a Caesar Salad.'

By the time she had finished her lunch, Catherine was bored of being suspended, so decided to go back to the flat. She could always surprise Emily by doing some housework or putting the washing on.

When she pulled into the car park under the apartment building, to her surprise, Emily's little red Mini was already there. Catherine looked at her watch to see that it wasn't even three o'clock. She blipped the lock for her car and made her way to the front door. When she got there, her key wouldn't turn the lock properly, and she ended up having to knock on the door of her own flat. Catherine swore to herself as she waited for Emily to come and open the door.

'Hi Catherine,' Emily said as she pulled the door open. 'You're back early? Everything okay?'

'Did you put the door on the latch?' Catherine asked as she walked past Emily and into the flat. 'And no, everything is not okay.'

'It must have slipped down by accident,' Emily replied in the voice that Catherine knew she used when she was lying through her teeth. When she glanced into the lounge to see Andy sitting there, sipping a cup of tea without a care in the world, Catherine's suspicions were confirmed.

'Slipped down by accident,' she muttered as she made her way into the kitchen. 'Like your knickers, you little slut.' Emily walked in behind her. 'I thought you looked a bit flushed,' Catherine said, which just made Emily's face redder.

'I, er, I finished my inspections early,' Emily stammered, 'and Andy got a couple of hours off as he got a big sale. So we thought we'd have a cuppa. Anyway, what's happened at work?'

'I'll tell you later, babes,' Catherine replied. 'When Andy's gone. It might take a glass of wine or two.'

'Oh, that's not good.' Emily's pretty face creased into a sympathetic frown. 'He's not stopping for long anyway. He's going back home for his tea. Chicken casserole, apparently.'

'Not a bad way to spend an afternoon, is it?' Catherine asked Emily. 'Come round here for a quick game of hide the sausage, and then back home for his Mum's casserole?'

'Shut up, Catherine,' Emily giggled. 'Don't say anything to him. You know how embarrassed he gets.'

'I won't, don't worry,' Catherine replied as they walked into the lounge to join him.

The three of them sat in an awkward silence for a little while. Catherine was desperate to say something to see how pink she could make Andy go, but she managed to keep her inner voice quiet for once. He got to his feet a few moments later, saying how he must be going as he had lots of stuff to do.

'What, like eat your tea?' Catherine said with a grin.

'See you later, yeah?' She left the lounge so that he and Emily could say goodbye to each other properly and fetched the washing basket from the bathroom. A few minutes later, the washing machine was loaded. When she went to put the fabric conditioner in, Catherine tutted.

'What's happened in the utility room?' Catherine asked Emily a moment later, back in the lounge.

'What do you mean?' Emily replied almost in a stutter, not looking at Catherine.

'Well I went to put the fabric conditioner in, and there was already a load of it spilt on the top of the washing machine.' There was no reply from Emily. 'Emily, babes?' Catherine paused for a second, thinking. 'Oh, you disgusting slapper,' she said. 'That's not fabric conditioner, is it?'

By the time she had finished scrubbing her hands in the bathroom, Catherine had almost finished laughing.

'I'm sorry, Catherine,' Emily said, leaning on the door. 'We thought you were out, and we didn't have any time to clean up.'

'Oh, well thank you for thinking of me,' Catherine replied. 'But the utility room? Really?'

'It's a game Andy wants to play. Sex in every room in the flat. We've only got the toilet to go.'

'That'll be easy,' Catherine replied. 'Just make sure you put the lid down.' Emily walked off when Catherine suddenly realised something. 'Ew, hang on. You've had sex in my bedroom?'

'Er…' Emily said. 'Well, now you see…' Her voice trailed off and she stared at the floor.

'You must have done if you've only got the toilet to go.'

'We did it on the floor.'

'That doesn't make it okay,' Catherine squealed.

'Oh, and the chair.'

'Jesus Emily, you used to be such a nice girl. Since you and him got back together you've been a right old slapper.'

'So, what happened at work?' Emily asked.

'Nice change of subject, babes. You're learning. I got suspended.'

'Really?' To Catherine's surprise, Emily laughed. 'The boardroom table? With those blokes that look like the Chuckle Brothers.' She paused for a second. 'Well, not the dead one. Like, when they were both alive.'

'How do you know about the boardroom table?'

'It's on YouTube.'

'Fuck off,' Catherine said. 'It's not, is it?'

'Bloody well is,' Emily replied. 'They've pixelated out all the good bits, but I'd recognise your tramp stamp anywhere. It's got loads of likes as well. You know Tina at your work?'

'Ten Tonne Tina?'

'Yeah. She's going out with Andy's mate Martin, from the supermarket. Tina told Martin, Martin told Andy, and Andy told me.'

'On the floor or in the chair?'

'Ha ha, Catherine,' Emily said with a look of mock annoyance. 'Anyway, being suspended's not that bad. It's happened to me loads of times. From the way you were talking earlier, I thought it was something really bad.'

'Well, it is for me. I've not been suspended before.'

'Only because you've not been caught before.'

'Fair one. Anyway, forget all that. You need to get your gym stuff out of whatever dark recess you've hidden it in. Me and you, babes, are going to the gym.'

'But I've already done some exercise,' Emily groaned.

'A knee trembler in the utility room isn't exercise, Emily. Besides, there's someone I want you to see.'

'Not again,' Emily said with a resigned sigh. 'Who is he this time?'

8

Andy sauntered down the road, hands in pockets and a spring in his step.

'Only the toilet to go,' he muttered under his breath. Quite how he was going to persuade Emily that sex in a toilet was the ultimate in erotica he didn't know, but he had a bet on with his mate Martin as to who could be first to tick off every room in their respective girlfriend's flats. It wasn't just money riding on it though, there was male pride and honour at stake.

He pulled his mobile phone from his pocket and tapped out a quick text to Martin. They'd arranged to meet in the pub a bit later on, but having ticked off the utility room, Andy was keen to get one up on him.

How's the challenge going mate? One less to go my end.

Andy finished the text with a winking emoji. It was only a few seconds before Martin replied.

2 mins mate

It wasn't quite two minutes later when Andy's phone buzzed. He glanced at the screen.

Kitchen's done

Andy grimaced as he realised what Martin must have been doing when he sent his first text. His phone buzzed again a few seconds later.

Pint in the Murderers?

Andy sat in one of the alcoves of the Murderers pub, one of their favourite haunts in Norwich. It had been a pub before the Romans had invaded, and looking around, Andy didn't think they'd done much to the place since then. Lick of paint maybe, but that was about it. Broad, darkened beams criss-crossed the ceiling giving it a medieval look, and an open log fire blazed away in an ancient fireplace. Andy put the two pints of lager he'd bought on the table in front of him and settled into the wooden bench to wait for Martin.

While he waited, he looked around at the other customers. It wasn't that busy — a few old men nursed pints while they studied what Andy thought was probably the racing form in newspapers — but Andy knew it would fill up in an hour or so with the after work crowd. He thumbed a text to Emily to see what she was up to, and almost dropped the phone in his lager when she replied saying that she was heading to the gym. In all the time he'd known her, his girlfriend had never been anywhere near the gym. Andy wasn't sure that Emily even knew where the gym was, let alone what to do when she got inside one.

'Hi mate,' a voice said. Andy looked up from his phone to see his best friend, Martin, standing in front of the table with a grin like a Cheshire Cat on his face.

'You alright?' Andy asked, shifting over on the bench to give Martin room to sit down.

'I am now,' Martin replied, picking up his beer. 'Cheers, buddy.'

'Cheers.'

Andy had known Martin since even before they were both interns at the supermarket. In some ways, they were like chalk and cheese. Martin was short, gangly, and by his own admission, a bit odd looking. Andy, by contrast, was utterly normal in every respect. According to Martin, that was one of the reasons he was so boring.

'So,' Andy said, putting his beer back down. 'Kitchen, eh?'

'Yep. Tick, job done. How about you?'

'Utility room. Had to get a shift on though. Her bloody flat mate turned up when I was on the tingle,' Andy replied with a wry smile. 'What you got left then?'

'Just the toilet.' Martin thought for a few seconds, studying the bubbles in his glass. 'Does the shed count?'

'Don't think so. It's outside, technically speaking.'

'Oh, okay,' Martin said. 'Done it anyway.'

'The shed?'

'Yeah. I did the Spiderman to her in there. She didn't think it was very funny.'

'The Spiderman?' Andy asked. 'What's that?'

'Look it up in the urban dictionary if you don't know, loser. What's wrong with having sex in a shed, anyway?'

'Nothing,' Andy replied, sipping his beer and deciding the urban dictionary could wait. 'Emily hasn't got a shed. Even if she did have one, I think that might be a step too far. We've only got the toilet to go as well. It's going to be tricky.'

'That's where Emily and Tina are different. I mean, don't get me wrong, I'm sure that once Emily defrosts, she's quite entertaining in the sack.' Andy frowned and opened his mouth to complain, but Martin just carried on regardless. 'But I bet she's not utter filth like my Tina.'

'Martin, can we not talk about my girlfriend like she's a frozen chicken?'

'Did I tell you why me and Tina got thrown out of Marks and Spencer? Tell you what mate, those changing rooms will never be the same again.'

'I don't want to know,' Andy said with a laugh, before changing the subject quickly so that Martin didn't have a chance to tell him the gory details of what had happened in Marks and Spencer. He told him about the elderly customer and the cock picture, and Martin laughed so much he spilt a bit of his beer down his trousers.

'Oh, great,' he said, chuckling. 'Now I look like I've pissed myself.'

The two men sat in a companionable silence for a few minutes. Andy's thoughts turned to toilets, more specifically, having sex in them. He'd never been inside Tina's flat. In fact, he only ever met the woman once. But Andy did remember Martin telling about the first time he and Tina spent the night together. Apparently, Martin had woken up to find Tina no longer in the bed, and when he went to look for her, he found her in the toilet having a pee with the door wide open. It turned out that when Tina was in the toilet, there wasn't enough room to close the door. It may have been quite a small toilet, but even so it was fair to say that Martin preferred the larger lady. The much larger lady.

'Penny for your thoughts, mate?' Martin interrupted Andy's thoughts. 'You're miles away, so you are.'

'Sorry,' Andy replied. 'I was thinking about the logistical difficulties of having sex with your girlfriend in the toilet.' Martin stared at him, his glass raised half way to his lips.

'You what?'

'Will you both fit in there?'

'Fuck off,' Martin grinned. 'Course we will. Shouldn't you be thinking about having sex in the toilet with your own girlfriend instead of mine, though?'

'I can't.'

'How come?'

'She's still defrosting.'

'Alright, point taken. Sorry. Anyway, listen. I've got an idea. We should coordinate.'

'What do you mean?' Andy asked.

'The toilet. We should coordinate a time, do the deed, and then we both win the wager. Then it's honours even, and we both win.'

'I really can't see Emily going for that.'

'Ten o'clock tonight.' Martin held out a hand for Andy to shake. 'Deal?'

Andy thought for a moment about Martin's suggestion. Catherine would hopefully be out, ten o'clock was a reasonable time for some hanky-panky, and Emily would be a glass or two of wine to the good. Reluctantly, he shook Martin's hand.

'Deal,' Andy said. 'Now fuck off to the bar. It's your round.'

9

Jack watched the black and white images on his computer monitor, waiting for Beth to run out of steam. He was sitting at the table in his farmhouse kitchen, a glass of fine malt whisky in front of him — just the one cube of ice so that the flavour was released the way it was supposed to be — and looking at the feed from the small camera mounted in the top corner of what was now Beth's bedroom. The room she was in was in fact a room within another room in one of the farm's outbuildings. Thick stone walls provided plenty of security and sound-proofing, and Jack was certain she couldn't get out. The outbuilding had originally been used as an abattoir and had been built to last. Even if there had been windows in the walls, Beth probably couldn't have fit through them anyway. Jack grinned at the thought.

The inside of Beth's room was functional if nothing else. The only furniture was an oversized commode with a stainless-steel bedpan underneath it and a bed. On one wall was a sink with a solitary cold tap, and in the middle of the sloping floor was a drain. Jack had loosened the cover so that his guest could take it off and do her business straight into it instead of using the commode, but he'd have to wait until she'd calmed down a bit before explaining that to her.

On the monitor screen, Beth was sitting on the commode with her arms and legs tightly wrapped to the steel frame with duct tape. She'd been awake for almost an hour, and all she had done since the horse anaesthetic had worn off was scream, cry, then scream some more. Jack had paid extra for a camera with a decent microphone, but he'd had to turn the sound down after a few minutes. There was no way he could listen to that bloody racket for long, but at least given the farm's isolated position, no one else would have to listen to it either.

His main concern was that she would tip the commode over and land in a heap on the floor. Jack had underestimated how difficult it was to manoeuvre a woman of her size around, and he thought he might have put his back out dragging her into the abattoir earlier. That was something he was going to have to address at some point. If his plan worked, she wouldn't be getting any thinner. He watched her for a few more minutes, finishing his whisky as her screams dropped to whimpers and eventually to silence. He wanted her tired, exhausted, and compliant.

'Hello, Beth,' he said when he opened the thick wooden door to the inner room of the abattoir twenty minutes later. 'I hope you're comfortable?' She looked at him and started screaming again, so he shut the door and waited outside until she'd calmed down. 'Are you going to behave now?' he said when he re-opened the door a few moments later.

'Who the fuck are you?' Beth screeched, staring at him

through almost closed eyes. 'What the fuck are you doing? Let me go!' She started sobbing. 'Please? I won't tell anyone, I promise.'

'Don't worry, Beth,' Jack said in a soothing voice. 'I'll look after you.'

'What's the hosepipe for?'

Jack looked at the green translucent tubing in his hand. Technically, it was aquarium piping as opposed to a hosepipe, but he didn't think it mattered that much. It wasn't quite as thick as a hosepipe, but wasn't far off it.

'This is part of the programme,' he replied, pulling a small pot of strawberry jam from his pocket. 'So is this.'

'Please, Aaron, just let me go,' Beth wriggled from side to side in the commode. Jack tried to ignore the jiggling of flesh that he could see wobbling through her clothes.

'My name's Jack,' he said. 'Sorry, I told a porky pie.'

'I don't give a fuck what your name is, just let me go.'

'All in good time,' Jack replied, opening the top of the jam jar and scooping a large glob of the thick jelly out with his index finger. Beth's eyes widened as he smeared the jam on the outside of the aquarium piping. 'My mother used to love jam,' he muttered under his breath as he took a few steps towards her.

'Where the fuck are you going with that?' Beth squealed, wringing the chair to try to get away from him.

'Now now, Beth,' Jack said. 'No need to be rude. Why don't you shut up, and open wide?'

Twenty minutes later, Jack was back in the main room of the abattoir, pacing up and down the flagstones. He was trying not be angry, but couldn't help it. Through the open door of the inner chamber, he could see Beth still taped to the commode, looking at him with undisguised anger. Her mouth and cheeks were covered in jam.

'You fucking come near me with that hosepipe again, and I'll fucking shove it right up your arse!' she shouted through the open door. Jack couldn't see how that was going to happen, but fair play to the woman. She wasn't going to give up without a fight, even if it was in her best interests to go with the flow. He crossed over to the large cylinder of halothane gas in the corner of the main room and wheeled it into the bedroom. Beth had been right earlier when she'd said you could buy anything on the internet.

Ignoring her shrieks, Jack picked up the rubber mask attached to the cylinder by a thin pipe and opened the valve. He jammed the mask onto her face and held it tight against her cheeks as she struggled against his grip. The jam on her face wasn't helping, but Jack just tightened his grip on the mask to make up for it. He had no idea how long the anaesthetic gas would take to work, but in the end, it was less than a minute. When he was sure that Beth was out for the count, he turned off the gas and dropped the mask to the floor. In his pocket was a laryngoscope, a weird bladed instrument with a little torch on the end used by anaesthetists to put medical breathing tubes down their patients' airways. That wasn't quite what he wanted it for, though. Jack tilted Beth's head back, pushed the laryngo-scope into her mouth and peered inside. When he saw Beth's vocal chords, he grabbed the jam smeared piping and slipped it behind them, pushing the tube deep into her stomach. Jack had another quick look with the torch to make sure that the tube wasn't in her lungs before shoving the laryngoscope back into his pocket and tearing off a strip of duct tape, which he used to secure the tubing to her cheek.

While he waited for Beth to come round, Jack wandered back into the main abattoir and poured himself another healthy glass of whisky. He swirled it round the glass, wondering if it was worth buying a small fridge to go in the abattoir so that he could have a cube of ice with his drink next time, and crossed to a counter by the wall. On the top of the counter was a sealant gun with several plastic tubes, each about the same size as a packet of ginger nut biscuits, next to it. Jack had emptied them of the sealant that had been in the tubes before putting them through the dishwasher and refilling them using a recipe of his own creation. It was a thick paste, loaded with as much fat and as many calories as possible. He'd spent ages perfecting the recipe, making sure that it was as nutritious as he could make it in weight gain terms. If Beth was going to fit into the dress in Jack's cupboard, his guest would need to put quite a few pounds on.

Jack could hear Beth stirring next door in the bedroom, so he picked up one of the tubes and fitted it to the sealant gun. Her eyes widened as he walked back into the room, and she made a half-hearted attempt to wriggle away from him. At least the thick tube sticking out of her mouth had stopped her screaming, Jack thought. He inserted the nozzle of the sealant gun into the end of the tube, and started squeezing the handle, watching with satisfaction as his special recipe started making its way down the tube and into Beth's stomach. She wriggled for all she was worth on the commode, but Jack grinned as he looked at her staring back at him with bulging eyes. As he squeezed the handle harder, he grinned at Beth and muttered under his breath.

'Nom, nom, nom, nom.'

10

'Come on babes!' Catherine shouted through the bathroom door at Emily. 'What are you doing in there?'

'I'm getting ready,' Emily's muffled voice came back through the door.

'Jesus wept,' Catherine replied. 'You're going to look like a sweaty mess within five minutes of getting there anyway, so what does it matter?'

Catherine jumped back as the bathroom door flew open. Emily was dressed in a sports bra and knickers, and a pair of socks. Her face was red, and from the look on it, Catherine could see that she was pissed off.

'What's up?' Catherine asked. 'You're looking, er, a bit flustered.'

'They don't bloody fit, Catherine,' Emily hissed through clenched teeth. 'Look, I've got flappy bits.' Catherine glanced down at Emily, but couldn't see much in the way of flappy bits anywhere on her body. In fact, she looked almost too thin. Bitch.

'You have not,' she replied. 'Besides, even if you did have rolls, that's just another reason to get to the gym, isn't it?' Catherine smiled, pleased with her logic.

'They've shrunk,' Emily replied, a look of exasperation on her face as she ran her finger underneath the bra.

'What?' Catherine asked. 'Your tits, or the bra?'

'Oh, piss off,' Emily replied, half closing the door. 'The bra, you fool.'

'Well, at least no one will notice if you pop out while you're doing a star jump.' Catherine started laughing as Emily closed the door in her face.

A little while later, they were in the car heading for the gym. Catherine glanced across at Emily in the driver's seat and managed not to laugh.

'It'll be fun, babes,' Catherine said. 'Just wait until you see him.'

'You still haven't told me who "he" is.' Emily glanced across at Catherine. 'This bloke you're dragging me out to look at.'

'I'm not sure what his name is,' Catherine replied. 'But I saw him the other day when I signed up for a free taster session. So I signed up for another one, and one for you as well.'

'Yeah, thanks Catherine. It's not like I had any plans for this evening after all.'

'Sorry, babes. What were your plans exactly? Was Andy going to come back round on the off chance I was out and make you look like a plasterer's radio?'

Catherine watched Emily think for a few seconds until she had worked it out.

'Oh, my God,' she replied. 'You are disgusting.'

'That's what Andy said about you.'

'When?' Emily barked, staring at her. 'When did he say that?'

'Only joking,' Catherine replied with a grin, nodding towards the windscreen of the car. 'Mind that bus.'

'Fuck,' Emily said, stamping on the brakes and missing the Number 24 from Thorpe St Andrew by inches. The driver's hand emerged from the window and waved at them with a middle finger.

'That's nice,' Catherine muttered. 'I should report him to his head office. I'm pretty sure the chief driver of Norwich Buses wouldn't be impressed with that.'

'I did nearly ram him from behind, Catherine,' Emily replied as she put the car back into gear and pulled away.

'Now, talking of ramming from behind, this fitness instructor bloke is like a bloody real-life anatomical sculpture.'

'Catherine, please!'

'Oh, don't be such a prude. Just wait until you see him until you pass judgement.'

'Bloody hell, Catherine,' Emily gasped, her face beetroot red as her legs whirred away on the stationary bicycle. 'Can we slow down a bit?'

'Nope,' Catherine replied, her own legs going just as fast. 'Got to work up a bit of a sweat so we look all healthy.' She wasn't going to say anything to Emily, but her legs were on fire.

'But I've got chest pain.'

'It's because your bra doesn't fit.' Emily didn't reply, but leaned across and turned up the resistance on Catherine's bicycle. 'Oi, bitch. What are you doing?' Just as she said this, Catherine's attention was drawn by a door opening on the far side of the room, and one of the fitness instructors walked through. 'That's him, that's him! How the hell do you turn this thing down?' she hissed as she fiddled with the dial on top of her bike.

'He's coming over,' Emily said. 'Quick, look healthy. Jesus, I see what you mean.'

'Hi ladies,' the fitness instructor said as he walked over to where Catherine and Emily were working out. Catherine looked across at Emily and realised that she'd managed to turn her own bicycle's resistance down and was sitting there like a bloody athlete. In contrast, Catherine felt as if her legs were about to fall off.

'Hi,' Emily chirped. 'How you doing?'

'Not too bad, thank you,' the instructor replied. 'I'm Jack, by the way. One of the instructors here.'

'I'm Emily,' she replied, putting out a hand for him to shake as Catherine swore under her breath. 'This is Catherine.'

'Hi,' Catherine gasped. She had been planning on saying a lot more, but couldn't get the words out.

'I would turn that down a bit if I were you, Catherine,' Jack said, extending a chiselled jaw towards the dial on top of the stationary bicycle. 'I think you're working a bit too hard.' He turned on his heel and walked away to talk to a couple of middle-aged overweight men who were trying to lift a barbell between them.

'You. Fucking. Bitch,' Catherine said in short, sharp breaths. She stopped cycling and rested her head on her forearms for a few seconds. When she had got her breath back, she continued. 'I can't believe you did that.'

'Did what?' Emily replied, her expression all sweetness

and innocence. 'You were the one who said we had to look all healthy.'

'Bloody hell, my legs are killing me.' Catherine nodded towards Jack, who was deep in conversation with a customer. 'What do you think? He's lush, isn't he?'

'I guess,' Emily said. 'Not really my type though. Too muscly for me. He probably spends longer in the bathroom getting ready to go out than you do.'

'Yeah, right,' Catherine laughed. 'You're a fine one to talk.'

Ten minutes later, Emily and Catherine were sitting in the health club's jacuzzi, having decided to cut their workout short on the basis that Catherine could hardly walk.

'This is more like it,' Catherine said. 'We should have just come in here. Not bothered with the gym.'

'It was your idea, not mine,' Emily murmured. She leaned her head back against the side and closed her eyes. 'So have you got a plan, then?'

'What for?'

'For Jack.' Emily opened one eye and looked at her before closing it again. 'You wouldn't have dragged me out here just to look at him. You must have a plan.'

'Well, sort of,' Catherine replied. 'Phase one was getting to speak to him, so that part is achieved. I was hoping for a longer conversation, but being able to breathe is kind of a pre-requisite for that.'

'But why did you need me for that?' Emily sat up, brushing water from her eyelids.

'So I didn't look too desperate.'

'But you are desperate.'

'He doesn't know that, does he.'

'Not yet he doesn't. Are you still breathless now?' Emily asked with a smirk.

'No, why?'

'You might be in a minute.' Emily looked over Catherine's shoulder. 'He's just walked out of the changing rooms in a yellow pair of budgie smugglers.' She paused, and her smirk widened. 'Don't look now, but he's walking over.'

11

Andy belched and looked at the empty pint glass in front of him. He was starting to feel decidedly woozy.

'Is it your round, or mine?' he asked Martin, who was looking much fresher than Andy felt.

'Mine, I think,' Martin replied. 'Might as well have one for the ditch.' Andy shifted over on the bench to give Martin room to get out.

'Can you get us a packet of dry roasted as well, mate?' Andy said. 'I'm bloody starving.'

'I thought you had dinner round your Mum's?'

'I did, but that was ages ago.'

'Got to keep your strength up, eh fella?' Martin laughed as he picked up the empty glasses and headed for the bar, wobbling his way through the customers who had filled the place up in the last hour. It was a typical after work crowd, all suits and laughter.

While he waited, Andy scrolled through his phone. Apart from some cat photos on Twitter and inconsequential updates from people he barely knew on Facebook, there wasn't much going on. He squinted at the screen and tapped out a text to Emily.

U still at the gyn?

'Oops,' he chuckled to himself when he read the message he'd just sent. He followed it up with a quick correction.

*gym.

Emily hadn't replied when Martin lurched his way to the table, a pint in each hand and a couple of packets of dry roasted peanuts between his teeth. He put the glasses down and spat the packets onto the table.

'Got us one each,' Martin said as he sat down.

'Cheers, mate.'

By the time Andy left the pub, it was almost seven o'clock. Emily still hadn't replied to his text messages, so she was either ignoring him or was still at the gym. Even though he was a bit pissed, he couldn't remember doing anything to annoy her, so he figured she must still be working out, or whatever it was people did in gyms. He was about as familiar with them as he thought Emily was. He stood, shivering, for a few moments as he tried to decide what to do. He could go back to his parents' house, but then his Mum would probably give out to him for being drunk. Or he could go to Emily's and wait for her to get back. But then she'd probably give out to him for the same reason. Deciding that Emily's wrath would be less fierce than his Mum's, he set off for her flat. Hopefully, by the time he got there, the fresh air and brisk walk would have sobered him up a bit.

The walk to Emily's started off okay. It was cold, but Andy just stepped up his pace a bit to get the blood flowing. As he walked along Yarmouth Road, he looked up at the stars, enjoying the clear night sky. But by the time he reached The River Garden — one of Norwich's less popular chain pubs that wasn't really close enough to the river to merit the name — he was bloody freezing.

'Pint of Stella, please,' Andy said to the bored-looking barman a moment later. While his pint was being poured, Andy rubbed his hands together. 'Chuffing freezing out there.'

'Is it?' the barman replied without the slightest trace of enthusiasm. 'Four pounds fifty, please.' He put the pint down on the bar and stared at Andy as he fished in his pocket for some money.

The next pub on the way to Emily's was called The Rushcutters. Andy hadn't got a clue why but assumed it was something to do with the Norfolk Broads. They certainly seemed to flood the place every couple of years, but Andy figured that they couldn't complain when they'd built the place right next to a river.

'Stella?' he asked the barmaid.

'Nope.'

'What else you got? Lager wise?' Andy listened as the barmaid reeled off a list of foreign sounding beers that Andy had never heard of. 'Which one's strongest?' he asked when she got to the end of her list.

'Leffe,' she replied with a smirk. 'That's from that Belgium, that one. Made by monks, or something.'

'I'll have a pint of that, then.'

'Are you sure? Most people only have a half. It's pretty potent.'

'Young lady,' Andy said, realising a few seconds later that the barmaid probably had about ten years on him, 'I would like a pint of monk's beer, and if I feel like it, I might even have another one.' The barmaid stared at him for a couple of seconds before raising her eyebrows and reaching behind the bar for two bottles. She poured the beer into a glass and slid it across the bar.

'Eight quid.'

'Bloody hell. Really?'

'Really.'

Andy paid for his drink and took it to a table that faced the bar. As he was about to sit down, he saw the barmaid staring across at him, so he took a long drink from the glass just to make the point.

'Fuck me, that's nasty,' Andy muttered to himself as he sat down with a thump and got his phone out of his pocket. There was a text message on the screen, and he smiled when he saw it was from Emily.

Where r u?

Andy tapped out a reply.

Rushcutters. Fancy a drink?

Emily replied almost straight away.

Me & Catherine are having a smoothie in the gym. I'll see u at mine. Should be back at 9. The text was finished with a smiley face, so it was all good and Andy knew that he didn't need to reply.

'A smoothie?' he muttered as he took another sip. 'A bloody smoothie?'

By the time he had finished the pint, which had got more palatable the farther down it he had got, Andy knew he had a decision to make. Emily lived in an estate on top of one of the few hills in Norfolk, and he was currently sitting in a pub by the Norfolk Broads. At sea level. It was, according to the clock on the wall, now just after eight. Twenty minutes to walk up to Emily's, which left him plenty of time to spare. Plus, there would be a requirement for sustenance to get him up the hill.

'Another one of those, please,' he asked the barmaid a second later. 'And have you got any dry roasted?'

'You sure you want another?' she replied. Andy looked at her, realising that she was a lot more attractive than she had been twenty minutes ago. He smiled, or at least tried to smile. From the look of disgust on her face, he wasn't sure that he'd got it quite right. This time, she didn't even bother to pour his pint, but just put the bottles on the bar. Andy looked at them and then at the barmaid. 'Penis?' he asked.

'What?' the barmaid's look of disgust turned into one of anger.

'I said,' Andy replied, taking more time over his words this time round, 'Peanuts. Do you have any dry roasted peanuts?'

'Haven't got dry roasted.'

'Have you got anything?'

'Got some wasabi flavoured ones.'

'Two packs, please.'

12

Jack parked his van outside the farmhouse and turned off the ignition with a satisfied sigh.

'Christ, what a day,' he muttered under his breath. It was a bit of an understatement, all things considered. He'd gone into work first thing after throwing Beth a multi-bag of crisps for her breakfast, and then hadn't stopped until lunchtime — not even for a quick protein shake. It was a real "can you just" day. Every time he tried to go and do something, one of the customers would walk up and ask him a stupid question that started with the words 'can you just'. He'd managed to get a quick thirty minutes of his own exercise in, earbuds tightly crammed into his ears to show everyone else that he was busy. Tuesday was always abs and glutes, but the fact that he'd missed his protein shake at breakfast and was doing an hour long set in half the time had left him feeling sick. His legs had taken most of the afternoon to stop shaking, but he was starting to feel a familiar burn in them now.

The strangest thing that had happened all day was an unexpected phone call which had resulted in what he hoped would be a very enjoyable evening. Jack had been towelling off after his post-workout shower, enjoying the admiring glances of the middle-aged and gone to seed crowd in the changing room when he'd heard the public address system crackle into life.

'Jack Kennedy to reception,' the receptionist's voice had said. Her already annoying nasal voice was made worse by the distortion, and Jack had wondered not for the first time why she was employed in a front of house role. 'Jack Kennedy to reception. Phone call.' He'd thought briefly about going out there wrapped in a towel so even more customers could admire him, but thought better of it. The last time he'd done that, the manager had gone apoplectic, so he decided not to chance it.

'Hello?' he had said, breathless, when he managed to get to reception.

'Hello,' a woman's voice had replied. 'Is that Jack Kennedy?'

'Yep, that's me. Who is this?'

'It's Lynne,' the voice said. Jack paused before replying.

'Lynne?'

'From the bank?'

'Oh, that Lynne,' Jack said, injecting a false note of enthusiasm into his voice. Ten minutes later, she knew that Jack hadn't yet met with the bank's mentor, had offered her services as an unofficial financial advisor, and invited herself over to the farm that evening. Jack didn't want to count his chickens, but he was pretty sure he was on a promise.

Inside the farmhouse, Jack hurried round and tidied up. Not that there was much that needed tidying. One of the advantages of living on his own was that when he put something somewhere — and everything had its own place — it stayed there. Jack thought his neatness was definitely from his father, whose study was immaculate. His dad had told him that it was a throwback to theological college when if the trainee vicars didn't keep their rooms tidy, the bishop would have what his father described as 'a proper fucking mardy' before 'getting all mediaeval on their arses'. Jack had never plucked up the courage to ask his father at the time, and it wasn't as if he could ask his father now, but he hoped he wasn't talking literally.

When everything was just as it should be inside the farmhouse, Jack wondered about checking on Beth before Lynne came round. He glanced at his watch, figuring that he had about an hour before the woman from the bank arrived. He could go and see Beth, or he could spend the time in the workshop before he needed to get freshened up for Lynne. That should be enough time to at least make a start on his latest, and most ambitious, creation yet. Still wrapped in tissue paper, there was a piece of acacia wood in his workshop that had taken him weeks to find on the internet. It was going to make a fantastic candlestick which, when finished, would be a priceless piece of art with its own place in history.

Right on time, Jack's doorbell rang exactly ninety minutes after he had got home. He checked his reflection in the mirror, making sure that his hair was in place and that he hadn't got anything stuck in his teeth, and opened the door.

'Lynne,' he said. 'Thank you so much for coming.' He let his eyes deliberately wander up and down her body, taking in her loose-fitting blouse with just a hint of white lace showing through the thin material, and her flowing skirt that wouldn't have looked out of place in an old people's home. 'Wow, look at you. If I'd known you were going to be dressed up, I'd have made more of an effort.'

'Well, you don't look too shabby to me,' Lynne said, walking past him and into the kitchen. 'Oh my God, look at this place. It's amazing.'

'Er, come in,' Jack replied with a laugh. 'Let me show you round.'

A couple of hours later, they were both sitting on the sofa in Jack's kitchen. He'd lit the log burner in the corner of the room, and they sipped from glasses of wine and stared at the crackling flames. Jack had given her a guided tour of the farmhouse, which hadn't taken long, and to his surprise the room that she'd been most interested in was his workshop. He'd spent a good half hour in there showing her his various tools, and demonstrating his new wood turning lathe. If she wasn't interested, she hid it well.

The discussion about finances had taken about twenty minutes in the end, and Jack thought that although Lynne had played the game pretty convincingly, it was obvious that she wasn't there to talk about profit and loss statements. That was fine by Jack. He wasn't interested in them either.

'So, Jack,' Lynne said, almost in a drawl. 'Carpentry.'

'What about it?' he asked.

'What's the appeal?' She leaned down and put her wine glass on the stone floor next to the still half-full bottle before sitting back and turning to face him. She wriggled on the sofa, pretending to make herself more comfortable. Jack noticed that she had shifted herself so that she was a good eight inches closer to him.

'I like creating things,' Jack replied. 'Taking my hands to something natural, and using them to make it beautiful.'

He paused before continuing, almost in a whisper. 'Desirable.' A faint smile played across Lynne's lips.

'Do you think I'm natural?'

'Very much so.'

'When you showed me round earlier,' Lynne said, 'you never showed me the bedroom.'

'Would you like to see it?' Jack asked, looking at her face in the firelight. They sat there for a few seconds in silence until, eventually, Lynne replied with a wry smile.

'Very much so.'

13

'Catherine, for God's sake,' Emily said, taking her eyes off the road for a second. Catherine was sitting in the passenger seat, staring straight ahead, her arms crossed firmly over her chest. 'Would you lighten up? It wasn't my fault.' Catherine didn't reply, but just tightened her arms.

Emily knew why Catherine was pissed off with her, but it genuinely wasn't her fault. When Jack had come up to them earlier, he'd squatted down next to the jacuzzi, giving Emily a completely unnecessary perspective of what was barely hidden by his budgie smugglers.

'Hey Emily,' he had said to her with a wide smile before turning to Catherine. 'Hey, er, sorry. What was your name again?'

'Catherine.'

'Of course it is,' Jack had said, his smile slipping a fraction before he turned back to Emily and hiked it back up again. 'Good workout? I noticed you were working pretty hard on your thighs.' Emily hadn't said anything at first, but had looked at Catherine for support. When she got nothing back from her friend, she had replied.

'It was okay, thank you.' Emily stared at a point over his shoulder as she spoke, desperate to look at anything but the yellow material fifty centimetres away from her face.

'So, are you two thinking of joining?' he'd said, but as he did so, his gaze was firmly on Emily.

'Er, possibly. Isn't that right, Catherine?' Emily replied, trying to draw Catherine into the conversation, but she was having none of it. Jack shuffled a bit closer to Emily, the yellow budgie smugglers taking up more of her peripheral vision. It was all she could do not to squeeze her eyes shut.

'Because don't tell the management, but I can sort you out with a special discount,' Catherine whined from the passenger seat in a passable impression of Jack. 'For fuck's sake, Emily.'

'I told you, it wasn't my fault. I didn't do anything.'

'Special discount, my arse,' Catherine continued, unfolding her arms and sitting back in her seat with a sly grin on her face. Emily glanced across at her, relieved. One of the things that she liked about Catherine was the fact that she couldn't stay pissed off for long. 'Did you see those bloody swimming trunks?' Catherine asked.

'I tried not to, but they were right in my face.'

'What did you think?' Catherine said. Emily paused before replying.

'Well, I think he's more of a grower than a shower.'

Catherine cackled with laughter and slapped Emily on the arm.

'So, you were looking, you grubby little slapper.'

'I might have accidentally peeped,' Emily said, and was rewarded with another raucous laugh from Catherine. 'But I told you, he's not my type. I don't really like him, to be honest. There's something a bit icky about him.'

'Oh stop being such a nun! Icky, my arse. He's bloody gorgeous,' Catherine replied. 'Just imagine him doing fifty press ups with you sitting on his back, squealing. I can't see Andy doing that.'

'Leave him out of this,' Emily said as she pulled up at a red light. She turned to look at Catherine. 'Don't you say a bloody word to Andy.'

'As if I would,' Catherine replied, examining herself in the mirror behind the sun visor. 'Hey Andy, you'll never guess what happened at the gym tonight.' She started giggling. 'This absolute stud-muffin of a fitness instructor came up and waved his cock in your girlfriend's face.'

'Oh, shut up, Catherine. That's not what happened.'

'Where is he tonight, anyway?'

'Who, Jack?'

'No, you little slut. Stop thinking about him and focus. Andy. Where is he tonight?'

'He was in the Rushcutters, but he's meeting me outside ours,' Emily replied, pushing the image that Catherine had just planted in her head to the back of her mind.

'Okay, cool,' Catherine said. 'You've got over your commitment issues then?'

'I don't have commitment issues,' Emily sighed, not wanting to go over this again. She'd made the mistake a few weeks ago of telling Catherine that she didn't think Andy was 'the one' and had regretted saying a word to her since. 'I'm just not convinced that he's the right man for a long-term relationship, that's all.'

'So just shag him until you get bored and move on.'

'I'm not like you, Catherine. I'm just thinking longer term, that's all.'

'You talk some bollocks sometimes, babes,' Catherine replied, examining her fingernails. 'You are shagging him though, aren't you? Not gone all platonic on his poor hairy arse?' Emily didn't answer, but felt herself smiling. 'I'll make myself scarce then,' Catherine continued. 'I don't want to listen to you two grunting.'

'We don't grunt.'

'One of you does.'

'Well at least I don't make a noise like a pig being slaughtered,' Emily retorted as she put the car into gear and moved away from the lights.

'That's harsh, that is.' Catherine flipped the sun visor away. 'Why don't you give him a key?'

'He's not asked for one, and I don't know if I want him to have one,' Emily replied. 'Not just yet, anyway.'

'What, you're frightened you might come back and find him dressed in your lingerie?'

'No,' Emily replied, turning on the indicator as they approached the road their flat was in. 'I can't see that happening. He'd have to wear yours. Mine wouldn't fit him.'

'Bitch.'

'I thought you said he was going to be outside the flat?' Catherine asked Emily as they stood outside the door to their block.

'He said he was,' Emily replied. 'He's probably still in the pub. Have you got the keys?' She pulled her thin coat around her shoulders. 'Hurry up, it's bloody freezing.'

'You had them,' Catherine said.

'Nope, you had them. You had to go back and check that you'd locked the door. Remember?'

'Oh, yeah.' Catherine patted her pockets. 'Bollocks, they're in the cup holder thingy.'

'Go on then,' Emily said, throwing her the car keys. 'Trot off and get them. I'm going to call Andy and see where he is.'

As Catherine flounced back to the car, Emily pulled her phone from her pocket. No text messages from Andy, which meant he was probably still in the pub. She scrolled down her contacts, remembering as she did so that at some point she really should add him to her favourites.

Emily prodded the call button on her phone a couple of times. Her fingertips were that cold that the first few stabs didn't register. She held the phone to her ear and listened for the 'bring bring' of Andy's phone. It rang for maybe ten times before she gave up.

'Emily?' Catherine's voice came through the dark. 'Babes, come here.'

'Fuck's sake,' Emily muttered as she set off down the path back towards the car. Catherine was standing half way down the path next to a tall hedge. 'What?' Her flat mate just pointed at the base of the hedge. 'What?' Emily repeated.

Catherine didn't reply, but pointed again in the same direction. Emily's eyes followed her finger and she squinted in the dark to see what she was pointing at. When she saw what it was, she sighed.

'What the fuck's Andy doing in the hedge?'

14

'What do you mean, fat?' Jack winced as Lynne shrieked at him from the other side of the bedroom. 'You arsehole!'

'I didn't say that.'

'You bloody well did.'

Lynne was standing beside Jack's bedside cabinet, wearing only a pair of knickers. Her arms were crossed over her ample breasts, and her head was darting from side to side as she looked for her clothes.

'Lynne, come on, please,' Jack pleaded. 'That's not what I said.'

'Yes you did,' she replied, bending over to retrieve her bra from the floor where it had been thrown less than ten minutes before, and a random thought about how many points the word 'pendulous' would score in Scrabble popped into Jack's head. 'The minute you got my top off, you said, "Blimey, there's a bit more of you than I was expecting." Didn't you, you bastard?' Jack paused, knowing that there wasn't a lot he could say to that. Those hadn't been his exact words — he'd used the phrase 'a lot more', not 'a bit more' — but the sentiment was the same. The thing was, it was true. Lynne had chosen her clothes well.

'That's not what I meant. Sorry, it came out wrong.'

'Bloody right it did. Jesus Christ, I've never been so insulted,' she muttered as she struggled into her bra. Jack doubted that but wasn't going to raise the point. 'I'm only a size ten.'

'Really,' Jack said, not able to stop himself laughing. That was a bit of an understatement, to put it mildly.

'Alright, a twelve in some shops. But that's not the point. You called me fat. I'm no stick insect, I'll give you that, but I'm hardly obese.'

As she reached for her top and slid her arms into it, Jack did some mental arithmetic. Given her height, and what he thought she weighed, he figured that she probably was obese, statistically speaking at least.

'Look, I'm sorry Lynne,' Jack said, trying to defuse the situation. 'I've just got a bit of a mental thing about fat, I mean ever so slightly overweight, women.' Her jaw dropped an inch at his words. A second later, she pointed at his crotch.

'Yeah, well so's Mr Floppy there,' Lynne said with a sarcastic laugh. 'As soon as my tits came out, he went into hiding faster than a chocolate gateaux at a Weight Wizard's meeting.' She crossed the room to get her skirt. 'I'm going home.'

'Thank fuck for that,' Jack said under his breath when she left the bedroom and headed for the bathroom.

When she came out of the bathroom, Lynne had composed herself and was looking just as business-like as she had done when Jack had first met her at the bank. She was staring at her mobile phone.

'Why can't I get a bloody signal?' Jack wasn't sure if the question was directed at him or the phone.

'It's the walls,' he said. 'They're too thick.'

'Not the only thick thing around here, are they?'

'I'll call you a cab.'

Lynne muttered a 'thank you' under her breath and walked over to the sofa, retrieving her wine glass from the floor where she had left it when they had fled for the bedroom. A few moments later, Jack joined her.

'It'll be twenty minutes or so,' Jack told her as he sat down.

'For fuck's sake, really?'

'It's quite isolated out here. To be honest, twenty minutes is pretty good.'

'Right.'

They sat in stony silence for a few minutes until Jack suddenly thought of something.

'This whole, er, unfortunate misunderstanding,' he said, speaking slowly. 'It won't affect my standing at the bank, will it?' Lynne turned to look at him, and her jaw dropped again. Jack wasn't a poker player, so he had no idea if he'd be any good at it or not, but he was pretty sure that Lynne would be much worse.

'Seriously?' she said, raising her wine glass and almost emptying it in one go. She picked up the bottle from the floor and refilled her glass. 'Seriously?'

'I mean, this is a personal issue,' he said, 'and the bank relationship is a business one.'

'Jesus,' Lynne replied, taking a large sip from her glass. Jack managed not to wince at the way she was getting through a bottle of wine that had cost him thirty quid earlier that evening. 'You've just insulted me by calling me fat. Then your fairly promising erection did a disappearing act that Paul Daniels would have been proud of, and you're worried about your relationship with the sodding bank? For fuck's sake.' She got to her feet, any semblance of composure that she had shown coming out of the bathroom long gone. 'Your relationship with the bank is well and truly fucked,' Lynne said, draining her glass. 'Unlike me.'

'No, you can't do anything to me at the bank,' Jack replied, more hopeful than anything else. 'I'll complain about you to the manager.'

'Mr Parsons,' Lynne said with a triumphant smile, 'would do anything I ask him to in exchange for a cheeky lunchtime blow job.' She walked towards the front door. 'I'd open an account somewhere else if I were you.'

'Are you not going to wait for the taxi?'

'I'll fucking walk back to Norwich if I have to,' Lynne replied as she opened the door. She slammed it behind her, and Jack thought for a moment about going after her. When he realised that if she was, in fact, walking back to Norwich then the taxi would have to drive right past her, he decided against it.

'Bollocks,' Jack muttered as he locked the kitchen door. Not quite the end to the evening he'd been hoping for, but he couldn't help biology or pretend that Lynne was something she wasn't. 'Size ten, my arse,' he said to himself as he poured the last of the wine into his glass. 'In your bloody dreams.' He looked at his watch, realising that it was earlier than he'd thought. He could get another hour or so in the workshop before an early night. Once he'd sorted Beth out, that was.

Jack crossed to the stove where a large saucepan of his special recipe had spent the day cooling. He lifted the lid to the pan, recoiling at the smell. The mixture might be very nutritious, but it stunk to high heaven, and he was relieved that the lid had kept the smell in while Lynne was in the kitchen. Not that it would have made much difference to the outcome.

'Feeding time at the zoo,' Jack muttered as he walked over to the dishwasher to retrieve the sealant tubes.

15

A ndy knew from the tight band across the back of his head, and the thumping inside it, that when he did eventually open his eyes it was going to hurt. He lay where he was for a moment, taking stock. The last thing he remembered from the night before was drinking some of that bloody awful Belgian beer, and eating some horrible green peanuts that had burnt the skin off the inside of his mouth. The only way he'd been able to make the pain go away was to drink some more Belgian beer. After that, it all got a bit fuzzy.

He was lying on something soft, wrapped up in a thick duvet. Bed perhaps, maybe a sofa? As he wriggled to see how much room he had, his arm came up against what felt like the side of a sofa just as a hot water bottle fell off his stomach and onto the floor. There was nothing else for it. He was going to have to open his eyes.

Andy started with one eye, inching it open. So far, so good. He opened the other eye and blinked a couple of times to try to get the room he was in to stop spinning. The first thing he saw when his vision stabilised was Emily. She was fast asleep in an armchair opposite him, snoring softly, and wrapped in a large fluffy dressing gown that he'd never seen before. The dressing gown looked as if it had seen better days, which was probably why it was new to him. Emily was nothing if not fastidious about what she wore in bed when they were together, and he couldn't see her leaping into bed with a grey dressing gown that looked as if it had been washed far too many times.

'Emily?' Andy said, his voice coming out as a pathetic croak. He cleared his throat and tried again. 'Emily?'

Emily jumped and opened her eyes, blinking for a few seconds as she looked at him.

'Hi Emily,' Andy said with a smile that split the dry skin on his lower lip. He tried not to grimace. 'You okay?' She stared at him for a moment before replying.

'You fucking bastard.' Not the greeting he'd been hoping for. 'You stupid fucking bastard.'

Ten minutes later, Andy was sitting on the edge of the sofa and sipping a cup of hot sweet tea. He could hear Catherine bustling around in the kitchen, singing the theme tune to 'The Snowman' at the top of her voice. Emily, meanwhile, was standing in front of him. She was still wearing her dressing gown, had her arms crossed firmly over her chest, and by Andy's reckoning, she was a bit pissed off.

'Emily,' he said, trying for a puppy dog expression. 'I've said I'm sorry. I didn't realise how strong the beer was.'

'Andy,' she replied, 'you're a grown man. Or at least, you're supposed to be. For fuck's sake.' She sat on the edge of the armchair and tapped her bare foot on the carpet. 'What if we'd not found you?' Andy didn't reply, figuring that it was probably a rhetorical question. 'Andy?'

'Er, I don't know.'

'You'd have bloody well frozen to death. I'd be sitting here talking to the Old Bill and explaining how much of a twat my dead boyfriend was.' Andy's discomfort at Emily's words was relieved by Catherine walking into the lounge.

'Right, you two lovebirds. I'm nipping out to the shop. I'll be back in about an hour.' She looked at Andy and gave him a theatrical wink. 'Plenty of time for you two to make up.' With that, she turned on her heel and walked out. Andy stared at his tea until he heard the front door shut behind her. He looked up at Emily, and to his dismay saw that she was crying.

'Oh, Emily,' Andy said, getting to his feet. Once he'd steadied himself, he walked over and knelt in front of her. 'I'm so sorry. I really am.'

'Yeah, of course you are,' Emily replied, wiping her cheeks with the back of her hand. She stood up and walked to the door, leaving Andy kneeling on the carpet. 'I'm getting a tissue.'

When she returned from the bathroom, Andy was sitting back on the sofa. He patted the cushion next to him, gesturing for her to sit next to him. She looked at him for a second with an inscrutable expression before sitting on the sofa about as far away from him as she could get.

'What can I say?' Andy asked. 'What can I do to make it up to you?'

'Andy,' Emily said in a low, determined voice. 'I bloody well thought you were dead. Seriously. When we first saw you lying under that bush, you looked like a Smurf you were that blue.' She started crying again. 'There's so many "what ifs" from last night. What if I'd not tried to phone you? What if Catherine hadn't been by the hedge when I did call. What if, what if...' Her voice tailed off as she started sobbing, and Andy knew that it was going to take more than a cheap bunch of flowers from the garage at the end of the road to sort this out. He decided that discretion was the better part of valour and remained silent.

After a few minutes, Emily had composed herself. She looked at him through tear-stained eyes and gave him a sad smile. Andy decided to seize the moment. He pulled the corner of the duvet back.

'We could always snuggle under here, warm up a bit more?' A millisecond later, as Emily's face dropped, he knew he'd made the wrong decision.

'Really?' she said, her eyebrows higher than he'd ever seen them before. 'Really?' She got to her feet, re-crossed her arms, and stared at him with a look that was a cross between pure anger and disgust. 'Look at you, for fuck's sake. Just look at you.'

'What?' Andy replied, realising that he had to say something.

'You're lying on my sofa with sodding leaves in your hair and reeking of booze after passing out under the hedge outside my flat. Where you nearly died of hypothermia.'

'Emily, come on, that's a bit dramatic.'

'Dramatic?' Emily said loudly, her voice higher by an octave or two. 'Fucking dramatic? Look at you. You're like a fat homeless person in my flat, and you think that a quick ten seconds of you grunting will make me all lovey-dovey? Get a grip, you melt. You're a disgrace.'

'I don't grunt,' Andy mumbled, knowing that he was on the ropes.

'One of us does,' Emily shot back. 'Now get out.'

'Emily, come on, let's talk.'

'No, I mean get out as in get the actual fuck out of my flat.' Andy frowned. Emily didn't swear that often. In fact, he thought she'd sworn more in the previous five minutes than in their entire relationship. 'Go on, off you fuck. Go home and lather up in the shower if you're that horny. Just tell your parents to look out for jellyfish when you're done.'

'Emily, please,' Andy tried to reason with her, but from the look on her face she wasn't having any of it.

'I'm not going to tell you again, Andy. I don't want this.' She waved her index finger at him. 'Just get out. I don't want to see you again.'

'What do you mean?'

'Andy.' Emily took a deep breath before continuing. 'We're done. You hear me? Done.'

A few minutes later, Andy was standing on the doorstep of Emily's flat, squinting in the bright morning sunshine. Emily had slammed the door behind him so hard that he thought one of his eardrums might have been damaged. He walked down the path, deliberately ignoring the hedge to the side of it, and pulled his phone from his pocket. There was no way he was going to walk all the way home, so an Uber would have to do. As he looked at the screen, he saw that there was a text from Martin, timed at two minutes after ten the night before. He groaned when he read what it said.

Boom. If you've not done the dirty in the toilet yet, I win.

16

U nusually for Emily, she was quite nervous. It wasn't because she was driving back to The Heartsease for the re-inspection; it was because her boss was sitting next to her in the passenger seat. Emily didn't think that Pete the landlord would say anything about her previous visit, but all it would take was one wrong word and she'd be deep in the brown stuff. Again.

'So, Emily,' Mr Clayton said, running his hand over his bald dome of a head. 'Based on the intelligence we've received, this is going to be a definite closure.' He shuffled some paperwork on his lap. 'The man who runs the place has got a history of violence as long as his arm, so the police are going to meet us there.'

'The police?' Emily glanced over at Mr Clayton. 'Really?'

'Yes, Emily, really. This chap is a nasty piece of work.' Emily thought back to her previous visit. Pete had certainly looked the part, but at the same time she quite liked the bloke.

After she navigated the roundabout outside the pub, Emily pulled into the car park next to a small white Ford Fiesta with the word 'POLICE' stencilled on the door in slightly wonky large red letters. There were no blue lights anywhere to be seen on the vehicle.

'Low priority job for the police, then,' Mr Clayton muttered as he got out of the car. Emily did the same and stood next to him as the door to the police car opened. In her pocket, she could feel her phone vibrating with yet another text message. If Andy kept this up, Emily was going to have to block his number.

The policeman who stepped out of the car didn't really look that much like a copper. If anything, Emily thought, he looked like a college student about to go to a fancy-dress party. He had more equipment hanging off his stab-proof vest than she'd ever seen, and she wondered how he managed not to stoop from the weight of it all.

'Bloody hell,' Mr Clayton whispered. 'Do you think his Mum knows he's out on his own?'

'Hello,' the policeman said, walking over to them with a broad smile. 'You must be the environment lot?'

'Yes, we're from the Food Standards Agency,' Mr Clayton replied, shaking the policeman's hand. 'Is it just you?'

'I'm William,' the policeman said, ignoring Mr Clayton's question and turning his attention to Emily. His smile broadened even further as he looked at her. 'Blimey, who are you?'

Emily felt her cheeks starting to colour as she shook his hand. He might be a bit on the boyish side, but he was a good looking young man. Quite fit looking under all the equipment, a nice smile, and lovely pale blue eyes. Just the job to take her mind off Andy, but it was a good job

Catherine wasn't here. She'd be all over the copper like a tramp on chips.

'I'm Emily. Emily Underwood,' she replied with a tentative smile, cursing her cheeks which she knew were getting redder by the second.

'So, how do you want to play this, er, William?' Mr Clayton asked with an exasperated look at Emily.

'Well, probably best if I stay out here. That's what my sergeant said, anyway. I can be a present.'

'Do you mean presence?' Mr Clayton asked.

'Oh,' William's face fell. 'Yeah, probably.'

Emily stifled a laugh as an image of the policeman wrapped in nothing but gift paper with a bow on top of his ill-fitting hat. He'd need unwrapping, of course.

'Emily?' Mr Clayton said a few seconds later. 'Are you still with us?'

'Sorry, Yes,' Emily replied, trying to shake the not unpleasant image from her head. 'I was miles away.'

'Obviously,' her boss said, irritated. 'Come on then, let's get this over with.' He walked across to the door of the pub and knocked loudly. A few seconds later, it swung open and a familiar young face looked out. As soon as Jimmy saw the police car, it swung shut and Emily heard him shouting inside.

'Uncle Pete? The fucking pigs are here again. And that fit bird from the food lot's back with her dad.' Emily pressed her lips together and glanced at her boss, but he hadn't seemed to have noticed what Jimmy had said.

Mr Clayton had just raised his hand to knock on the door again when it opened, properly this time. Pete was standing behind the door. He looked at Mr Clayton and at William standing by the police car. To Emily's relief, when he looked at her there wasn't a hint of recognition on his face.

'Are you from the environment?' he asked, his voice hoarse.

'Food Standards Agency,' Mr Clayton replied, holding up his identification card. 'Here for your annual inspection.'

'Please,' Pete stepped back from the door with an approximation of a smile. 'Come on in.'

Inside the pub was just as Emily remembered, apart from the cloying smell of air freshener. At one table in the corner were two men with cups of coffee in front of them. Emily wasn't sure if Norwich City had ever had a crew of football hooligans back in the eighties, but if they did, these two would have been front and centre. They wouldn't be looking over Pete's shoulder at the opposition either. From the look of the two men who were staring at Mr Clayton with undisguised hostility, Pete would be looking over theirs.

'Bit early for customers, isn't it?' Mr Clayton said. 'Your license only lets you sell food and beverages from ten, and it's only just gone nine.'

'They're the cleaners,' Pete replied with a snarl. 'But if you want them to leave, just ask them.' One of the men leaned forwards and cracked his knuckles

'No, no, that's fine. If they're staff, they can stay,' Mr Clayton said, his voice a notch higher. 'Can we see the kitchen area please?' Pete fixed Mr Clayton with a stare that would have wilted most men and pointed to the back of the bar.

'Through that door there,' he said. Mr Clayton thanked him and set off towards the door. As soon as his back was turned, Pete looked at Emily and winked at her.

Emily followed Mr Clayton towards the door behind the bar. As she walked through the hatch in the bar, she looked over at the join between the bar and the wall.

Where there had been a hole in the wall the last time she'd been here was now a fresh patch of plaster. Above it was a cardboard sign with something scrawled on it in a child's handwriting.

RIP Mr Chips. Mudered here in cold blud.

17

The minute Jack heard the doorbell ring, he instinctively reached out and turned the monitor of his computer off. Even though he had positioned the large screen in a corner of the kitchen where no-one would be able to see it, even if they were physically in the kitchen itself, old habits died hard.

He got to his feet and lumbered across the flagstone floor to the front door of his farmhouse. The driveway had been relaid a few weeks before, but he hadn't appreciated the advance warning the stones that were there before had given him of visitors. Jack opened the door to see a small man in his late-fifties standing on his doorstep, a large white van parked behind him in front of the farmhouse.

'Mr Kennedy?' the delivery driver said in a nasal whine.

'That's me.'

'Got a delivery,' the man replied, nodding at the vehicle behind him. 'In the van.'

'Right,' Jack sighed, wondering not for the first time what it was with people from Norfolk that made them want to state the bleeding obvious. 'I need it down at the building over there.' He nodded towards a low group of buildings a couple of hundred yards away from the farmhouse.

'Right, no problem.' The driver turned and started walking back to his van.

'Hey,' Jack called after him. 'Can I get a lift down there?' The driver didn't even look back at Jack as he replied over his shoulder.

'No, sorry. Health and Safety. Might have an accident and you wouldn't be insured.'

By the time Jack got to the outbuildings, he was out of breath. The driver had managed to get the van down the track without having an accident, which was hardly surprising as the nearest vehicle was probably about a mile away. He was sitting on a low wall, smoking. Jack tutted as he walked over to him. He hated smokers.

'Do you want to put that out and get my delivery?' Jack asked. The driver looked at him through a cloud of blue smoke before grinding the cigarette out on the floor.

'Sure,' he whined before walking to the rear of the van. Jack heard the doors of the van open, and a few seconds later, the driver was back. 'Give us a hand, would you? It's bloody heavy.'

'Sorry,' Jack crossed his arms over his chest. 'Health and Safety. I might have an accident.'

By the time the delivery driver had managed to get the delivery out of the back of the van, he was sweating profusely. Jack even thought he could hear him wheezing as he pushed the large box on a sack barrow towards the door of the outbuilding they were standing outside.

'Bloody hell, that weighs a ton,' the driver said,

upending the barrow and depositing the box outside the door of the outbuilding.

'Right,' Jack replied. There was a pause as the two men looked at each other.

'What's in there, then?' the driver asked, looking at the outbuilding.

'It used to be an abattoir.'

'Looks more like a bloody prison to me.' Jack watched the other man take in the doors and windows that had only been fitted a couple of weeks before. He'd paid a fair bit extra for security, and then a little bit more on top to persuade the workmen who'd fitted them not to say a word about the job. There was another pause in the conversation, if it could be called that.

'Was there anything else?' Jack asked after an awkward silence. The driver shifted his weight from foot to foot.

'Er, well, I don't know how you feel about a tip?' the driver whined through his nose.

'Yeah, sure,' Jack replied. 'I'll give you a tip.' The look of gratitude on the driver's face was short lived. 'How about you get the fuck off my farm?'

A few minutes later, Jack had managed to get the box inside the abattoir. The interior of the building was minimal to say the least, and partitioned off into two sections. The main section — where Jack was standing — was tiled throughout with a sloping floor and drain in the middle from the building's previous life. The second section was smaller, and was originally used for gassing pigs with carbon dioxide before they were slaughtered. It was, when it needed to be, completely airtight apart from a vent in the ceiling that was controlled from the main section of the building. The only alteration that Jack had made to that section was to wall up the original outside door, using the same foot thick stones that the rest of the building was made with.

Jack was sweating by the time he had manhandled the box into the middle of the room. The delivery driver hadn't been joking when he said the delivery was heavy, and Jack was impressed that he'd managed to get the box off the van and to the door. He used a Stanley knife to open it, and a moment later was looking at his latest purchase. According to the sticker on the side of the large metal contraption, it was a Prism A-320B Bariatric Aluminium Mobile Hoist. Jack didn't really care what the thing was called. All he cared about was what it could do. Which, according to the website, was lift people up into the air. Not just any people, but rather large people. The maximum weight it could lift was apparently 320 kilograms, or fifty stone in old money. That was, even by modern standards, pretty hefty.

He spent the next few minutes fiddling with the hoist, trying to work out how the sling attached to it and what the various buttons and levers did. There wasn't an instruction leaflet with it, which was hardly surprising seeing as it was second-hand, but he managed to work it out pretty quickly. It had taken him ages to find this particular model on the various internet auction sites he'd been looking at. Fortunately for him, a nursing home on the outskirts of Norwich had recently closed down. Or, more specifically, had been closed down by the Care Quality Commission for feeding their already overweight customers food that wasn't even fit for consumption by animals, let alone humans.

Satisfied with his purchase, Jack left the abattoir and locked the heavy doors behind him. He shivered in the early evening chill and set off at a brisk pace back to the farmhouse. There was plenty more to be done before he was ready for the first visitor to his fitness suite, and not much time to get it all in place. Jack smiled to himself as he walked down the track, muttering an old nursery rhyme under his breath.

'This little piggy went to market…'

18

Catherine sighed and looked around the interior of the flat. Since Emily had left for work that morning, Catherine had done the washing up, put a load of laundry into the machine, and had just finished with the hoover. She thought briefly about going to the supermarket and buying some furniture polish and a duster, but to be honest, there wasn't a great deal in there that needed dusting. Catherine walked into the kitchen, straightened up a tea-towel that was hanging off the cooker, and put the kettle on for a cup of tea. Being suspended was, Catherine thought, a bit shit, and also a bit pointless. All over a stupid video that wouldn't even get many views on a free website for adults, let alone if it was behind a paywall. At least it was nearly lunchtime.

By the time the kettle had boiled, she'd gone all the way through the contacts in her phone to see if there was anyone who might be free to meet up, but as far as she could tell they would all be at work. Catherine made a cup of tea and plonked herself down on the sofa in the lounge to see what rubbish was on television. She had just settled on a re-run of an utterly pointless game show involving some very strange contestants and equally bizarre host when the doorbell rang.

'Thank fuck for that,' she muttered as she muted the television. 'Human company.'

Standing on the other side of the front door was Andy, half hidden by a large bunch of flowers.

'Hi Catherine,' he said. 'Is she in?' Catherine tried to read his expression, but other than looking sheepish and embarrassed in equal measures, she wasn't sure what he was thinking.

'No, she's at work,' Catherine replied. 'Where did you think she'd be?' Andy's face fell.

'Er, I don't know. I thought maybe she might have taken the morning off or something?'

'Sorry, Andy, that came out wrong. I didn't mean to be snappy. Come on in.'

Catherine went back to the kitchen and opened up a few cupboards to see if they had anything to put flowers in. In the end, she settled on their largest saucepan. It was about the only thing big enough for the flowers which were, she thought with a touch of envy, a rather nice bunch. It was a long time since anyone had bought her flowers.

'Do you want a cuppa?' she asked Andy. 'Kettle's just boiled.'

'That'd be great, thanks. White with two, please.'

'Two sugars?' Catherine laughed. 'No wonder you're a bit heavy round the middle.' Andy didn't reply, but just stared forlornly at the flowers in the saucepan. Catherine sighed, and decided to change the subject. 'You not working today, then?'

'I don't start until one,' Andy replied. 'So, I thought I'd pop round with these on the way in.'

'Good idea, mate,' Catherine said as she threw a teabag into a cup. 'She was a bit pissed off with you earlier.'

Andy didn't reply until they were both sitting in the lounge.

'Did she say anything to you?' he asked her in a quiet voice. Catherine thought for a few seconds before replying.

'Andy, you must know by now that I can't break the sisterhood code.'

'The sisterhood what?'

'Oh, never mind,' Catherine waved a hand at him and then lied through her teeth. 'She didn't say anything about it, so don't worry.' The truth was that Emily had spent the time between Andy leaving and her going to work with a right face on. She'd gone on and on about what an utter loser he was and that they were done. It was game over with no re-spawn. Catherine hadn't really said anything, leaving Emily to get it out of her system, but from the look in her eyes, Emily was deadly serious. But Andy didn't need to know any of that.

'Really?' he asked, looking like a lost dog.

'Yeah, really. She'll get over it.' She waved her hand again.

'Can I ask you something?' Andy said. Catherine stifled a sigh.

'Sure.'

'Do you think she's really dumped me, or if she was just saying that?'

'What?' Catherine did what she thought was a reasonable impression of surprise. He really was quite thick sometimes. Emily had told her word for word what she'd told him, but the message didn't seem to have sunk in. 'Why'd you say that?'

'I've never seen her so angry.'

'Probably shouldn't have tried to shag her on the couch then.'

'So, she did talk to you,' Andy replied, his face suddenly dark. 'You said she didn't. What else did she say?'

'Jesus,' Catherine said. 'Listen Andy, what Emily and me talk about is between us. That's how women work.'

'I knew it,' Andy blew his breath out of his cheeks and sat back in the chair. 'She's going to dump me.' His bottom lip started quivering, and for a second Catherine wished that she hadn't invited him in but just taken the flowers and told him to sod off.

'Andy,' she said, more sharply than she'd meant to. 'Andy?'

'What?' he replied, looking at her with puppy dog eyes.

'Man the fuck up.'

'What?'

'You heard. Man the fuck up. Sort yourself out.'

'How, exactly?' he asked. At least his bottom lip had stopped quivering.

'Get a haircut, some new clothes, a new job, and go to the gym to tighten yourself up a bit.'

'Easier said than done, Catherine. Haircut and clothes is one thing, but a new job might be a bit tricky, and I don't even know where the gym is.'

'At least try,' Catherine replied. 'Then she'll know you're serious about improving yourself.' She watched him look at his mug of tea, deep in thought. 'And I can take you to the gym. In fact, I know one of the trainers up there. Kind of.'

'Yeah, but I can't exactly go to the gym and then walk back in here shirtless and say, "Oi Emily, look at these guns — they're sick" can I?'

'Give it a few weeks and you might be able to.'

'You think?'

'Emily'll know you're trying,' Catherine replied, 'and that while you might be a bit of a melt now, you won't be forever.' She saw the ghost of a smile start to creep across his face.

'Okay, why the hell not.'

19

E mily sat back in her chair and looked at Mr Clayton and Pete who were deep in conversation across one of the pub tables. To say that the inspection had been a surprise was a bit of an understatement. Emily wasn't sure who was more surprised though — her or Mr Clayton. He'd been convinced that the place was an absolute pig sty, so convinced that he'd even arranged for the police to be on standby outside the pub in case things turned nasty. Although, Emily thought, the copper who had turned up probably wouldn't have been able to do much except call for backup if it had all kicked off. Especially if the cleaners had still been there. Emily had been quite relieved when they'd left. It wasn't their size so much as the aura of violence just under the surface, and Emily would have hated to see anything horrible happen to that nice young policeman.

'Well, Pete,' Mr Clayton said. 'Is it okay if I call you Pete?' The landlord smiled, reminding Emily why she was glad she didn't smoke.

'Of course,' Pete replied. 'That's my name.' Mr

Clayton had just opened his mouth to reply when there was a loud metallic crashing noise from outside the pub. Both Emily and Mr Clayton jumped, and as Emily pressed a hand to her sternum she saw that of the two of them, he had jumped much higher.

'What the hell was that?' Mr Clayton gasped. 'Jesus, that made me jump.'

'Accident on the roundabout,' Pete replied with a nonchalant expression. He waved a hand at the window of the pub. 'Happens all the time. It'll be fine, don't worry about it.'

'That is a horrible roundabout,' Emily said. She looked at the window, but realised that she wouldn't be able to see anything through the frosted glass.

'Thank you, Emily,' Mr Clayton replied, with a glance at her that she knew meant she should shut up.

'Good for business,' Pete said.

'How come?' Emily asked, ignoring Mr Clayton for the moment.

'If it's a bad one, then we get a flood of people in here for a pick-me-up.'

'Oh, right,' she said, not sure what to say next. Maybe Mr Clayton was right after all.

'There was an old girl got knocked off her bike by the Number 24 from Thorpe a few months ago. Went right over her legs, so it did.'

'Crikey,' Mr Clayton said. It could have been Emily's imagination, but she was sure he'd just gone a bit pale.

'Had the whole bus in here after. Cracking lunchtime it was.'

'What happened to the old lady?' Mr Clayton asked. He was definitely a touch on the pale side. It hadn't been Emily's imagination.

'No idea,' Pete said. 'Brown bread, probably.

According to one of the passengers, there was a big bit of bone sticking right out of her–'

'Could we get back to the inspection perhaps?' Mr Clayton interrupted him. Emily had to stifle a giggle at the look on her boss' face. He was starting to look as if he was about to throw up.

'Are you okay, chap?' Pete asked, noticing his discomfort. 'Do you want a glass of water or something?'

'No, I'm good, thanks. Just a bit warm in here, that all.'

'Let me know if you change your mind.' Pete glanced over at Emily, his eyes widening for a second. She looked away and bit her lip so hard that it hurt, but at least it stopped her bursting into laughter.

Ten minutes later, Mr Clayton had managed to compose himself and was looking a lot brighter. He'd taken Pete up on his offer of a glass of water in the end and was shuffling the inspection paperwork on the table in front of them.

'Well, Pete,' he said with the briefest of smiles. 'I'm pleased to tell you that you've got a very good rating. Five stars, in fact.'

'Excellent stuff,' Pete beamed. 'That's great news. Do I get a sticker?'

'A sticker?' Mr Clayton asked.

'Yeah, for the window. The chippy opposite has got one, but he's only got three stars, so it'd be good to rub his face in it.'

'Emily? Have you got any stickers?'

'Er, yep,' she replied. 'I think so.' Emily rummaged in her briefcase to see if she could find one. As she did so, Pete got to his feet.

'I think this calls for a drink. What do you fancy?'

'Oh, nothing for us, thanks. We're still on duty,' Mr

Clayton replied. Pete wandered off towards the bar, and Mr Clayton leaned in to whisper to Emily. 'There was nothing, was there? I didn't miss anything, did I?'

'No,' Emily whispered back, pulling a green sticker from the briefcase. 'The kitchen was spotless. Everything as it should be.'

'It's almost as if he knew exactly what we'd be looking for, isn't it?' Emily stared into her briefcase and kept silent, not daring herself to look at her boss. When she did eventually glance up at him, to her relief he was fixated on making sure the paperwork was all in order. They said goodbye to Pete, leaving him with a large scotch and an equally large smile as he looked at the brand-new sticker in the window of the pub door.

When they stepped out into the car park, there was a scene of minor chaos going on. In the middle of the roundabout, on its roof, was a small red Nissan Micra. Even though they were upside down, the learner plates on the back of the car were still clearly visible. Traffic was crawling around the roundabout as everyone slowed down to have a good look at the accident.

In the car park of the pub was a young woman, sitting on the kerb near Emily's car with tears streaming down her face. An older man in a suit was standing next to her, and kneeling down next to the bawling woman was the policeman, William. They were all staring at a small machine in William's hand. Emily and Mr Clayton were just walking over to them when a green light flashed on the machine, and William smiled.

'All clear,' he said, looking up at Emily. When he realised it was her, he smiled broadly and gave her a slightly effeminate wave with his free hand.

'I told you I've not been drinking,' the young woman sobbed.

'Miss Netherton,' the man standing next to her said. 'I'm sorry to have to tell you but you've not met the standards laid down by the Driving Standards Agency.' He glanced at the car in the middle of the roundabout just as a car full of young men drove past it, laughing. 'So I'm afraid that you've failed your test on this occasion.'

The young woman's sobs became louder as Emily and Mr Clayton tip-toed past them to Emily's car.

20

'It's your choice, Beth,' Jack called through the thick wooden door as he watched her on the camera feed on his phone. 'Either sit on the chair and be nice, or we're going to end up having an argument.'

'Why are you doing this?' he heard her tinny voice through the speaker of his phone. 'What have I done to you?' That wasn't a question he could answer. She obviously hadn't made the connection between the web site that she worked on, and his attraction to her. Mind you, it wasn't the sort of attraction that she would have been expecting. Most of the visitors to the site, Jack guessed, were there for sexual kicks because they liked watching large women eat. He used the website to watch large women get larger, but the main problem was that on the internet they didn't get big very quickly. That was why he'd decided to take matters into his own hands.

Jack glanced across at the sealant tubes he'd spent ages preparing after finishing work that afternoon. After Beth had managed to keep down three full tubes last night, he'd decided that she could probably take a couple more tonight.

'Sit on the chair, Beth,' he said into his phone, trying to inject an authoritarian note into his voice. Beth didn't reply, but a few seconds later, he grinned as he saw her wobble her way over to the commode. 'That's it, now put your hands on the armrests and keep them there. I'm going to come in the door and put some tape round your wrists to keep you safe. Okay?' She glared at the camera in the corner of the room, making eye contact with him via the camera on the wall, but then did as he asked.

Jack opened the door and walked in, wheeling the anaesthetic cylinder behind him, the mask trailing on the floor. He crossed to the chair, and gingerly wrapped duct tape around her wrists, taking care not to tie it too tightly. There wasn't much point taping her ankles as well. It wasn't as if she was about to sprint for the door. When he was happy that she was secure, he sat on the edge of her bed and looked at her.

'Did you sleep well?' he asked. The last thing he'd done before leaving the bedroom last night was to cut the tape so that she could get from the commode to the bed. He'd watched her from the comfort of his kitchen, enjoying the fact that he could see her on his computer monitor instead of a tiny screen.

'Why are you doing this, Aaron,' Beth asked before correcting herself. 'Jack. Whatever your fucking name is?' Jack tutted. He didn't like her swearing. Jack's mother never swore, and neither should Beth.

'I want you to be beautiful,' he replied, ignoring her foul mouth for the moment. There'd be time to correct that later.

'Some people think I am already.'

'I don't doubt that,' Jack said, admiring her confidence

under the circumstances. 'And in a sense, you are. But you could be so much more.' He held up the green aquarium piping, which was almost clean after a session in the dishwasher. 'And this will help you.'

'Is that your programme then? A poxy bit of hosepipe?' Beth regarded the tube with disgust. 'I can't see how that's going to help me lose weight.'

'The programme's not designed to help you lose weight, Beth,' Jack replied. 'Au contraire.'

'Eh, what?'

'It's French. It means, on the contrary.'

'Well fuck me,' Beth snarled. 'You're not only a kidnapping fucker, but a bilingual one.'

'Mind your tongue,' Jack replied. 'I don't like bad language.'

'Oh, fuck off. You're happy to kidnap a woman and abuse her, as long as she doesn't swear?'

'Whatever,' he said. 'If it makes you happy, swear away. But it won't make any difference.' He waved the tube at her. 'Now, are you hungry?' She looked at him through piggy eyes before replying.

'A bit.'

'Just to be clear, in a few moments time, this tube is going to be in your stomach,' Jack said. 'Now, you can swallow it, or I can put you under like last night. Either way, the end result's going to be the same. Your choice.'

'I don't want the gas again,' Beth said a few seconds later. 'But I can't just swallow the hosepipe.'

'Sure you can,' Jack replied. 'They do it in hospitals all the time.'

'Can I get jam on it?'

'Why not,' he said with a grin as he reached into his pocket.

A few moments later, Jack was dangling the jam-coated tube above Beth's mouth. She had her head tilted back like a small bird waiting to be fed, and he inched it into her mouth.

'Just swallow a couple of times, like you're eating a fresh fancy,' he whispered, touching the tube to the back of her throat and taking a step towards her. Just as he did so, Beth's arm shot up and her fingers clamped around his testicles like a vice. A second too late, Jack realised that he'd not taped her arms tightly enough.

'Oh, you fucking bitch,' Jack gasped, dropping the tube and grabbing her wrist. Beth looked at him, and to his surprise, started giggling.

'You let me go, and I'll let you go,' she said, increasing the pressure on his crotch. Jack wasn't sure, but he thought he could feel her fingernails piercing his scrotum through the thin material of his jogging trousers. It couldn't be more painful if he'd put his testicles in the vice in his workshop and tightened it. He let go of her arm, and scrabbled behind her for the rubber mask, trying to ignore the fire between his legs. As he spun the valve on the top of the cylinder, there was a sickening tearing sensation in his groin. For a horrible second, Jack thought he was going to be sick, but he jammed the mask over Beth's face and tried to take a deep breath.

'Jesus wept,' he whispered, the beginnings of tears forming in his eyes as he opened the valve to the maximum. 'Jesus, would you let go, for the love of God.'

Twenty, maybe thirty, seconds later his prayers were answered. It was the longest twenty or thirty seconds in Jack's entire life. Beth's entire body flopped in the chair as did, to his relief, her fingers. He glanced down at her hand, noting the fresh blood under her fingernails before letting go of the mask and picking up the tube from the floor. He tilted Beth's head back, tempted for a moment to grab her hair and wrench it until she was in the position he wanted. He resisted though — he wasn't a monster, after all — and opened her mouth with trembling fingers. At the last moment, he realised that the laryngoscope was back in the farmhouse, so he just shoved the tube into her mouth and kept on pushing it in until it was at the same level as it was last night.

Knowing he only had a few moments before she came back round, he re-wrapped her wrists with duct tape, making sure that they were tight against the arms of the chair this time. As an afterthought, he did the same thing to her ankles just in case. The final touch was a strip of tape to secure the tube against her face.

Jack tried to ignore the excruciating dull pain in his testicles as he connected the sealant gun up to the tube. He was fairly sure that he could feel blood dripping down the inside of his thighs, but he had more important things to attend to. It wasn't until the third cylinder was almost empty that Beth's eyes started flickering. She made a half-hearted attempt to move, but Jack paid no attention to her at all, concentrating instead on the rapidly emptying sealant tube. He needed to feed her, and then he needed to pay some attention to whatever trauma she had caused him. Another couple of tubes to go, and then he could get back to the farmhouse and assess the damage.

21

Andy tried as hard as he could to concentrate at work, but his heart just wasn't in it. He had managed to sell a couple of phones, which at least would keep the manager off his back, but he couldn't get what had happened that morning out of his mind. Every few minutes, he checked his phone to see if Emily had texted him, but the last contact he'd had from her had been her flat door slamming in his face when she'd thrown him out that morning. He knew she couldn't really use her phone when she was at work, but he was desperate to know that everything was okay between them.

'Excuse me, mate?' Andy heard a man's voice say in a broad Norfolk accent. He slipped his phone back into his pocket and hiked a smile on his face as he looked up to greet the customer. 'Do you buy phones as well as sell them?'

'Yeah, we do,' Andy replied, looking at the customer. He was maybe mid-thirties, scruffy, and had wiry long black hair tied back in a loose ponytail. 'What've you got?' Andy managed to keep the smile on his face despite the customer's appearance and the fact that the commission on second-hand phones wouldn't even get him a pint at the Murderers after his shift.

'It's an iPhone,' the customer said, reaching into the pocket of his battered leather jacket. 'Latest one, I think.' He put what looked to Andy like a brand-new phone on the counter. It even had a toughened cover and gorilla glass screen protector.

'Nice,' Andy replied, his mood lifting. Maybe the commission on this would get him a pint after all. He picked up the phone and examined it, flipping off the cover to get to the battery compartment. 'Is it unlocked?'

'Not sure, mate,' the customer replied, shrugging his shoulders. Andy popped the battery out and squinted to look at the label inside the phone.

'Box? Charger? Any of that sort of stuff?'

'Er, no.'

'Okay, no worries,' Andy said, tapping at the keyboard on the counter in front of him. He was putting the IMEI number into their system, hopefully without the customer noticing. A few seconds later, a silent alert from the Mobi-Code website popped up on his screen.

Reported Stolen.

'Everything okay, mate?' the man asked. Andy looked at him and noticed that he was shifting his weight from foot to foot.

'Is it nicked?' Andy replied. The customer paused for a moment before leaning forward and replying.

'It is, mate, yeah,' he said. 'I'll just take whatever you can give me. I don't need a receipt or nothing.'

Andy realised that his boss was looking over to see what was going on.

'I'm sorry, sir,' Andy said, putting the phone back on the counter. 'But we can't accept stolen property.'

'Er, no, it's not stolen.'

'You just said it was.'

'No I didn't. I said it's Nick's.'

'Who's Nick?' Andy asked, managing to keep a straight face.

'Er, well, he's my brother.'

'Sorry, we can't take it.' Andy nodded at the computer on the desk, hoping that the customer would get the message. 'Computer says no.'

'Bollocks,' the customer said, lowering his voice. 'And there was me thinking that people who worked in phone shops were dead inside and didn't care anyway. Any ideas where I can get rid of it?' Andy looked across to see if his boss was still looking over, but he was busy with another customer.

'You could try the smoking area at the back of The Heartsease pub up in Thorpe,' Andy whispered. 'But don't take less than a hundred for it. It's worth five times that even if it is dodgy.'

'Cheers mate,' the customer replied, a broad smile on his face. 'I owe you a beer if I ever see you up there.' Andy doubted that debt would be paid any time soon.

Just over an hour later, having finished his shift without taking a single pound in profit for the phone shop, Andy was sitting in the Murderers pub and nursing a pint of lager. He checked his phone again, but there was nothing except an e-mail from a woman called Helga in Russia who'd seen his profile and was keen to cam with him. Andy sighed and deleted the e-mail before drifting into a daydream that involved Helga being real, willing, and sitting in his bedroom waiting for him when he got home.

'Fuck me, you look miserable.' Andy snapped out of

his daydream just as it was getting to an interesting bit to see Martin standing in front of him, grinning. 'You look like a man who needs a beer. Same again?'

When Martin came back with a fresh pint for himself and a refill for Andy, he sat down heavily on the seat.

'Think you owe me something, fella,' Martin said. Andy sighed and reached into his pocket for a crumpled ten pound note. He tossed it on the table where it landed between the drinks.

'There you go,' Andy said. 'You win.'

'Thank you very much,' Martin replied, sweeping the note up and stuffing it into his own pocket. 'Emily a bit too posh for sexy time in the toilet then, I take it?'

'Oh, mate,' Andy sighed. 'Where the fuck do I start?'

22

'Bloody hell, Catherine,' Emily said to her flat mate as she breezed into the lounge and threw her briefcase onto one of the armchairs. 'What the hell's happened in here?'

'What do you mean?' Catherine asked from her position on the sofa where she was wrapped up in an oversized dressing gown in front of the television.

'It's a bit, er, clean. Isn't it? Have we been broken into by a bunch of obsessive-compulsive burglars?'

'Bugger off, Emily,' Catherine sighed. 'Just because I've put the hoover round doesn't mean that you have to take the piss.'

'Seriously?' Emily laughed, looking at her. 'I didn't think you knew we actually had a hoover.' She glanced at Catherine's almost empty wine glass on the coffee table. 'Do you want a glass of wine?'

'Does the Pope shit in the woods?' Catherine replied with a giggle. She picked up her glass and held it towards Emily. 'Fill her up, babes.'

Emily filled both their glasses, and picked hers up

before walking into her bedroom. She slipped her shoes off and massaged her feet for a moment before getting changed into her most comfortable pyjamas. They'd been washed so many times that they were almost falling apart, and the only other person who'd ever seen her wearing them was Catherine, but putting them on was like getting a hug from an old friend. Completing the outfit with a pair of slippers that were of a similar vintage, Emily went into the kitchen to sort out the wine situation.

'Catherine?' Emily asked a few moments later when she had settled into the sofa, legs curled underneath her.

'Yes, babe? Make it quick. *Celebrity Ice Dancing in the Jungle* is about to start.'

'How come there's a big bunch of flowers simmering in a pot in the kitchen?' Catherine's head snapped round, her eyes wide.

'Fuck,' Catherine said. 'I must have put the ring on.' She started to get to her feet, and Emily started laughing.

'Don't worry, I turned them off. They look cooked.'

'Jesus, sorry.'

'Are they from Andy?' Emily asked, even though she knew that they were from the charred card that was attached to the flowers.

'Yeah, he brought them round earlier.'

'Right,' Emily replied, pressing her lips together. 'Nice try.' On the television, the two presenters from the ice dancing show were trying to warm their remote audience up, helped by a massive amount of canned laughter.

'So, what's going on with you two?' Catherine asked. Emily turned to see her flat mate looking at her with a very serious expression. 'Have you dumped him?'

'No,' Emily sighed, taking a sip from her glass. This wasn't really what she wanted to talk about. 'Not officially.'

'Are you going to?'

'I don't know. Maybe. Last night, this morning, was just pathetic.' She took another sip, a much larger one this time. 'Not a good indicator for a long-term relationship, is it?'

'So, take a break,' Catherine offered. 'Take a month off. Get yourself run through by as many young stud-muffins as you can, and then go back to Andy with a big smile on your face and some new tricks in your repertoire.'

'Jesus, Catherine,' Emily said. 'We really do have different ideas about what fun is, don't we?'

'An orgasm's an orgasm, babes,' Catherine replied with a wry grin. 'Doesn't matter where, who, or what it comes from.'

'Do you want to watch this, or not?' Emily barked, nodding at the television. One of the male presenters, recently caught by the press coming out of a hotel first thing in the morning with a woman who not only was not his wife but also had an eye-watering hourly rate, was waving his arms about inanely.

'Just don't string Andy along, Emily,' Catherine said. 'That's all I'm saying. He's a decent bloke and doesn't deserve that.'

As they watched a bunch of people Emily didn't recognise mugging for the camera and trying to revitalise what were presumably flagging careers, she told Catherine about the inspection at the Heartsease. By the time she got to the bit about the learner driver and her upside-down car, they were both in stitches.

'The funniest thing was,' Emily giggled, 'was the look on the stupid woman's face when the inspector told her she'd failed her test.'

'Seriously?' Catherine asked. 'You think she thought she'd passed?'

'Yeah, I think so,' she replied with a grin. Emily

thought back to the car park, and remembered William. 'The policeman was quite nice, though.'

'Really? Nice as in friendly, or nice as in easy on the eye?' Emily thought for a second before replying.

'Both, I guess. You see what I mean?'

'Er, no.'

'Why can't Andy be more like him?' Emily took a sip of her wine. 'I'm not saying Andy's not bad looking, but the copper was very well turned out. Fit, no beer gut, decent job with prospects.'

'Andy's not got much of a beer gut though, has he?' Catherine asked.

'A little bit when he gets his kit off,' Emily replied. 'But he's only in his twenties. If he's got a bit of a paunch now, what's he going to be like in ten or fifteen years' time?'

'Jesus, you're thinking about ten or fifteen years' time? I can't even think past this coming Saturday night, and what to wear.'

'Yeah, well,' Emily sighed. 'See, if I stay with Andy, ten years' time he might be an assistant manager in a phone shop, and we'd be in our own shitty little two up two down in the arse end of Norwich somewhere.' Catherine wriggled to the edge of the sofa and grabbed the bottle of wine to fill up their glasses as Emily carried on. 'Whereas with someone like William, I could be in a little cottage in the country while he's an Inspector Superintendent or something.'

'Who's William?' Catherine asked.

'The copper.'

'He's called William?'

'Yeah, what's wrong with that?'

'Old Bill?'

'Oh,' Emily said, grinning. 'I'd not thought of that.'

'Do you want me to find out a bit more about him?'

Catherine asked. 'I know a few coppers.' Emily looked at her friend and smiled.

'I'm sure you do,' she replied. 'Probably more than a few, knowing you.'

'Now now Emily, be nice.'

They sat and watched the rest of the show, both comfortable with each other's company. At one point, a morbidly obese woman who was apparently a reality television celebrity fell flat on her face on the ice rink, prompting explosive laughter from the pair of them.

'For fuck's sake,' Catherine laughed. 'I can't believe they showed that.'

'At least it proves it's live, I suppose,' Emily replied.

'So have you been in touch with him at all, then?'

'Who, William? No, I've not got his number.'

'Not the policeman, you little slut bucket,' Catherine said. 'Andy? Your boyfriend?'

'No.'

'Are you going to?' For some reason, Catherine's question brought a lump to Emily's throat and she felt tears pricking at the back of her eyes.

'I don't know.'

23

'Mr Jack Kennedy?' He didn't hear the nurse calling his name the first time round. It was only when she called it again that Jack realised it was his turn. 'Mr Jack Kennedy?'

'That's me,' he gasped, staggering to his feet and making his way across the waiting room of the Norfolk and Norwich Emergency Department.

'This way,' the nurse said, opening the door to a small room in the corner of the waiting room. 'In here, please.' Jack limped past her and sat in the chair inside the small room.

'I'm Sister Harvey,' the nurse said when she had closed the door and sat down. 'The triage nurse. Now, let me have a look and see what brings you here.' While the nurse scrolled through a complicated looking screen on her computer, Jack looked at her. Sister Harvey was a kind looking woman, maybe late forties, but with a hardness behind her eyes that suggested she'd seen it all before. 'It says here you have a personal problem,' she said, staring at the screen before looking at him with a not very kind expression. 'Is that right?'

'Er,' Jack stammered. 'Do you have any male nurses available?'

'No.'

'Oh.'

'But I guarantee that whatever your problem is, I've seen it before.'

'I doubt it,' Jack muttered, making a conscious effort not to clutch his groin.

'Something stuck?' the nurse asked.

'Sorry?'

'Have you been walking round the kitchen naked, and slipped perhaps? Straight onto an upturned carrot, or a rather large King Edward?' On one level, Jack admired the woman's ability to keep a straight face. On another level, he was disgusted that she obviously thought he was the sort of bloke who enjoyed that sort of thing.

'No,' he said, firmly. 'Nothing is stuck anywhere. I've just had a bit of an accident, that's all.'

Nurse Harvey got to her feet and twiddled a dial next to the windows to the small room, closing the blinds and cutting off the view to the waiting room.

'Up you get then, sunshine,' she said in a business-like voice. 'Drop them and let's see what we've got.' Jack got to his feet and slowly undid the front of his shorts.

'Oh my Lord,' Nurse Harvey gasped when Jack pulled his underpants down. 'Jesus, Mary and Joseph, you poor man.' She crossed herself before reaching with trembling fingers for some latex gloves. When she had snapped them on, the nurse picked up some gauze swabs and passed them to Jack. 'For the love of God, cover that mess up, would you.' She reached for a phone on her desk. 'Can I get a doctor to the Triage Room please?' There was a pause before she continued, this time almost shouting. 'No, not in a minute. I need one now.'

Jack closed his eyes and listened to the rhythmic sound of the paper bag inflating and deflating. It was punctuated with Nurse Harvey's gentle reminders to *Breath In* and *Breathe Out*. The sound of the bag, and her voice, were almost soporific. If it weren't for the stabbing pain in his testicles, he would be asleep.

He opened his eyes and looked at the junior doctor with his head in his hands on the chair opposite him in the Triage Room. Nurse Harvey was pressing a bag to the doctor's face and rubbing the back of his white coat.

'That's it, Josh. Breathe in, relax, and breathe out,' she said, like a mother soothing a child. 'And again. Breathe in, and now breathe out.'

Nurse Harvey glanced up at Jack and gave him what he thought was supposed to be a reassuring smile before returning her attention to the junior doctor.

'Would you like me to call the urology registrar for you?' The doctor didn't reply, but just looked at Jack briefly.

'Yes please,' the junior doctor sighed as he closed his eyes and returned his attention to the paper bag.

'So, this was a sexual accident, yes?' the unflappable looking man in the white coat asked. At least this one looked old enough to be a doctor, Jack thought as he lay on the couch baring everything to the world. Not like that muppet back in the Triage Room. 'Is that correct?' The urology registrar had a slight foreign accent which suited his pristine appearance perfectly. He looked mid-forties, but with a shock of white hair that was swept straight back from his forehead. Jack wondered what had turned it white, but then thought if the doctor had to deal with injuries like his every day, it was no wonder.

'Yes, that's right,' Jack croaked. 'I was in bed with, er, my girlfriend. She was enjoying it so much that she got a bit carried away.'

'Carried away, hmm?' the doctor replied, leaning forwards and looking at Jack's injuries. He extended a gloved finger and prodded Jack's scrotum, making him wince loudly. 'I was going to ask if you could feel that, but you obviously can.'

'I did feel that, yes.'

'Okay, well I've got good news and bad news,' the doctor said. Jack didn't like the sound of the bad news part, but the man in the white coat was smiling so it couldn't be that bad, could it? 'The good news is that there's no permanent damage. Everything is, how do you say, hunky dory?' It hadn't looked hunky dory the last time Jack had looked between his legs, but maybe all the blood just made it look worse than it was. 'The damage is all fairly superficial, and all the important parts are where they should be.'

'What's the bad news?' Jack asked. The doctor didn't reply, but turned his back on Jack and started fiddling with some equipment that was hidden from his view. Jack heard the metal clatter of instruments banging together, and he felt his mouth go dry and his macerated scrotum contract in protest.

'Well, Mr Kennedy, the bad news is that,' the doctor said before he turned around with a syringe in his hand.

Jack stared at the huge needle on the end of the syringe, complete with a bubble of what looked horribly like pre-ejaculate on the end, with horror. 'This is going to sting quite a bit.'

24

E mily peered through the windscreen at the long line of red brake lights in front of her. The traffic into Norwich was even worse than it was most mornings. A light rain was falling, and she was getting annoyed with her windscreen wipers. If she put them on full, then they started squeaking after a couple of goes over the screen, but if she put them on intermittent then she couldn't see properly after a few seconds.

'Bloody hell, come on,' she muttered, drumming her fingers on the steering wheel. There was a team meeting first thing, and then Mr Clayton had something planned. He'd mentioned it on the way back to the office last night, but not told her what. At least if she was stuck in traffic, the rest of the office probably was as well.

When they'd got back to headquarters yesterday, one of the other food inspectors — a big nosed woman from Marketing — had made a snide comment in the toilets about the amount of time that Emily and Mr Clayton were spending together. That was all Emily needed. A nasty rumour going around the office about her. She'd not said anything to the other inspector, but she would if she had to. Emily just wasn't sure exactly what she would say, but she was pretty sure Catherine would help out on that front if asked.

By the time she'd parked and run through the rain to the front of the office, it was only a couple of minutes before the meeting was due to start. She grabbed a cup of coffee from the machine in the foyer and made it to the meeting room with seconds to spare.

'Emily,' Mr Clayton said as she burst into the room. The entire food inspection team were there, and they turned as one to look at her. So much for all of them being stuck in traffic. 'Nice of you to join us. Is it raining?' Too late, Emily realised she should have nipped to the Ladies to check her face and hair. She was soaked. The rain had picked up by the time she'd parked the car, and her umbrella was back in the flat.

'Hi Mr Clayton,' Emily said with what she hoped with a bright smile. 'Sorry, the traffic was awful.' As she sat down, Emily caught the inspector from the toilets giving her a withering look.

The meeting took about an hour, and was as dull as every other team meeting she'd ever been to. Mr Clayton gave a breakdown of complaints over the previous few weeks, showing a slide that highlighted a cluster around a hot dog van that was popping up in various places around the city. It seemed to appear, sell some very dubious hot dogs to the locals, and then disappear before the food inspectors could get to where it was parked up.

'This is a photograph of the van in question,' Mr Clayton said, pushing a button on the computer in front of him. The cluster map that had been projected onto the screen disappeared, and a slightly out of focus picture of a rusty looking hot dog van replaced it. The van had 'Norfolk Dogs' painted on the side in bright yellow letters. A ripple of laughter ran around the room, and the man sitting next to Emily whispered to her.

'Serves them right buying food from something looking like that.' Emily nodded in agreement.

'It won't be funny when a pregnant woman dies from listeria poisoning, will it?' Mr Clayton said, visibly irritated. 'How would that look on the front page of the Eastern Daily News?' The room quietened. 'We need to find this van, and quickly. If you do see it, get the number plate and we'll get the police on the case to track it down.'

The mention of the word 'police' sent Emily into a not unpleasant daydream about William, and his slightly crooked hat, which managed to entertain her until the end of the meeting. As everyone else got to their feet and started shuffling towards the door, Mr Clayton called out.

'Emily? Could I borrow you for a second please?' The inspector from the toilets gave Emily a knowing look as she walked past, and Emily was tempted to stick a foot out and trip the nasty little bitch up.

'Sure Mr Clayton,' Emily replied. She walked to the front of the room where he was packing his laptop away. 'What can I do for you?' Mr Clayton flashed her a quick smile.

'Would you join me for lunch?'

'Er, yeah, okay. Where, in the canteen?'

'I was thinking about going out somewhere. Maybe that new pub that's opened up on the way to Thetford?' It could have been her imagination, but was he a touch nervous? And why would he want to go to a restaurant that wasn't even in their patch, but belonged to the Kings Lynn office?

'Sure, why not,' Emily replied, looking at him more closely. He looked relieved at her reply, and she realised that he had been nervous. 'Any particular reason you wanted to go there? Have you heard something about it?'

'Only that the menu's supposed to be amazing,' Mr Clayton replied. 'We'll leave at half eleven.' Emily frowned as he walked away. That wasn't the usual reason that food inspectors visited places.

A few minutes later, Emily was sitting at her desk and finishing off the report for the Heartsease pub so that it could be uploaded onto the Food Standards Agency's website. She grinned as she remembered Mr Clayton's amazement at the kitchen, and Pete's pleasure at his sticker. Emily wondered if Pete had mentioned it to the chippy over the road yet, and thought that he'd probably been straight over as soon as they'd left.

In her pocket, her phone buzzed with an incoming text. She grabbed it and looked at the screen, annoyed and relieved in equal measures that it wasn't from Andy, but was from Catherine.

What are you doing for lunch, babes? We could meet up?

Sorry, I've got plans. Mr Clayton's taking me out somewhere. Emily replied. A few seconds later, Catherine replied.

Business or pleasure? Emily thought for a moment before tapping out a reply.

Not sure.

She had just finished her report and saved the file when her phone buzzed again.

Babes - DO NOT, I repeat, DO NOT shag your boss. Emily tutted at Catherine's text. That was just bloody typical of the woman. Everything had to be about sex.

I don't think Mr Clayton wants to sleep with me, Catherine. Emily replied, hoping that the use of her full name in a text would give Catherine the message.

Of course he does, babe. Who else does he think about when he's having some 'me time'???

Emily tapped out a fast reply.

You disgust me. A few seconds later, Catherine replied.

I know. Be careful. xxx

25

The first thing Andy did when he woke up was look at his phone in case he had missed a text or call from Emily. When he saw there was nothing on his screen, he sighed and lay his head back on the pillow.

'Bollocks,' he muttered as he wondered what to do. He'd done the flower thing, but that didn't seem to have made any difference, even though he'd spent ages with the woman in the shop where he bought them. According to her, the bunch that he bought was almost guaranteed to make any woman's heart melt. Mind you, he'd not told the woman in the shop exactly why Emily was so annoyed with him, but that hadn't stopped the old crow taking fifty quid off him for the privilege.

The smell of bacon filtered through his bedroom door, and he could hear his mother bustling about in the kitchen downstairs. She insisted on cooking what she called a 'hearty' breakfast pretty much every morning. Bacon, sausages, fried eggs, black pudding, and beans. It was the same every day. When Andy's Dad had been diagnosed with high blood pressure a few years ago, the eggs had been poached for a while, but that hadn't lasted.

Andy got up and went to the bathroom. He looked at himself in the mirror, pinching the fat around his waist. According to the websites he was looking at last night, he had what was called truncal obesity. Which basically meant he was fat round the middle, like a middle-aged man. Except he wasn't middle-aged.

'Time for action,' he said to his reflection as he lathered shaving foam over his cheeks. 'It starts today.'

An hour later, still bloated from what was going to be his last cooked breakfast, Andy was sitting on the bus heading into Norwich. His mother had given him a knowing smile when he told her that he was stopping the fry-ups in the morning, telling him that his Dad said that every time he came back from the doctors. Andy didn't normally get the bus into the city this early even if he was working, but he had some shopping to do and wanted to beat the crowds doing their Christmas shopping. Even though it was still November, the city was getting busier and busier every day.

The young lad in the sports shop that he went to first was, to Andy's relief, in much worse shape than he was. He had a nasty case of truncal obesity that started below his chin and ended above his knees. By the time the lad had rung all of Andy's purchases through the till, the cashier had a right sweat on which wasn't helped by the nylon shirt he was wearing.

'One hundred and sixty-five pounds eighty, please,' he said, breathless from the exertion of pressing the buttons on the till. Andy handed over his credit card, managing not to wince at the cost. It wasn't as if he used the credit card very often, but even so, the sports kit he'd just bought had cost almost an entire week's wages. At least he could pay it off over a couple of months.

Andy was just walking back to the bus stop when his phone buzzed. He stopped, fished it out of his pocket, and read the text from Catherine that he'd been expecting.

Got to nip into work quickly. Pick you up at two, yeah? Andy typed out a quick reply to confirm. When he started walking again, he realised that he was right outside the Food Standards Agency building.

'Bollocks to it,' he said, clenching his teeth.

Inside the building was a security guard sitting behind a desk, his nose in a book. He barely looked at Andy as he walked into the foyer and over to the desk.

'Good book, mate?' Andy said brightly, determined to make friends with the man.

'Yeah, is okay,' the guard replied. 'Supposed to be a legal thriller, but I don't think the author's ever been in a courtroom in his life.'

'Well, that's fiction for you. Anyhow, I'm here to see Emily Underwood, one of the inspectors?' Andy said.

'Fourth floor,' the security guard said, nodding at the lifts.

'Can I ask you a really big favour?' The guard stared at him for a second before raising his eyebrows a couple of millimetres. 'Could I leave these bags here, just for a few minutes?' The last thing Andy wanted to do was to walk into Emily's office looking like a homeless person with his life's belonging in carrier bags, especially after her earlier comment.

'Sure,' the guard said, returning to his book. Andy stashed the bags to the side of the desk, figuring that they would be safe enough, and crossed to the other side of the foyer.

As the lift approached the fourth floor, Andy checked

himself in the full-length mirror on the wall and sucked his stomach in. He had no idea what he was going to say to Emily when he saw her. The lift pinged, and the doors started to open. No time to rehearse anything now. He would just have to improvise. Make her see that he was sorry, really sorry, and was going to change. That he loved her. Andy shook his head.

'Don't go overboard, mate,' he said under his breath, psyching himself up.

Andy walked into the large open plan office and looked around. He'd never been in here before, but Emily had told him it was like working in a call centre. As he looked around, he could see what she meant. The office was about half full of people, most of them on the phone or tapping away at keyboards. There were several signs hanging from the ceiling, and when he saw one with 'Food Inspection Department' on, he made his way over to the desks underneath it. But there was no sign of Emily.

'Can I help you?' a woman's voice said. Andy turned to see a beak-nosed thin woman looking at him.

'Er, I'm looking for Emily. Emily Underwood?' The woman pointed at an empty desk.

'That's where she sits, but she's gone out for lunch in Thetford,' she said, 'with her boss.'

'Oh, right,' Andy said, deflated.

'Well, that's what she said, anyway. They could be parked up in a lay-by somewhere so she can work on her promotion,' the woman continued. 'That's what the old office jungle drums are saying.'

'Jungle drums?' Andy repeated, momentarily lost for something to say.

'Office gossip. You know, that he's slipping her a bit more than a pay check at the end of the month.' The woman smiled, but it wasn't a friendly smile. Far from it. 'Can I leave her a message for you?'

'No,' Andy replied, suddenly feeling ridiculous standing there. He let his stomach sag back out. 'No message, thank you.'

26

C atherine sat in the uncomfortable plastic chair in what passed for the outer office of the Head of Human Relations of her firm. In reality, it was little more than an extended cupboard with a couple of chairs that would get blown over if they were outside when it was a bit windy. She shifted in the chair, laughing when the friction between her skirt and the plastic made a farting noise, and she was trying to recreate the effect when the door to the main office opened.

'Catherine,' the Head of Human Relations said. She was an overweight menopausal woman called Miss Bloor — first name unknown — who had probably never had a meaningful relationship with another human in her life. 'Come on in.'

Inside the office there was a man who Catherine had never seen before sitting behind Miss Bloor's large dark wooden desk. The Head of Human Relations took a chair to the side, giving Catherine a rough idea of the pecking order. So much for the boutique agency only employing women, then.

'This is Mr Cummins,' Miss Bloor introduced the stranger. 'He's from Head Office.' Catherine looked at the man. He was maybe mid-fifties, dressed in a well-tailored suit and starched shirt, and had a smug smile on his face. He'd seen the video then, Catherine surmised.

'Is he your boss?' Catherine said, ignoring Miss Bloor for the moment and looking at Mr Cummins with what she hoped was an enigmatic smile. If he had seen the video, then he'd seen more of Catherine than she'd seen herself, so maybe she could play on that a little.

'Yes, I am,' he replied in an unusually deep voice, the smirk still fixed to his face.

'Mr Cummins has very kindly come all the way here from Kings Lynn to help us with this disciplinary issue,' Miss Bloor said with a frosty look at Catherine.

'Where's Mrs Cave?' Catherine asked. 'Shouldn't she be here as well? She is my boss, after all.'

'I'm afraid Mrs Cave is implicated in this sordid little affair,' Miss Bloor replied, 'and as the victim in one of the allegations, she can't be involved.'

'Victim?' Catherine couldn't help herself. 'What do you mean, victim?'

'She claims you sexually assaulted her at a staff party.'

'She was no bloody victim. Far from it. In fact,' Catherine paused, thinking on her feet, 'in fact, this whole thing has got sexual harassment written all over it. She got me drunk, and then seduced me on the photocopier. I'm the victim here.'

'Catherine, please,' Mr Cummins said in a rich baritone. 'No matter what happened in the stationery cupboard, there is the other far more serious matter of the boardroom. It looked fairly consensual on the video, and I really can't see you claiming to be a victim standing up in an employment tribunal.' So he had seen it then, the dirty pervert. Mind you, according to the number of views and likes the video had on YouTube, quite a few people had despite the pixels.

'But she's my boss. She told me that if anyone found out about it, I'd be sacked.' Catherine was lying through her teeth, but this whole situation wasn't looking good.

'Well she got that right,' Catherine heard Miss Bloor mutter under her breath.

'Eh, what?' she asked. 'What did you say? I'm being sacked?'

'Ladies, ladies,' Mr Cummins intervened. 'That's enough.' Next to her, Miss Bloor crossed her arms and stared at Catherine from underneath knitted eyebrows. 'Now, Catherine,' the man from head office continued. 'You're not being sacked, but we are restructuring Mrs Cave's department following a continuous improvement exercise. The outflow revealed a surplus in headcount that we need to rationalise.'

'Sorry, what was that?' Catherine asked, not entirely sure what Mr Cummins had just said. 'Can you run that past me again, maybe a bit slower?'

'What Mr Cummins means,' Miss Bloor said with an evil smile, 'is that you're surplus to requirements, so we're letting you go.'

'So you are sacking me?'

'No,' Mr Cummins replied. 'We're restructuring, and you're no longer needed.'

'You can't bloody sack me, you bastards. After everything I've done.'

'The only thing you've done is put us on the front page of the Eastern Daily News for all the wrong reasons,' Miss Bloor countered.

'Bollocks,' Emily replied. 'The agency was trending on

Twitter for at least a couple of days. You can't tell me that didn't bring us plenty of free advertising.'

'What was the hashtag, do you know?' Mr Cummins asked. Catherine looked at him carefully. He didn't look like the sort of bloke who would use Twitter, so she could try to bluff him, but equally he might know full well that the hashtag was #officeorgasms.

'Catherine,' Miss Bloor said. 'We don't need filth like you in this agency. That's the bottom line.'

'Miss Bloor,' Mr Cummins said through thin lips. 'Could you give Catherine and I a few minutes please? I'll take it from here.' Miss Bloor got to her feet reluctantly and left the office without another word. It was just as well really, as Catherine wouldn't have been able to come up with a retort on the spur of the moment. She'd never actually been sacked before and wasn't sure what she was supposed to do.

'Listen, Catherine,' Mr Cummins said when Miss Bloor had slammed the door behind her. He relaxed back into his chair and steepled his fingers. 'We can go one of two ways here. We can in fact sack you for gross misconduct, and then of course you'd be entitled to challenge it in the courts. You'd lose of course, but you'd still have your day in the limelight — and the newspapers. Which the agency would rather avoid for obvious reasons.'

'Or?'

'Or you can accept redundancy as part of our organisational restructuring. No package, but you could walk away with a clean slate and a reference for another position.'

'I can't see that maudlin cow giving me a reference,' Catherine replied, nodding at the door that Miss Bloor had walked through.

'It wouldn't be from her,' Mr Cummins said. 'It would

be from me, and as far as I'm concerned, you've been a model employee.'

Catherine remained silent for a few moments, thinking through her options. The redundancy option was by far the better one, both for her and for the agency, but there might be a third option if she could pull it off. She sat back in her chair, sighed, and tried for a little-girl-lost expression.

'Are you sure there's no way to sort this out?' Catherine asked, twirling a finger through her hair and widening her eyes slightly.

'No, Catherine.' She wriggled her buttocks forwards on the chair and leant forward slightly. Hopefully, the man from Head Office would be able to see right down the top of her blouse.

'Are you absolutely sure?' she said, lowering her voice to just above a whisper. 'If there was some sort of arrangement we could come to, even if it was just between the two of us, I think you'd find I could be very flexible.'

'Nice try, Catherine,' Mr Cummins replied with a thin smile. 'But you're not my type.' Time for one last throw of the dice, Catherine thought.

'But I could be,' she said softly, closing her eyes for a second before opening them again and giving Mr Cummins the best fuck-me look she could muster.

'Not unless you've got a cock hidden under that skirt, you're not,' Mr Cummins said, his smile broadening. 'And I couldn't see one on the video.' Catherine sat back in her chair and, despite the situation, started to laugh.

'Oh fuck, seriously?' she asked.

'Yep.'

'Bloody didn't see that one coming.'

'Nice try, though,' he replied, still grinning.

27

E mily flicked on the indicator on her Mini and pulled into the half-empty car park. She'd not been to this pub before although she'd driven past it loads of times. It was a fairly new building, but built to look rustic. At least, Emily supposed, that was what they had been aiming for. She wasn't quite sure it had worked though. It looked exactly like a new building that had been built to look old, and the large sign outside advertised reasonable rooms in the hotel, and an unbeatable 'cordon-blue' menu in the restaurant. Emily wondered for a second if she should correct their spelling when they got inside, but thought better of it as they were still in Norfolk.

'Here we are,' she said to Mr Clayton. He looked up from the paperwork he'd been engrossed in since just after they'd left Norwich about twenty minutes ago.

'Ah, excellent,' he said, tucking the papers back into his briefcase. 'Looks okay, doesn't it?'

'Er, yeah,' Emily replied. 'It's a bit beige, though.'

'Okay,' Mr Clayton replied. 'I'd not really noticed to be honest.' Emily looked again at the building. The walls were painted a light brown, with the odd wooden beam here and there painted dark brown. Through one of the windows, she could see that the walls were painted magnolia, which as far as Emily was concerned, was just a different shade of beige.

They walked across the car park to the main door, which Mr Clayton held open for Emily.

'Thank you,' she said as she walked through into the lobby. He walked in after her and over to the main reception desk where a bored looking young woman was busy doing something very technical with her nails. When she saw Mr Clayton standing in front of her, she jumped and hid a well-used emery board underneath an equally well-used copy of Cosmo.

'Hi, sorry,' she said with a broad smile that showed off some very white teeth. 'Do you have a reservation?'

'Yes, we do,' Mr Clayton replied with a tight-lipped smile at Emily.

'Let me guess,' the receptionist said with a knowing look at Emily. 'The bridal suite, right?' Emily felt her stomach lurch. Perhaps Catherine had been right after all?

'No,' Mr Clayton said. 'We've got a reservation for lunch. Twelve thirty? The name's Clayton.'

'Oh, I'm so sorry,' the woman said with a fake laugh. 'You need the restaurant. This is the hotel reception.' She pointed a bright pink nail at a door off the foyer. 'Just through there.'

As Emily and Mr Clayton walked over to the restaurant door, Emily whispered to him.

'How does she pick her nose with nails like that?'

'Maybe she doesn't, Emily,' Mr Clayton replied with a grin. 'But if she scratched her arse, she'd probably draw blood.'

Twenty minutes later, they were sitting in a bay window with a fantastic view of the A11 dual carriageway. The head waiter had treated Mr Clayton like an old friend, insisting that they have the best seats in the restaurant. Even though there were only four other customers in the whole place. Emily had winced when she saw the menu, or more specifically, the prices on the menu. Mr Clayton had picked up on this, telling her that she should have whatever she wanted. It was, he had said, his treat after all.

'Are you sure?' Emily had said. 'It's a bit pricey.'

'Emily, please,' Mr Clayton had replied. 'I insist.' She put down the children's menu with the cheesy chips on that she'd been considering, and ordered thrice-cooked pork belly with bacon and sage potato purée, sautéed leeks, whole grain mustard reduction and a selection of vegetables. It was a bargain at just under thirty quid, and he had insisted after all. To his credit, Mr Clayton didn't bat an eyelid when he placed her order, along with a cheese and ham panini for himself.

They were sitting there, enjoying a cup of coffee after eating, when Emily realised that there might be a price to be paid for having such an expensive — and filling — meal. She was just thinking how she'd eaten far too much for a lunchtime and would really like to have a little lie down somewhere when Mr Clayton got down to business.

'Emily,' he said, fiddling with a small biscuit that had come with the coffee. 'Can I talk to you, but on a personal level?' She sat up in her chair, suddenly not that sleepy any more.

'Er, yeah. Of course.'

'I thought I could,' he replied, eyes fixated on his coffee. He looked up her with intense eyes. 'But can I trust you not to say anything to anyone?'

'Okay,' Emily said, starting to feel slightly nervous.

'I mean, whatever you think of what I'm going to say? No matter how outraged or offended you might be, do you promise not to breathe a word?'

'Sure.'

'You promise?' His eyes were boring into her, and she shifted on her seat.

'Pinky promise.'

'I don't know what that is,' Mr Clayton said.

'It means I won't say anything to anyone,' Emily replied. 'So, you don't need to worry.'

'It's just I need to talk to someone, and you seem like the perfect person. This can't get back to work. It would finish me, but I like you. Everything about you is perfect. The way you look, the way you act, the way you're just so, I don't know, feminine.'

Emily looked at him picking at a bit of skin next to one of his fingernails. She had a horrible feeling she knew where he was going, and didn't like it one bit.

'Can you not talk to your wife?' she said, just as a reminder to her boss that he was married. Just in case he was going where she thought he might be. She'd read an article in some women's magazine about just this type of scenario. The power play of a male boss and an apparently vulnerable young woman. Except she wasn't vulnerable. Quite sleepy, yes, but not vulnerable. It would take more than an expensive helping of pork belly to get her into bed.

'She doesn't understand me,' Mr Clayton said with an air of finality. 'She has no idea of my wants, my needs. Even after twenty years of marriage, she doesn't know who I really want to be.' He fixed her with a stare. 'But I think you might understand.'

Bollocks, Emily thought. This wasn't going well. Not only that, but she had absolutely no idea what to do about it.

'I'm not sure I understand, Mr Clayton,' she said. She took a sip of her coffee, but despite the fluid, her mouth was still dry.

'I'm trapped, Emily,' he said. 'Completely trapped.'

That was the title of the article that Emily had read. She remembered being in the hairdresser's, waiting for a tint, reading about men who claimed to be trapped in love-less marriages so that they could justify a bit of extra-curricular activity. Catherine had been right. Emily thought for a moment before replying.

'Mr Clayton, I'm flattered. I really am.' She was about to find out if there was a God, and if lightning could come through beige walls. Emily crossed her fingers under the table to try to ward off any divine intervention from the bare-faced lie she was about to tell. 'But I'm a strict Catholic, and even thinking about infidelity is a mortal sin.'

'Infidelity?' Mr Clayton said, and then to Emily's surprise, he started laughing. 'Who said anything about infidelity?'

'You said you were trapped?'

'I am, Emily,' he replied. 'I'm trapped in a man's body.'

28

J ack handed over his credit card to the woman behind the pharmacy counter. He'd managed to persuade the urology registrar to write him a prescription for something strong, based mostly on the conversation that they'd had while the doctor was stitching him back up about how much it was going to hurt when the anaesthetic wore off. They'd only given him a few tablets when he left the hospital the night before, and as soon as he'd got back to the farm, he'd taken them all and fallen into bed. Jack hadn't bothered checking on the bitch in the abattoir. It wasn't as if she was going to starve to death, was it? He didn't trust himself not to do something stupid, so didn't even bring up the camera feed in case it sparked him off.

'That's going to be twenty-four pounds eighty please,' the pharmacy woman said, looking at Jack. She was quite pretty, and under any other circumstances, Jack would have tried to strike up a conversation with her.

'Yep,' Jack replied. 'No problem.' Her eyebrows went up a couple of centimetres.

'Blimey, most people complain like mad about the price.'

'Honestly, I'm not fussed as long as they work.' The woman looked at the label on the package.

'They're quite strong, they are.'

'Hope so,' Jack muttered, just wanting her to hurry up so that he could get out of the place.

'Two tablets with water, every eight hours, no more than six in twenty-four hours,' the woman recited as she fiddled with the credit card machine. 'No drinking, no driving, no operating heavy machinery. PIN number?'

'Three four one six,' Jack replied.

'No, silly,' the woman laughed and put a hand over her mouth like a naughty schoolgirl. 'You're not supposed to tell me what it is. You're supposed to put it in the machine.' He looked at her again, thinking about he might come back and see her at some point when he didn't feel like he'd been kicked between the legs by an elephant.

'Sorry, bit distracted.'

By the time Jack had got into work, the dull ache in his testicles was just beginning to develop into a full-on throbbing pain. He hobbled through the reception area, ignoring the curious look that the receptionist gave him, and fetched himself a cup of water from the cooler.

'Two tablets at a time, my arse,' he mumbled as he pressed four tablets out of the foil packet and threw them into his mouth. The doctor had said to wait until the sensation started to return before taking any painkillers, but Jack wished that he'd ignored his advice and dosed up before driving in that morning. If his boss wasn't such a cock, Jack would have phoned in sick, but he wanted to keep the manager on his side in case he needed any extra time off for Beth.

He sat at his desk and pretended to check his e-mails while he considered what to do about his guest at the farm. After the attack yesterday, she obviously couldn't be trusted. Jack's mind wandered to what the building she was in used to be used for, and he had an idea. If they used to gas pigs with carbon dioxide in that room, then maybe he could do the same thing to calm her down a bit. Knock her out before he had to go near her, perhaps? He was just googling where to buy carbon dioxide cylinders from when his boss walked past his desk.

'Kennedy, what are you doing arseing about on the bloody internet? Get in the gym and do what I pay you for.' Jack sighed and waited until the manager was out of earshot before he muttered a reply.

Inside the gym there were only a couple of customers. Jack walked about, waiting for one of them to ask him a stupid question like they usually did, but none of them seemed interested. He was just wondering what effect doing some work on his arms might have on his damaged testicles when he saw a couple walk in. It was the woman from the other day, but she didn't have her fit companion with her this time. She was with a bloke this time. Jack narrowed his eyes and looked at her friend — he needed some help, that much was for certain.

'Can I help you?' Jack said as he walked over to them before focusing on the woman. 'You were in here the other day, weren't you?'

'Yes, I was,' she smiled, obviously pleased to be recognised by someone like him. If Jack had the faintest idea what her name was, it would help, but try as he might he couldn't remember her name, just her friend's. Emily.

'Well, welcome back,' Jack replied with a fake smile. He turned to her companion. 'But you're new, aren't you?'

'Yep, I am. Not been here before. I'm Andy anyway, and this is Catherine.' Good lad, Jack thought before replying.

'Oh, I know Catherine,' he said with a wink in her direction. 'How could I forget?' While she simpered at the attention, he turned his interest to Andy. 'So, Andy. You've not been to a gym before, have you?'

'Er,' Andy replied, sucking his stomach in. 'Well, I have been to a gym before. Just not for a while.'

'Okay, no worries.' Jack was fairly sure from the look of Andy that he would probably come for a couple of weeks and then sack it. But if he could be persuaded to sign up for a monthly plan, then he might just forget about the direct debit like most of his sort did. It was time, Jack thought, to turn on the charm. 'You're in pretty good shape from the looks of you, nothing that a bit of tightening up won't solve.' Jack could tell from the look that Andy gave Catherine that he'd hit the mark. 'Let's get you started on the treadmill.'

Ten minutes later, Jack left Andy to it on the treadmill. He'd set it up so that he would start on a gentle run which would then increase in pace and incline over the next few minutes. At least it would give Jack something amusing to watch. From the huffing and puffing that was going on, even on the lowest settings, it wasn't going to take long. What Jack hadn't told Andy was that if he used the stop button on the machine, it set a raucous alarm off that meant everyone in the gym would stop whatever they were doing and stare at him.

'Excuse me, can you help me?' Jack heard a voice say next to him. He turned to see a short middle-age man complete with an impressive paunch looking at him. 'I want to use that hip abductor machine thing over there. Can you give me a demonstration please? I've not used it before.' Jack sighed before plastering a smile on his face.

'Sure, of course I can.'

29

'Bloody hell,' Andy gasped. 'Is this thing getting harder?' His legs were burning, and he actually had pain in his lungs. Next to him, her arms crossed over her chest, Catherine smirked before reaching over and fiddling with the buttons on top of the treadmill.

'I've heard a fair few blokes saying that, but never in public,' she replied.

'Very funny,' Andy said. 'Have you turned it down a bit?'

'Yep, don't worry. Mr Steroids over there had put it on a high intensity programme.' Catherine got onto the treadmill next to Andy and started it up at a gentle walk. As his own treadmill whirred its way to something similar to Catherine's speed, Andy shot a glance across at the fitness instructor.

'Bastard,' he muttered. On the other side of the gym, the instructor was sitting on a weird looking machine and talking to another customer. 'What the hell is that thing he's on, anyway?'

'It's a hip abductor,' Catherine replied. 'You sit on it

and it pushes your legs apart. You're supposed to close your legs against the resistance and work your hips.'

'Bollocks to that,' Andy said. 'Looks bloody painful to me. I'm sticking with the treadmill.'

'Yeah, don't blame you.'

They walked in silence for a few moments. Andy was a hell of a lot happier with the new settings on his machine.

'This is more like it,' he said, glancing over at Catherine. She was just staring across the gym, completely zoned out. 'Are you okay?' Andy asked. They'd talked in the car on the way to the gym, and she'd told him about losing her job. He was desperate to talk to her about Emily, but sensed that now probably wasn't the time.

'Sorry, miles away,' she said with a quick smile.

'Bit shit what happened, isn't it?'

'Yeah, you could say that.'

'But you have got a reference out of them, haven't you?'

'Technically I have,' Catherine replied. 'But the human resources gossip factory is legendary. The chances of me finding something else in Norwich are pretty bloody slim.'

'You could find something else? Use this as an opportunity for change, maybe?'

'I'm sure I've heard that somewhere before just recently. Can we talk about something else?' she asked him. Andy saw his opportunity, and decided to seize it.

'Can I ask you something about Emily?'

Catherine laughed, and Andy couldn't tell if she was genuinely laughing or taking the piss out of him.

'You've been bloody itching to ask me about her since you got in the car,' she said.

'I didn't think you'd want to talk about her and me, what with you being sacked and everything?'

'I thought I asked you if we could change the subject.'

'I'm trying to,' Andy replied with a quick glance at Catherine. She had a thin smile on her face, so he thought everything was cool.

'Go on then,' she said. 'Ask away.'

'I went into her work today, to apologise properly and everything, but she wasn't there,' Andy said. 'I spoke to one of her work mates, who said she was shagging her boss in a lay-by somewhere.'

Catherine reached out and pressed down on a button on her treadmill. When it had ground to a halt a few seconds later, she turned to look at Andy with a serious expression on her face. If he knew which was the right button to press on his own treadmill, Andy would have done the same thing.

'Andy, would you listen to yourself?' Catherine asked him. 'Do you really think Emily's that sort of woman? I mean, she won't even have sex with her boyfriend in the toilet. Or possibly ex-boyfriend before you bloody ask and no, I don't know.'

'Did you say ex-boyfriend?' Andy replied. Catherine cursed under her breath, partly for saying that but mostly because Andy could be as thick as mince sometimes.

'No, I didn't say that,' she replied. 'I said I don't know. My point was that she's not the sort to be shagging her boss in a sodding lay-by in the middle of the day. Besides,' Catherine couldn't help herself. She started giggling. 'Emily's got a Mini.'

'What's that got to do with it?'

'Have you ever tried to have sex in a Mini?'

'Nope, and from the way you're talking, I never will.'

'Oh stop being such a mardy arse, Andy,' Catherine giggled. She tried to stop laughing, but when she looked at him, she found she couldn't. He had an expression on his face that made him look like he'd been sucking lemons which just made her worse. She leaned over and turned the speed up on his treadmill, hoping that he wouldn't be able to run and whine at the same time.

A moment later, as they ran next to each other at a sedate pace, Andy turned back to Catherine.

'Would you speak to her for me,' he said between puffs. 'Please?' Catherine thought for a second. Although he was being pathetic at the moment, there was something about Andy that was quite endearing. In a sense, he was perfect for Emily. Just a bit needy, not too bright, but quite amiable. They were made for each other in Catherine's opinion.

'Of course I will, Andy,' she said. 'Leave it with me. I'll see what I can do. No promises, mind.' They ran on in silence for a moment and Catherine was just thinking about sacking it and going to sit in the jacuzzi for as long as she could when there was a loud crash from the other side of the gym.

'Bloody hell,' she heard Andy exclaim next to her. 'Did you see that? Mr Steroid just fainted on the abductor machine.'

30

'Fuck, fuck, fuck,' Emily muttered as she saw the blue lights in her rear-view mirror.

'Emily, language please,' Mr Drayton replied. They were the first words he'd spoken since they'd left the pub about ten minutes ago. Emily had been toying with what to say to the man other than sorry for laughing when he'd revealed his secret to her. In fairness, it had been a nervous reaction to his confession. It wasn't at all what she'd been expecting him to say, but try as she might, she couldn't think of a way to explain it to him. Then she'd seen the blue lights behind her.

They'd started out way in the distance, and the length of time that it had taken them to catch up with her had made her think it was an ambulance, or maybe fire engine. But now that they were right behind her, she could see that they were on top of a car, and the car was sitting right behind her making no effort at all to overtake. She couldn't hear a siren though, which didn't make sense.

'There's blue lights behind me,' Emily said with a glance over at Mr Clayton. 'What should I do?' He craned his neck round and looked through the rear window of Emily's Mini.

'It's the police, I think,' he said. 'In a little white car with a blue bubble light on top. There's a lay-by just up here. You'd better pull over.'

Emily did as instructed and parked the car with a sigh. Behind her Mini, the police car pulled in right behind her. She looked in the wing mirror to see a policeman get out, but she couldn't see his face. Even though she was expecting a knock on the window, Emily still jumped when the policeman rapped on the driver's side window. She pressed the button to wind the window down and looked up.

'Hello again,' the policeman said with a broad smile. It was the one from the Heartsease inspection. The rather good looking one. Emily frowned, trying desperately to remember what he was called.

'Hi, erm, officer,' she replied, giving up on his name. 'Have I done something wrong?' He leaned forward and looked in the window. When he saw Mr Clayton in the passenger seat, the smile disappeared from his face. 'Could you step out of the vehicle and join me in mine please, Madam?' he asked her before turning and walking back to his car.

'Bollocks,' Emily said. 'Oh, sorry for swearing, Mr Clayton. I meant to say bugger.'

'His name's William,' her boss hissed as she undid her seatbelt and opened her car door. 'Try and make friends with him.'

Emily's heart was thumping as she walked around to the passenger side of the police car. She'd never been pulled over by the police before and had no idea what to expect. Her fingers were trembling as she opened the door and got in. When she turned to look at William, his smile was back.

'Would you like a Polo?' he asked, offering her a crumpled tube of mints. 'They've been in my pocket which is why they're a bit warm, but they're ever so nice.'

'Oh, thanks,' Emily replied, taking one of them and popping it into her mouth. She sat in silence for a moment, sucking her mint, and wondering what was going to happen next.

'Isn't it lovely today?' he said eventually. 'Not going to last though. It's supposed to rain at the weekend, and I've got to go to the football. Norwich are at home again.'

'Okay, well that'll be nice.'

'Not really. I don't like football. It's too rough, and some of the fans are really rude just because I'm a policeman.' Emily tried to make a sympathetic noise, but it came out as a loud 'tut' because of the mint. They sat there for a few seconds before Emily decided to try to get whatever was coming over with.

'So, er, have I done something wrong?' she asked.

'Don't think so.'

'Oh. But you pulled me over.'

'Well, I saw you going round the roundabout back there and I thought "there's that nice young woman from the Food Standards lot." This is the first time the Sergeant's let me bring the blue light out, so I thought I'd use it to see if you'd fancy a chat?'

'It's William, isn't it?' Emily asked slowly. His face broke into a broad smile.

'You remembered! Fantastic. Sorry it took so long to catch up with you, but Percy the police car here's not very quick.' He patted the dashboard with the palm of his hand.

'Are you allowed to do that?'

'Do what? Use the bubble light? The sergeant said I could if it was urgent.'

'I'm just not sure if you're supposed to pull cars over with it because you want to have a chat with the driver.'

'They do it on *Police Interceptors* all the time, though. Pull people over to talk to them. Would you like another Polo?' He pushed the packet of mints in her direction, and she noticed his hands were shaking more than hers.

'I'm good, thanks.'

'Can I ask you a question?'

'You're a policeman. Of course you can,' she replied. 'I don't think you have to ask, though. I thought you'd just want to take my particulars down or something.' The minute the words were out of her mouth, Emily realised how that statement could be interpreted. She felt the colour flush to her cheeks.

'Have you got a boyfriend?' William asked. That was not what she'd been expecting him to ask her at all.

'No, er, yes,' she stammered, caught off guard. 'It's a bit complicated.'

'Only I was wondering, if you haven't, whether you'd like to go out for a drink or something?' Emily looked over at him, but he was examining his Polo mints with a forensic stare.

A few moments later, Emily was back behind the wheel of her Mini. As she pulled out of the lay-by and back onto the A11 dual carriageway towards Norwich, Mr Clayton broke the silence.

'What was all that about, then?' he asked. Emily thought for a second before replying.

'He just wanted a quick chat about my driving. I took that last roundabout a bit quickly.'

'Really?' Mr Clayton asked. 'Is he a traffic copper then? Only I didn't realise they drove Ford Fiestas.' Emily clamped her lips together to hide a smile before replying.

'I think he'd like to be at some point.'

'Well, he seems to like you,' Mr Clayton replied, 'and unless I'm mistaken, you quite like him as well.' Emily gave up trying not to smile.

'What makes you say that?' she asked.

'The fact that you've got his phone number scribbled on the back of your hand?'

31

'Is this it?' Catherine peered at the farm track in front of her.

'Yep, just up the track. That's my place at the end,' Jack replied. 'Thank you so much for giving me a lift back home.'

'Well,' she said, pulling her car onto the track, 'it's not as if you could drive, not with that bang to the head.'

'Oh, God,' he groaned. 'That's so embarrassing.'

'No, it's not. You can't help fainting.'

'The paramedic said it was a collapse, not a faint.' Catherine paused before replying, not sure what the difference was. 'But there was no way I was going to go to the hospital. Not after what they did to me last time.' She paused again, desperate to ask him exactly what had happened to make him faint, or collapse, or whatever. That was something he'd been very tight lipped about, even when he was semi-conscious on the floor of the gym.

Catherine parked her car outside the farmhouse, and Jack got out gingerly.

'Do you want a coffee?' he asked her. 'It's the least I

can do.' Catherine pretended to think for a moment before replying as she'd thought he wasn't going to offer her anything. She got out of the car, stood in front of the farmhouse and looked around.

'Oh, go on then,' Catherine said. 'If you insist.'

She followed Jack as he made his way up to the farmhouse door, fishing in his pocket for his keys as he did so.

'Have you lived here for long?' she asked, more for the sake of something to say than because she was genuinely interested. Catherine knew all about the history of the place, but she wasn't about to start a conversation about it with Jack just in case he didn't know.

'About a year,' he replied, slotting the key in the door and swinging it open. 'Come on in.' Catherine followed him into the kitchen and looked around the modern interior. It was obviously a man's kitchen, with no sign at all of a woman's touch, but it was immaculate. Not so much as a mug draining next to the sink. The walls were painted with an eggshell blue colour, cool but not cold, and modern appliances were dotted around the dark granite worktops.

'Wow,' Catherine said, genuinely impressed. 'This is lovely.'

'Thanks,' Jack replied, tossing his keys into a stainless-steel dish in the centre of the kitchen table. 'I had the whole farmhouse gutted just after I bought it and redone. It was in a bit of a state, but I got it for a decent price. Give us your coat and I'll hang it up.'

'Must have cost a bloody fortune to get all this done,' Catherine said after she'd shrugged off her coat and handed it to Jack. She ran her hand over one of the worktops. Jack didn't reply, but just nodded towards a comfortable sofa that sat in front of a log burner in the corner of the room.

'Make yourself at home,' he said. 'I'll just get some logs

in from outside and get the burner on. Unless you'd prefer the central heating?'

'A fire sounds great,' Catherine murmured, running her hand over one of the granite worktops as Jack hung her coat up on a stainless-steel coat rack. She smirked as he walked back out of the kitchen door, watching his muscular frame. This could turn into quite a romantic evening.

Ten minutes or so later, they were both sitting at opposite ends of the sofa. Catherine was sipping a cup of fantastic coffee. One of Jack's appliances was a futuristic looking coffee machine and she had watched him, impressed, as he bustled around the machine with obvious ease. She glanced across at him, but to her disappointment, he was just staring at his phone. The screen was angled away from her, but even if it wasn't, he had his hand cupped around the phone to stop her seeing what he was looking at. Strong but silent type then, she thought. After another minute or so, she decided to take the initiative.

'So, I take it being a fitness instructor's pretty well paid then?'

'How do you mean?' Jack finally put the phone away in his pocket and looked over at her, frowning.

'Well, all this can't have been cheap,' Catherine replied, waving her hand aimlessly around the kitchen. He looked away from her and back at the fire. 'Sorry, I didn't mean to offend you.' In truth, Catherine wasn't that bothered if she had offended him. Although the coffee and log fire was very nice, she was starting to get bored. She didn't even think he had a television. At least, if he did, it wasn't in the kitchen. Maybe he just spent his evenings staring at the fire, hopping up every once in a while to do some press ups or star jumps.

'I bought it with my inheritance,' he said quietly, 'after

my father died.' He dropped his voice to just above a whisper, and Catherine had to listen carefully to what he said next. What she heard shocked her to the core. 'He was murdered.'

'Oh, Jack,' Catherine said, reaching across the sofa to stroke his arm. 'I'm so sorry to hear that.'

'That's okay,' Jack replied. 'You weren't to know.' They sat in silence for a moment

'Your mother's not around anymore either then, I take it?' Catherine asked, figuring that if she was, Jack wouldn't have inherited anything at all. She jumped as his head snapped round. The first thing she noticed was the look of fury on his face. The next thing was the single tear rolling down his cheek. Oops.

Jack brushed the tear away and leapt to his feet, leaving the kitchen without a word. Catherine sighed.

'Bollocks,' she muttered, draining her coffee. 'Guess it's time to go.'

Catherine was standing by the kitchen door, buttoning up her coat when Jack walked back in from one of the doors off the kitchen. To Catherine's surprise, he was clutching an unopened bottle of whisky and two cut glass crystal tumblers. Jack didn't even seem to notice that she'd put her coat on.

'Do you drink whisky?' he asked her.

'Er,' she replied, momentarily lost for words. Catherine glanced at her watch. It wasn't even four in the afternoon. 'Well, it's a bit early and I'm driving.'

'But you can still have one, can't you?' She looked at him, noticing that any sign of anger had disappeared. If anything, he looked lost. 'You weren't going, were you?' he asked, nodding at her coat.

'Well, I was,' Catherine said. 'I thought I'd upset you.'

'No, you haven't upset me at all,' he replied with a weak smile. 'I don't need any help at all with that.'

Catherine slipped her coat back off and hung it on the coat rack. A few seconds later, they were back where they had been a few minutes before. She noticed that Jack wasn't quite as far away from her on the sofa as he had been, which she took as a promising sign. He had poured her a finger of the dark brown whisky and then added a couple of minute drops of water from a small jug before handing her the tumbler.

'It helps release the flavour,' he'd said with a faint smile. Catherine kept silent to see if Jack would say anything else about his parents. She was intrigued, but didn't want to ask anything else. Perhaps he would open up if she kept quiet? While she waited, she glanced at him a couple of times from under her fringe. Jack was turning out to be nothing if not enigmatic. Physically fit, good looking, sophisticated after a fashion, and vulnerable. There was, Catherine thought, a lot to like about the man. He was just staring at the flames of the fire through the glass door of the log burner until eventually, he spoke.

'I don't really talk about my parents much.' Catherine gave him a moment to see if he'd say anything else. When he didn't, she decided to chance another question.

'Do you mind if I ask what happened to your parents?'

'Well, like I said, my dad died not that long ago.'

'And your mother?'

'She's not around.' There was a finality to Jack's statement that gave Catherine pause for thought. 'She's in prison.'

32

A ndy sat back on the doorstep, leaning his back up
against Emily's front door. He knew he was being
ridiculous, waiting here for her to come back from work,
but he wanted to sort this out for once and for all. If Emily
was going to actually dump him, then the least she could
do is say it to his face properly instead of just screaming at
him before slamming the door.

He wrapped his coat around himself and shuffled to
try to get comfortable. Andy could feel the cold of the
stone step he was sitting on coming through his jeans, but
he didn't care even though he was desperate for a pee.
While he waited, he scrolled through his phone, reading an
article on the Eastern Daily News website about a missing
woman from Dussindale. Despite the fact she was missing,
Andy stifled a laugh when he saw a photo of the woman. It
was hardly flattering. She was a bit on the large side, and
the camera had caught her with a mouthful of what looked
like a sausage sandwich. Then he carried on reading and
realised that she was properly missing as opposed to just

not gone home one night, and immediately felt bad for laughing.

A few moments later, the pressure in his bladder was getting to the point where if Emily didn't come back soon, he was going to have to nip round the side to the alley. It wouldn't look good if the first words out of his mouth when she turned up were, 'Can I use the loo, please?'. While he waited, he thought back to the incident at the gym earlier. The fitness instructor, Jack, had gone down like a sack of spuds. He'd spoken in the changing rooms to the strange little man Jack had been instructing. Apparently, one minute he'd been demonstrating how using the machine worked your inner thighs, the next Jack had gone white as a sheet and gone down. At least Catherine had done a first-aid course, or at least she said she had. It had been pretty obvious to Andy from the minute that the fitness instructor had walked in that Catherine hadn't taken him to the gym purely out of friendship.

Andy sighed and got to his feet. He couldn't hold on any longer. He tucked his phone into his pocket and skipped down the steps, determined to be as quick as he could. In the alley to the side of Emily's flat, he unzipped himself and sighed loudly at the relief. A cloud of steam rose up from the puddle he carefully directed into the corner between the gate and the wall.

'Jesus wept, I needed that,' he said under his breath as he tucked himself away. Andy was desperate to get back into his sentry position and was struggling with his zip as he walked around the corner. His fingers were that bloody cold that he couldn't feel the thing properly. He managed to get the zip done up most of the way, and looked up at Emily's door to see her staring back at him, her mouth open and her hand frozen half way to the door with the key extended.

'Please tell me you weren't having a piss down the side of my flat?' she said in a tight voice.

'Er,' Andy replied, all the opening phrases he'd spent rehearsing what to say when he saw her disappearing from his head in an instant. 'Er…'

Emily muttered something he didn't hear, and put her key in the lock. Before he could react, she'd unlocked the door, stepped through it, and closed it behind her. Andy was left staring at the outside of the door.

'Fuck's sake, that went well,' Andy said, his breath clouding in front of his face. He had got absolutely no idea what to do next, so he just stood there. A few seconds later, he saw a flash of light on the small lawn he was standing on and he realised that Emily had opened her lounge curtains. He turned to see her opening the window and leaning out of it.

'What do you want?' she said. 'You'll catch your death, standing out there in the cold like that.' As if Andy needed reminding.

'I came round to say something, Emily,' he replied, trying and failing not to sound desperate.

'Well hurry up and say it, then,' Emily said. 'I'm freezing, and I've got the kettle on for a hot chocolate.'

Andy wracked his brains for something to say. Something memorable. He thought back over the films that they'd been to see together. If he could just pull something out of the bag to make her listen to him. He tapped his fingers against his leg. There was a phrase floating round in his head, out of his reach but very close. Emily looked as if she was just about to shut the window when it popped into his head.

'Emily, wait,' he said, sharply. She stared at him with her eyebrows raised. He paused for a second, going over a drawling American accent in his head, then he looked her in the eyes.

'I wish I knew how to quit you,' he said carefully, trying to pronounce it just like the bloke in the film had. It didn't sound quite right to him, but from the smile that ghosted across her face, he thought he'd hit the mark.

'Andy, do you remember what film that quote's from?' she asked.

'Er, nope,' he replied. 'But I remember we saw it together.' She nodded in agreement, and her smile grew broader. Bingo, Andy thought. Or was it a homerun? He wasn't sure, but he was feeling good about this. The next thing she said brought him right back to earth with a crash.

'So, Andy,' Emily said, crossing her arms. 'Let me get this straight. You come round to my flat, urinate down the side of it, and then stand in my front garden quoting lines from a gay cowboy film at me?' Too late, Andy remembered the film. 'What part of the phrase "we're done" are you struggling with exactly?'

Emily slid the window closed and pulled the curtains across. With a lump in his throat, Andy turned and walked down the path towards the road, not even glancing at the hedge that had started all this. He knew in his heart that this was the last time he would be walking down this path, and as he walked down the road away from Emily's flat, he pulled his phone out of his pocket. Andy was just about to call for an Uber when it buzzed in his hands. For a split second his heart soared. Emily must have relented and was texting him to get him to go back to her flat for a cocoa.

Fancy a pint? the message from Martin read.

33

The minute the words were out of Jack's mouth, he froze. He'd not told anyone round here about his parents. Even though he'd not told Catherine that much, it was still more than he told most people. His parents were the main reason for moving to this God-awful part of the country — so the story couldn't follow him like a bad smell. So why had he just told a woman he barely knew?

'Sorry,' he said to Catherine. 'I'm not sure why I told you that.' He turned to look at her, and saw her staring back at him with a look of astonishment.

'Are you serious?' she said, her sincerity obvious. 'Oh, my God. That must be awful for you.' He didn't reply, but just nodded.

'Yeah, it's pretty shit to be honest,' Jack replied with a wry smile. 'But looking on the bright side, if it weren't for that, then I wouldn't have all this.'

'Right,' Catherine said, frowning. 'Do you mind if I ask why she's in prison?' Jack didn't reply as he couldn't think of anything to say. He should have kept his mouth shut, but it was too late to do anything about that now, so he just shook his head.

'I'd rather not talk about it, to be honest.'

They sat in silence for a while, both engrossed in the flames of the log burner. Jack offered to fill up Catherine's glass, but she put her hand over the top of it saying that she was driving. He was disappointed, but even if she was up for any nonsense, he certainly wasn't given the gauze wrapping between his legs. Even if she had been up for it, Jack still wasn't sure she was his type.

'Well,' Jack said a moment later. 'That killed the conversation, didn't it?' Catherine blew a breath out of her cheeks.

'It's not something I was expecting you to say, that much is true.' She put her glass on the stone floor and turned to face him, folding her legs up underneath her on the sofa. 'Are you sure you don't want to talk about it? I'm a pretty good listener.'

'Not really,' Jack replied. 'Like I said, I'm not sure why I told you. It kind of slipped out.'

'Must be the bump to the head,' she said, smiling. 'How's it feeling?' Jack relaxed into the sofa, pleased that she'd changed the topic.

'It's a bit sore, but not too bad.' He raised his glass in her direction. 'This'll cure it, I'm sure.'

'I'm sure there's plenty of things that would take your mind off a bump to the head.'

'I'm sure there are,' he replied, taking a sip. That answered that question then, and it had only taken a single whisky with no additives. Catherine was starting to grow on him. 'If I didn't have a blinding headache, and needed about ten hours sleep, then I'd agree with you.' No point throwing the baby out with the bathwater, after all. The sly grin on her face told Jack she'd got the message.

'I guess I'd better be going then,' Catherine said, unfurling her legs and getting to her feet. 'Maybe we could carry on the conversation when you're feeling a bit better?'

'I'd like that a lot,' Jack replied, surprising himself. He looked at her standing in front of him like a shy schoolgirl. It might have been the flickering light from the fire, but she was a lot better looking than he'd thought earlier. She wasn't wearing baggy clothes like that stupid cow from the other night, and although she might have been carrying a few extra pounds than he'd normally like, there was nothing he could see that he couldn't get to grips with. Once his stitches had come out, that was.

'Can I maybe get your mobile number?' Catherine asked, giving Jack a shy smile. 'Might make things a bit easier?' Jack returned her smile and scribbled his mobile number down on a Post-It note before giving her the pen and the yellow block of sticky paper so that she could do the same. Numbers exchanged, they stood for a few seconds looking at each other like teenagers on a first date, neither of them sure what to do next.

A few moments later, with nothing more than a chaste kiss of his cheek and a hug with an air gap, she was gone.

Jack stood at the window of the farmhouse until he saw the red tail lights of Catherine's car disappear down the main road. When he was sure she had gone, he crossed to the sink and opened the drawer next to it. Inside the drawer, wrapped in a tea-towel that helpfully had pictures of garden birds on it, was a dark, metallic object. He picked it up and went back to the sofa to pour himself another shot of whisky. He was going to need some Dutch courage.

The gun was a Glock 19, a smaller version of the Glock 17 pistol favoured by law enforcement officers and criminals around the world. Large enough to pack a punch, but small enough to be carried as a secondary weapon or concealed somewhere like an ankle holster according to the website he'd been looking at. It had taken him ages to buy it, what with the gun laws in the United Kingdom, but eventually he'd managed to pick it up at the market in Snetterton. It had cost him a fair bit, but at least he knew there would be no trace anywhere of him buying it. Snetterton market was that kind of place.

'Right then,' he muttered under his breath, weighing the gun in his hand. It was time to teach that bitch in the abattoir a lesson she wouldn't forget.

34

'What do you mean, sacked?' Emily shouted through Catherine's bedroom door. 'They can't sack you.'

'They already did,' Catherine replied, opening the door a couple of inches. Emily peered through to see her getting changed into her pyjamas, even though it was still early evening. She obviously wasn't going out tonight, then.

'Bloody hell,' Emily said. 'You should have told me earlier. I would have tried to get off work early or something.'

'It doesn't matter. Besides, I was busy and I knew you were out with your boss.'

'Even so, Catherine. You could have texted me or something.'

A few moments later, they were sitting in the lounge, each holding a large glass of wine. Emily was trying not to be annoyed with Catherine, not for losing her job, but for not telling her. They were supposed to be best friends, after all.

'What are you going to do, then?' she asked Catherine.

'Not sure yet,' she replied. 'I've got some money saved up, so won't be homeless just yet. Something'll turn up, probably not in Human Resources though. I'm a bit too much of a people person for that field, I think.'

'You'll probably get on better if you keep your clothes on,' Emily said, a smile spreading across her face. 'I mean, it's not as if anyone's going to pay you to take them off, is it?'

'Cheeky cow,' Catherine replied. 'Like I said, something will turn up. I'll start looking in the morning. Worst case, we can turn the flat into a brothel. You can manage the appointments, I'll manage the punters.' Emily laughed for a few seconds at the idea before remembering that she was supposed to be annoyed with Catherine.

'So, what were you so busy with that you couldn't even text me earlier?' Emily asked. Catherine smirked in response. 'Or is that who, not what?'

'Might be a "who",' Catherine replied. 'You never know.'

'Come on, spill the beans.'

'How about if I told you he was quite fit?'

'No way! Not the instructor bloke from the gym?' Catherine's smirk broadened and she waited until Emily was just about to take a sip of wine.

'He's got a lovely house,' Catherine said, causing Emily to splutter into her wine glass.

'You've been round to his house?' she asked, wiping her chin with the back of her hand.

'Yep.'

'Bloody hell, Catherine,' Emily replied. 'The other day he barely even looked at you, and now you're in his sodding bed.' Catherine could be generous with her affection at times, but not normally when she was sober.

'I wasn't in his bed,' Catherine said. 'Just his house. He lives in that Hill Top Farm place. You know, that one…'

'Yeah, I know the one.'

'He's done it out lovely, though. It's been gutted and completely redone. There is something a bit mysterious about him though.'

'Good for him,' Emily said. She didn't have many happy memories of Hill Top Farm and couldn't see how it being re-decorated would make it any more appealing. 'Who were you at the gym with?' she asked, not wanting to talk about the farm any more. Catherine didn't reply, and when Emily looked at her she was frowning. 'Catherine?'

'Er, Andy,' she said after a long pause.

'My Andy?'

'Yep.'

'He was round here earlier, being all weird. I've never known him go the gym, though. He hasn't even got a pair of trainers.'

'Well, he has now.'

'Okay,' Emily said, trying to process the information. 'Right.'

'He wants to get into shape,' Catherine replied. 'Be a bit less, well, a bit less like Andy.'

'Not going to make any difference,' Emily muttered into her wine.

'What?'

'I said, it's not going to make any difference.'

'Oh for God's sake, Emily,' Catherine said. 'You bloody idiot. He's the best thing that's happened to you in years.' Emily didn't look at Catherine as she said this, knowing that she would have her earnest expression on. A few seconds later, Emily glanced over at Catherine.

'I just can't see a long-term future with a man who works in a phone shop.'

'Who said anything about a long-term future?' Catherine replied, picking up the bottle of wine and refilling Emily's glass. 'What's wrong with Carpe Diem?'

'What have fish got to do with it?'

'Sorry?'

'I don't get the carp reference.'

'Jesus, Emily. Carpe Diem. It's foreign for live in the moment, or something like that.'

'Catherine, can you shut up for a moment.'

'Why?'

'Because if you don't then I'm going to start crying,' Emily said, knowing from the lump in her throat that it was probably going to happen anyway, 'and I don't really want to do that.' She managed to hold it together until Catherine shuffled down the sofa to hug her. That was then Emily started crying in earnest.

'I don't get,' Catherine said a few moments later, 'why you're upset when it was you that dumped him.' Emily wiped her nose and bunched the tissue paper into the sleeve of her jumper.

'It's not that simple,' she replied with a loud sniff. 'I can't just live for the moment, Catherine. I'm not like you.'

'So what's the plan, then? Are you just going to shag about for a bit and then welcome him back when you've got it out of your system?'

'I said I'm not like you, Catherine,' Emily replied with a smile. 'I haven't got a plan. I'm just going to take a break, and have a bit of a think.'

'Well just don't think for too long,' Catherine said. 'Andy's not made of wood, after all. You might try to welcome him back to your skinny little bosom and find he's been sowing his wild oats around half of Norwich.'

'I doubt it,' Emily mumbled.

'Yeah, me too,' Catherine replied. 'But just be careful,

that's all I'm saying.' She nodded at Emily's hand. 'You
might want to write that number down somewhere before
your snot wipes it off completely.' Emily looked down at
her hand to see the policeman's phone number starting to
fade. She grabbed a pen off the table and wrote the
number on the back of an advert for solar panels before
turning to see Catherine staring at her, eyebrows raised.
'And whose number is that, exactly?'

'Oh, God, I never told you about lunch, did I?'

'Don't avoid the question.'

'I'm not, I'll tell you later,' Emily replied, even though
she had no intention of telling Catherine about the incident with William. 'What size are you again?'

'What?'

'Ten on top, twelve on the bottom?'

'Cheeky bitch,' Catherine retorted. 'Just because you're
upset doesn't mean I won't poke you in the eye with a
fingernail.'

'Seriously, what size are you?'

'Depends on the shop, but you're not that far off the
mark. Why? What has my dress size got to do with
your lunch?'

'It's Mr Clayton,' Emily replied, grinning. 'He told me
something today, in the strictest confidence so I can't say a
word to anyone.'

'Which was what, exactly?' Catherine asked, leaning
forwards and giggling.

'I can't say what. I promised. But can he borrow some
of your clothes? Mine wouldn't fit him.'

'Seriously?'

'Seriously,' Emily replied. 'I'm on make-up, you're on
clothes.' She watched as Catherine realised that she wasn't
joking.

'Blimey, I wasn't expecting that.'

'Neither was I,' Emily muttered, taking another sip of her wine.

35

'Don't shoot, don't shoot!' Jack tried, and failed, not to jump when Beth screamed after seeing the gun in his hand. He tightened his grip, hoping that his hand wouldn't shake too much. 'Why have you got a gun?' she shrieked. 'We're not in bloody America. This is England, for fuck's sake.'

'Just sit on the commode and put your hands on the arms,' he said, as calmly as he could. 'Nice and slowly.' He watched as Beth made her way from the bed to the chair, never taking her eyes off the gun.

Jack had sat in his van outside the abattoir for a good ten minutes, plucking up the courage to actually threaten the woman with the gun. He didn't really want to have to use it, but the ache in his testicles told him that she couldn't be trusted, and he couldn't think of another way to subdue her. He'd finally managed to pluck up the courage to get out of the van and into the building. He was in charge, after all. Even more so now that she knew he had a gun.

When Beth was sitting on the commode, her hands clutching the arms so tightly that her knuckles were white,

Jack stepped into the abattoir. He looped heavy duty tie wraps around her wrists — not too tightly as he didn't want to leave any marks on her skin — and made sure that they were secure before he tucked the gun into his belt and knelt down to restrain her ankles the same way. Even though they were extra-large tie wraps, they only just fit around her legs. It was, Jack noticed, difficult to tell where Beth's calves ended and her ankles began.

'Why are you doing this?' she asked him as he sat on the bed and looked at her. 'What have I done to you?'

'Nothing, Beth,' Jack said with a sigh. 'Don't take it personally.'

'Don't take it personally?' she replied, her voice high. 'You've kidnapped me and you're force feeding me like a fucking goose, and I'm not supposed to take it personally?' Jack glanced at the tube and sealant gun on the table just outside Beth's bedroom.

'Are you peckish?' he asked, ignoring her question.

'Bloody starving,' she said. 'But I don't want the gas. Can't I just drink that stuff you're giving me?'

'No, it won't work that way,' Jack replied. 'It's got to go down the tube. It's too thick to drink.'

'Well, I'll swallow the tube then,' Beth said, closing her eyes for a second. 'Like you tried that first time. With the jam?' Jack remembered her staring at him with her face covered in his mother's favourite jam and thought for a few seconds.

'Okay,' he said, getting to his feet and leaving Beth's bedroom to get his things.

'That's it, swallow,' Jack said, inching the tube into her mouth a bit more. He'd lathered the end of the pipe with as much jam as he could, leaving several large blobs of the red jelly on the floor. 'And again.' He pushed the tube further in as he saw Beth's neck working. She made a gurgling sound, and her eyes widened. 'Once more.' The minute he saw her neck start to move again he pushed the pipe, sliding it down her throat until he felt a bit of resistance. The pipe was either deep in her stomach, or jammed into her lungs. He'd find out in a minute. 'There you go, all done,' he whispered, watching her carefully. Any signs at all that she was starting to go blue, and he'd have to take it out and get the gas. 'How you doing?' Seeing as Beth had a large pipe sticking out of her mouth, it was a slightly unfair question, but she nodded her head a couple of times.

It didn't take him long at all to feed her. Jack wondered as he squeezed the sealant gun whether he could water down his special recipe so that she could drink it, but he didn't think that she'd be able to get as much volume in her stomach as he could cram in with the sealant gun. He'd prepared five tubes for tonight's session. High in fat, high in calories. The perfect meal for weight gain, and although he needed to weigh her again at some point, Beth was going to have to put on a fair few more pounds until she would fit into the dress.

By the time he'd emptied the fifth tube, Beth's eyes were starting to glaze over. He pulled the pipe out, making sure that it didn't touch him, and she belched loudly. Jack reached into his pocket for his pliers, and used them to snip the ties. Ankles first, then Beth's wrists. She barely moved at all as he back tracked to the door to her bedroom, closing the door firmly behind him and locking it.

Ten minutes later, he was safely in his workshop. Jack watched his phone screen as Beth made her way from the chair and over to the bed. She was rolling herself onto it as he unwrapped the tissue paper from the piece of wood that he'd lovingly fastened into his vice, and by the time he was happy the acacia was secure, Beth looked as if she was fast asleep.

Jack had already used a gouge chisel to get the wood to the rough shape that he wanted. He didn't use any designs or pencil markings to guide his creation. He didn't need to. He knew exactly how he wanted the candlestick to look, and he didn't want to sully its beauty with any pencil marks. For the next half an hour, he carefully took off shaving after shaving, enjoying the way that the wood started to turn from a block into something much more beautiful. Jack stroked the wood before unfastening the vice, lifting the wood out, and crossing to the lathe. Once the wood was secure in the lathe, he glanced over at the phone screen to make sure that Beth was sound asleep, before turning the lathe on and picking up a straight skew chisel. When Jack touched the chisel to the fast spinning piece of wood, he felt a familiar thrill of excitement course through him as a thin sliver of wood shaving peeled itself away from the main block, leaving the smoothest of grooves in the wood.

'Perfect,' he muttered to himself as he readied the chisel in his hands for another sliver.

36

C atherine took a large sip from her mug of tea as she stared at the laptop screen. When Emily had left for work earlier that morning, Catherine had promised her that she would start looking for a job. Emily hadn't said anything, but Catherine knew she was concerned that there weren't that many decent jobs in Norwich. Just before they'd gone to bed last night, Emily had started muttering phrases like 'there might not be much out there' and 'it's not as easy as you think.' The problem was that Emily was right. Catherine scrolled through the jobs on the website she was looking at — apparently the home for every available job in Norfolk — and there really wasn't much about at all. Unless she wanted to flip burgers or wash pots in a pub kitchen, she was buggered.

She looked briefly at an advert for a 'customer services assistant' that turned out to be not much more than a cleaner in a grotty nightclub on Riverside, and was just reading the description for a call centre operative' that sounded like a thinly veiled phone sex line when her phone buzzed.

Fancy the gym today?

It was from Andy. Emily's ex-boyfriend Andy, although Catherine still wasn't clear on whether or not he actually realised that yet.

Sure. she replied. *What time?*

After lunch okay? At least that gave Catherine some time to keep looking for something, she thought as she told him that she would pick him up at one o'clock. She switched tabs on her laptop to bring up Linked In, and toyed with the idea of changing her employment status to 'available', but she couldn't stand the thought of all the e-mails she would get from gloating ex-friends asking her what had happened.

Thirty minutes later, she had downloaded a few application forms for various jobs that didn't look too demeaning and even got as far as filling one of them out. The problem was that she didn't really fancy the idea of being an office junior again. Sighing, she got to her feet and closed the lid of her laptop.

'You okay, babes?' Catherine called to Andy through the open window of her car as she pulled up next to him. He was standing on the pavement outside his parents' house, looking particularly miserable in his shorts and running top with a battered hold-all in his hand.

'I've had better days,' he said as he opened the passenger door after throwing his gym bag into the boot. 'How about you? Life on the dole treating you well?'

'I'm not on the dole, Andy,' Catherine grinned. 'I'm just in between jobs at the moment.'

'Of course, sorry,' he replied, mirroring her smile. 'Lady of leisure, so you are.' She felt her smile slip a notch.

'Not for long, hopefully.'

'You've not found anything yet then, I take it?'

'Jesus, Andy. Give me chance,' Catherine shot back, instantly irritated. 'I only got sacked yesterday. Bloody hell, you're worse than Emily.' As soon as she said her flat mate's name, Catherine realised her mistake. 'Sorry, I didn't mean…'

'She told you then,' Andy replied, looking away from Catherine and out of the passenger window.

'Yeah, she told me.' Catherine reached across and rubbed Andy's arm. 'She's my best friend, babes. Of course she told me.'

'You got any advice, then?' he asked a moment later.

'For you or for Emily?'

'For me,' Andy replied with a quick laugh. Catherine thought about her advice yesterday to Emily about shagging about for a bit, and decided not to suggest the same thing to Andy just in case he took her literally.

'Give her time,' she said. 'She said it's a break, yeah? Not that she never wants to see your ugly mug again.' Andy nodded thoughtfully. 'Like on *Friends*.'

'I don't watch it,' Andy said. Probably just as well, Catherine thought. It hadn't worked out that well for Ross and Rachel if she remembered right. 'I could have a look and see if it's on Netflix, I suppose.'

'No, no, don't do that,' Catherine said quickly. 'It's not very funny. Really girly. You wouldn't get it. Besides, Emily hates it.'

They drove on in silence until Catherine pulled into the gym car park, reversing into a space next to a battered van with blacked out windows.

'That's a right serial killer van, that is,' Andy said as he retrieved his gym bag from the boot. 'You wouldn't get in it if you were hitch-hiking, would you?'

'Probably not,' Catherine laughed, getting out of the

car. 'Right then,' she asked him as they walked across the car park, 'what are we going to work on today? Just cardio, or maybe a few weights as well?'

'Er, just cardio I think,' Andy replied. 'One step at a time.'

'Look at him,' Andy said from his position on the treadmill next to Catherine's. He nodded at the other side of the gym to where Jack was effortlessly curling dumb bells in front of a full-length mirror. Catherine didn't need Andy to point Jack out to her. She'd been watching the fitness instructor for the last ten minutes. 'Bloody loves himself, doesn't he?'

'Mmm,' Catherine replied. Although Andy was right, there was something mesmerising about the way Jack was working his arms, which were displayed for everyone to see courtesy of a thin singlet. His arms went up, and down. Up, and down. Up, and again, down.

'Catherine?'

'Yeah, sorry,' she replied, looking over at Andy. The contrast between him and Jack was quite marked. 'I was miles away.'

'Yeah,' Andy replied, shooting a glance at Jack. 'I thought women were more about personality and depth than personal grooming and muscles?'

'Generally speaking, we are,' Catherine replied with another dreamy look at Jack. 'But grooming and muscle helps a bit, that's all.'

'Right,' Andy said, leaning forward and increasing the speed on his treadmill. 'Maybe I will do some weights after all.'

37

'You've not told anyone about our conversation, have you Emily?' Mr Clayton looked at her over the top of his reading glasses. She was sitting in his office, fidgeting in the chair opposite his desk, and preparing the lie.

'No,' she said, her voice coming out in a squeak. 'No,' she replied, this time an octave lower. 'Of course not.' He sat back and steepled his fingers, staring at her. Although she could feel the colour rising to her cheeks, Emily made a conscious effort to stop fidgeting. Mr Clayton paused for a few seconds, his eyes boring into hers before continuing. Emily was sure she heard the door behind her opening, but she couldn't turn round and look while he was staring at her.

'Do you know, afterwards the only thing I felt was relief,' Mr Clayton said, rubbing the bridge of his nose. 'It's been like a bloody pressure cooker building up inside me.' He leaned forward and grabbed Emily's hand in his own, making her jump. 'But then that moment with you in the hotel, the relief was incredible. Like a volcano erupting.' She looked at him and saw him glance sharply behind her over her shoulder. Mr Clayton's entire expression changed in an instant, and he let go of her hand as if it was red hot. 'Can I help you, Miss Daniels?'

Emily turned to see the hook-nosed cow from Marketing standing at Mr Clayton's office door, her mouth open. Her eyes flicked between Mr Clayton and Emily, and she managed to close her mouth for a second before it fell open again. She'd obviously heard what he had just said.

'Er,' Miss Daniels said, recovering. 'Sorry to interrupt, Mr Clayton. But your one o'clock appointment is waiting for you in the main conference room upstairs.'

'Thank you, Miss Daniels,' Mr Clayton replied. 'I'll be there in a moment.' He stared at her for a second. 'That'll be all.' The woman from Marketing gave Emily a sly smile that only lasted for a fraction of a second before turning on her heel and walking out of the office.

'Great,' Emily muttered. 'That's all I bloody need.'

By the time Emily was in her car driving to her next inspection, she'd managed to put the whole incident pretty much to the back of her mind. When the cow from Marketing had interrupted them, they'd only been talking after all. It wasn't as if they were having sex on Mr Clayton's desk, was it? Emily thought about Catherine and the reason that she'd been sacked from the agency, and started laughing. If you had to get sacked from a place, you might as well go out with a bang.

She parked outside the pub she'd come to inspect — a dreary looking place on the way out of Norwich that got most of its trade from football traffic — and reached for her phone. When she unlocked it, she realised that she'd had a text message from an unknown number. Frowning, she prodded at the screen with a finger.

Hey Emily. Would you like to go out for a drink or maybe a meal this evening? Just for a chat, not for sex or anything.

Her frown deepened. One thing Emily didn't do was give out her number to anyone she didn't actually know. She thought for a second or two before replying.

Who is this? She typed before adding *please* to the message. No reason to be rude after all. Emily picked up her briefcase from the passenger footwell when the phone buzzed.

It's me.

'Oh, for God's sake,' Emily muttered. Andy must have got a new phone from work. She could imagine him and Martin, sniggering in a pub somewhere. Andy had probably gone to the bar to get a round in, leaving his phone on the bar for Martin to pick up and abuse. It had happened several times before. At least Martin had toned it down a bit, which told Emily that Andy had told his friend about them being on a break.

The last time Martin had got hold of his phone, she and Andy had had a big argument. It was, in fairness to Andy, mostly him trying to explain that he didn't actually want to tie her up and paddle her backside until she was red raw. When they'd both realised what had happened, it had descended into another argument about the fact that — according to one of the other text messages at least — Martin seemed to think that Emily had a cute little arse that was just begging to be reddened. At least Catherine had found it funny when Emily had explained it to her, and had managed to persuade Emily to apologise to Andy for being such a nun about it.

Emily put her phone on silent and threw it into her briefcase before making her way into the pub. She stopped for a few seconds on the threshold, knowing that she would be walking out a couple of hours later leaving nothing behind but a sticker with three stars for their window. It was the same every time. It wouldn't be good enough for anything more, nor would it be quite shit enough for anything less.

Sure enough, that was exactly how it played out. By the time she handed the sullen landlord his certificate and sticker, she couldn't wait to leave the place and get back to her flat. Her mood brightened as she walked back over to her car. Emily was day-dreaming about a very hot bath, followed by a nice cup of cocoa if Catherine hadn't found Emily's secret supply, and then an early night with nothing more exciting going on in her bed than a good book. She blipped the lock of her car doors and was just settling into the driver's seat when she heard her phone buzzing in her briefcase. When the buzzing continued, she realised it was an incoming call, so fished her phone out and looked at the screen. It was Andy, on his new number, no doubt calling to apologise for letting Martin get hold of it. Emily's thumb hovered over the red cross that would reject the call for a second before she relented. Hearing him all apologetic wouldn't be all bad, she thought as she made a conscious effort to sound angry.

'What?' Emily barked into the phone when she raised it to her ear.

'Hello? Is that Emily?' a male voice asked. Her heart sank when she realised it wasn't Andy.

'Who is this?'

'It's me.'

'Can you give me a little bit more to go on than that, perhaps?' she replied, the annoyance in her voice genuine.

'William.' William? Emily asked herself. The policeman?

'The policeman,' the voice said.

'Oh,' she said, not quite sure how to feel about his

earlier text message. The one about wanting to meet for a drink or a meal, but not necessarily sex. 'Hi.'

'Hi,' William replied, his voice brightening. 'Did you get my text message?'

'Yeah, I did,' Emily said.

'So,' he drew the word out. 'What are you doing this evening?' Emily thought for a moment. Washing her hair was too obvious, and she wasn't about to confess that her actual plans were a bath, cocoa, and a book. Not to a man who was, if she remembered correctly, rather nice looking and had a proper job. For an instant, Emily's mind drifted back to Catherine's advice about being more like her and having some fun. She pushed a brief thought of Andy to the back of her mind — they were on a break, after all.

'Can you pick me up at eight?'

Emily stared at the phone after William had ended the call, arranging to collect her at eight on the dot. Her fingers were trembling, and she could feel her cheeks were red. If she felt like this after a phone call, what would it be like if...

'Oh my God,' Emily muttered under her breath. 'What did I just do?'

38

'No, mate,' Andy said, crossing his arms to show Martin that he meant business and staring at the closed door on the other side of the road. 'I'm not going in there.'

'Oh, come on,' Martin replied, shifting a large stuffed cuddly elephant that was on his lap. 'It'll be a laugh.'

The two of them were sitting on a bench on the seafront in Great Yarmouth. For some reason, the bench faced away from the sea and towards the town, but it did give them a very good view of the building opposite them. As they watched, a man shuffled up to the small grey door, looked in both directions to see if anyone was watching him, and then knocked on the door. A second later, the door opened, and the man walked through it. The door shut behind him with a bang that they could hear from their vantage point.

'Nope,' Andy said. 'Waste of bloody money.'

'I told you, I'm paying.'

Andy and Martin had spent most of the day in Great Yarmouth, getting the train from Norwich so that they could both have a skinful. At least, that's what Martin had told Andy when he'd said that they were going to paint the town red. Andy had told Martin about the fact that he and Emily were 'on a break', and Martin had sprung into action with a plan to take Andy's mind off it all. That was why the two of them were sitting on Yarmouth seafront, staring at a door.

"Martin, listen,' Andy said with a sigh. 'The Sea Life Centre was great, especially the penguins. The amusement arcades were excellent, and we've got something to show for it.' He nodded at the elephant on Martin's lap. 'Fish and chips in Harry Ramsden? Bloody London prices for a bit of battered cod and soggy chips, but very nice even so.'

'If you'd not put so much vinegar on your chips, they wouldn't have been soggy. You're itching to say something beginning with but though, so spit it out.'

'It's been a great day, Martin,' Andy continued, 'but where I do draw the line is spending the rest of the evening at Fallen Angels.'

'Andy, it's–'

'Yeah, I know,' Andy interrupted. 'It's Great Yarmouth's premiere lap dancing venue. You've told me that I don't know how many times, and it's on the sides of virtually every bloody bus in Norwich.'

Martin pulled his phone from his pocket and swiped at the screen.

'Look at this one,' he said, waving the phone at Andy. The phone was moving too quickly for Andy to see the screen properly, but he didn't need to. It was at least the third time that Martin had tried to show him this partic-ular dancer. 'She'll take your mind off Emily. She's on most of the Yellow Line buses to Wroxham, she is.'

'Let me see,' Andy replied, reaching out to steady Martin's arm. When he looked at the woman on the screen, a pouting face stared back at him. The photo was washed out, as if the flash had been too strong, and the woman had a faintly startled expression behind the horn-rimmed glasses she was wearing. 'Bloody hell, Martin. She's rough as anything.'

'It's not the best picture, I'll give you that,' Martin replied. 'But just imagine her shaking her wobbly bits in your face.'

'I'd rather not, mate,' Andy said. 'Can we not just go to a pub and watch the football? Norwich is on Sky later. We could get the train back to Norwich and go to one of the pubs on Riverside.'

'How's that going to help you forget about Emily?'

'It's not,' Andy replied. 'Not any more than that fat slapper jiggling round on my lap would.'

The two of them watched as another lone man slipped in through the door of the lap dancing club. Martin leaned in towards Andy and lowered his voice even though there was no-one else in sight.

'They do extras, mate,' Martin whispered. 'That's what I've heard.' He looked at Andy and winked. 'If you know what I mean?'

'Oh well in that case, what are we still doing here?' Andy replied, putting as much sarcasm into his voice as he could as he crossed his arms.

Twenty minutes later, Andy was shivering on the bench when the door to the club opposite flew open, and Martin came out, assisted by a burly hand from a bouncer Andy could just see inside the door. Martin slipped on the pavement and was still trying to regain his balance when the door slammed behind him. He recovered, and by the time he walked back over to where Andy was sitting, Martin had a wry smile on his face.

'Can we go now?' Andy asked, getting to his feet. 'Kick off is in about an hour. I think we should find somewhere here.'

'Yeah, okay,' Martin replied. 'I could do with a pint.'

'So, how was she?'

'Who?'

'Whoever you just exchanged fluids with?'

'Oh,' Martin replied, his smile broadening. 'They don't do extras.' Andy looked at his friend and started laughing at his expression as Martin continued. 'Nor do they like you asking, so it turns out.'

'I think you probably had a lucky escape, to be honest,' Andy said, glancing at the grey door. They both stood and started walking along the promenade. 'You'll catch more than a cold in there, I reckon.'

'Premier lap dancing club, my arse.'

'What I don't understand,' Andy said as the train left the station and started gathering speed, 'is how there isn't a single pub in the entire town of Great Yarmouth that's got Sky.' Martin cracked open the top of a can of Stella, passing it to Andy before opening another one for himself.

'It's because the whole town is shit,' Martin replied as Andy took a hefty swig of tepid lager. 'The only thing that's great about Yarmouth is the train back to Norwich.'

'That bloke got a right arse on though, didn't he?'

'Well we were sitting in his garden on his patio chairs trying to watch the footy through his window,' Martin said with a laugh that blew a large bubble of frothy lager from the top of his can. It landed on the table between them.

'Even the off-licenses are shit,' Andy said. 'Call me a

pedant, but I prefer lager that's been in a fridge at some point in the last couple of weeks.'

'Paedo.'

'What?'

'You just told me to call you a paedo,' Martin replied, 'so you're a paedo.'

'I said pedant.'

'Same thing, isn't it?' The two of them laughed raucously, ignoring the disapproving looks of the other passengers on the train. Martin turned to a middle-aged woman who was sitting on the other side of the train carriage, trying to read a newspaper. 'Excuse me?' The woman looked at him with barely disguised hostility. 'Excuse me?'

'What?' she barked in an unusually deep voice. Martin pointed at Andy who was trying to empty his can in one long slug.

'Never, ever,' Martin said, extending a finger in Andy's direction, 'let that man there babysit.'

The woman glanced between Andy and Martin before sighing.

'Don't worry, I won't,' she said as she raised her paper in front of her face.

39

'Can you at least try and sit still for a bit?' Jack said. He was beginning to get a bit annoyed with Beth, who was currently spinning slowly round. She was suspended in a large canvas sling, but the weighing scales on the hoist wouldn't settle because she kept wriggling in the canvas.

'But it's uncomfortable,' Beth whined. 'The material's going right up my arse.'

Jack focused on the LCD screen with her weight on it. It kept flipping between numbers, and every time she moved the numbers changed.

'Well if you don't bloody sit still then you'll be hanging there all evening.' Jack glanced at Beth, but she currently had her back to him. A few seconds later, she'd swung back round and was looking at him through piggy little eyes. Even though she looked innocent enough, swinging there like a carcass, Jack didn't trust Beth an inch. His tattered bollocks were testament to that.

'Alright, princess,' she said. 'Keep your hair on. I don't want to be here all night any more than you want me to be. I'm bloody starving.' Just as she said this, the numbers on the LCD screen flashed a couple of times before staying constant. Jack squinted at the numbers and wrote them down on a notepad.

'Excellent, Beth,' he said with a grin. 'You've done really well. That's almost seven kilograms in the last few days.'

'Oh, good,' Beth replied. 'Can I get down now, please?'

Jack pressed a button on the hoist, and the metal arm that was holding her up in the air complained as it lowered her to the floor. He took a few steps backward, checking behind his back to make sure that the gun was still where it was supposed to be in his waistband. Jack hadn't needed to even show her the gun when he'd opened the door earlier, but he suspected that might have been because he also had a large carrier bag with him that was full of biscuits. The minute Beth had seen what was in the bag, she'd become quite compliant.

The hoist deposited Beth onto the stone floor, and she rolled herself onto her knees before finally managing to get to her feet. Breathless, she made her way over to the commode and sat on it, clamping her hands onto the arms.

'Come on then, big lad,' she said, arching an eyebrow in Jack's direction. 'Bring on the pipe.'

Jack had still fastened Beth's arms and legs to the commode before he fed her. She'd not complained once, and had even opened her mouth as he approached her with the jam covered pipe. By the time he'd emptied the fifth sealant tube into her stomach, she was almost asleep. Jack cut the tie wraps and retreated to the door as Beth lumbered to her feet. She glanced at him briefly as she picked up the carrier bag and made her way to the bed, rolling onto it and opening a packet of dark chocolate

Hob-Nobs in one motion. As he closed the door and secured it from the outside, he could hear her tucking into the biscuits like she'd not been fed for days.

Back in the farmhouse, Jack perched his phone next to his lathe and put his safety goggles on. On the screen of his mobile, Beth was barely moving. If it weren't for the occasional movement of her hand from the carrier bag to her mouth, Jack would have thought she was asleep. He picked up a chisel and was just about to touch it to the candlestick that was now spinning in front of him when his phone buzzed with an incoming text message.

Hey you. What are you up to? It was from Catherine. Jack smiled, remembering the conversation they'd had the other night as he composed a reply.

Doing a bit of wood working.

Jack took a deep breath as he inched the chisel towards the candlestick. He touched the rapidly spinning wood and gasped as a thin sliver of wood shaving pared away from the main block. His phone buzzed again and he sat back, momentarily distracted.

Maybe I could come round and help you work with your wood?

Jack laughed, wondering how intentional Catherine's double entendre was. His laugh dwindled as he realised it was probably entirely intentional. Nice idea, but with a few days to go before his stitches came out, it wasn't going to happen. But once the stitches were out and he was back up to full operating capacity, maybe he could offer her some splinter free wood then? Jack wasn't sure, but he was fairly sure that she wouldn't be that impressed with a scrotum that looked like a Frankenstein experiment gone wrong. Nor did he want to rip his stitches open mid-shag.

Sure. Jack replied. If she threw herself at him, and Jack

wouldn't blame her if she did, then he could just deal with that then. *You know where I am.*

Thirty minutes.

Exactly twenty-two minutes later, Jack heard his doorbell ring. He stopped the lathe, smiled, and detached the block of wood from the machine. If Catherine had been in Norwich when she'd texted him earlier, she must have broken several speed limits. After wrapping his creation in tissue paper and putting it in the corner of his workshop, he opened the front door and greeted her with what he hoped was a disarming grin. She smiled back at him and kissed him on the cheek.

'Hey you,' she said as she breezed past him, leaving a faint trace of perfume as she walked into the kitchen. 'Busy day?'

'Not too bad,' Jack replied. 'Can I get you a drink?'

'Ooh, you read my mind. Have you got any wine?' He went to the fridge and pulled out a bottle of cheap white wine he'd picked up from the garage near the Thickthorn roundabout.

'Will I put some music on?' Catherine nodded enthusiastically.

'Any requests?' he asked Catherine.

'I don't mind,' she replied. 'How about you put on a song that describes you? Then we can have an interesting conversation about why it's that one.'

'Alexa?' Jack called out. 'Play my song.'

A few moments later, they were sitting in the same positions on the sofa as they had been the other night, the only real difference being that Jack hadn't lit the log burner yet.

Dusty Springfield was singing about how the only man who could really please her just happened to be the son of a preacher man.

'Seriously?' Catherine said. 'Son of a preacher man?'

'Yeah, well,' Jack replied. 'My old man was a vicar.'

'Oh,' she said in a quiet voice. From the look on her face, Jack realised that she was thinking about what he had told her the other night. 'Can I ask what actually happened?' The first word that sprung to Jack's mind, not for the first time and certainly not for the last, was extreme violence.

'I'd rather not talk about it, to be honest.'

'Okay, that's cool. Would you rather talk about something else?'

'Yeah,' Jack replied, relieved that she'd decided to change the subject before he had to.

Jack had poured Catherine a glass of wine, and even though he didn't really drink it, one for himself as well. Catherine was busy telling Jack about how she'd left her job at the human resources department she'd been working at because of what she called 'creative differences' between her and her immediate boss. He was doing a good enough job of pretending to be interested, or at least he thought he was, but his mind kept drifting back to Beth, and how much more weight she would need to put on before she fit the dress.

'Are you okay?' Catherine asked, interrupting his thoughts. Too late, he realised that she'd finished talking about her job. 'You look miles away.'

'Er,' Jack replied, thinking on his feet. 'I was just thinking about something, that was all.' He flashed her a quick grin, hoping that she wouldn't ask him what he was thinking about.

'Sorry, I talk too much' she said, leaning towards him

and plucking the wine glass from his hand. She bent over and put the glass on the floor, and when she sat back up, she was much closer to him than she had been a few seconds before. 'I think you should kiss me to shut me up.'

Jack thought for a second about his tattered scrotum before he answered her.

'Just a kiss?' he asked her.

'To start with,' Catherine replied as she moved even closer. 'Then why don't we see what happens.'

40

'It's only a meal,' Emily muttered at her reflection in the mirror as she tried to decide whether or not to go all out on the make up, stay subtle, or just go naked. From a make up perspective. In the end, she chose the middle ground, and applied a thin layer of foundation and some neutral coloured lipstick. 'Only a meal.'

Emily glanced at her watch. It was almost quarter to eight, so she didn't have long to wait. Since she'd spoken to William earlier that afternoon, she'd picked up her phone several times to call or text him and cancel, but each time she'd bottled it. It was far too late now to do anything, so she was going to have to go through with it. Catherine would be proud of her, but she wasn't about and hadn't replied to any of Emily's text messages. Which meant, if past experience was anything to go by, whatever she was doing probably involved sexual activity of some sort. Emily was in fact quite pleased that Catherine wasn't in — she would be fussing around, making sure that Emily had got the right sort of lingerie on as opposed to the Bridget Jones style underwear she was actually wearing, and offering pointless and unwanted advice straight from the pages of Cosmopolitan magazine. Emily was feeling bad enough already about going out for a meal with William without Catherine making it worse, no matter how well intentioned she was.

The doorbell rang, and Emily jumped. *Bloody hell*, she mumbled to herself. *He's sodding early.* She scooted through to the kitchen and grabbed the already open bottle of wine from the fridge. No time for a glass, she told herself as she glugged a couple of large mouthfuls direct from the bottle.

When she opened the front door a few seconds later, William was standing on the doorstep clutching a bunch of daffodils in his hand. He was wearing a pair of brown corduroy trousers, black slip on shoes, and a burgundy tweed jacket over a bright yellow shirt. It was, Emily thought, an interesting combination of clothing. He thrust the flowers at her, smiling widely.

'Look, I brought you some flowers.'

'Oh, how lovely of you,' Emily replied, looking with suspicion at the sad looking flowers in his hand. They were tied up with an elastic band as opposed to wrapped in anything. She took them from him and returned his smile.

'Do you mind if I use your loo? I'm bursting.' William hopped from foot to foot, still with a huge grin plastered on his face.

'Of course,' Emily replied. 'First on the right, just there.' She nodded over her shoulder. 'I'll go and put these in some water.'

While William used the lavatory, Emily took the daffodils into the kitchen and filled a pint glass with water. As she put the flowers into it, she realised that the bases of the stems were ripped, not cut.

'I love your bathroom,' Emily heard William call out. She glanced at the bathroom door, and realised that it was open. 'It's very blue, isn't it?' A few seconds later, he stepped through the door, still zipping up his flies. Emily frowned but decided not to mention the whole hand washing thing. When she walked past the still open bathroom door and noticed that the seat was still down, her frown deepened. Unless she was very much mistaken, William's aim wasn't particularly good. If nothing else, that would give Catherine a surprise when she got back if Emily was still out.

'So Emily, you just go on and choose whatever you want from the menu. Don't worry about the price. I'm paying for everything, so have whatever you want.'

Emily looked at William over the table between them. Her already bad feeling about the whole evening was getting a whole lot worse. In fact, when they'd walked into the restaurant, she'd been on the verge of turning round and walking straight back out again.

'Okay,' she said, looking back at the menu. 'Can I have a bacon double cheeseburger meal please. With coke.'

'Do you want to supersize that?' William asked. 'It's only an extra one pound thirty, and you get loads more bacon and a massive bag of fries?' He pointed at the relevant part of the plastic covered menu

'No, William,' Emily replied through thin lips. 'I don't want to supersize that.'

As William scampered across to order from the counter, Emily looked over at the door to the Burger Queen they were sitting in. The restaurant was in the middle of Castle Mall, which at one point had been Norwich's only shopping mall. When it's bigger and better competitor had opened elsewhere in the city, it had started going downhill and never really recovered. There was a cinema upstairs that she could go and hide in if she did do a runner.

'They're going to bring it over,' William said as he sat back down, and Emily realised she had left it too late for an escape. 'That's why I love this place so much. They really do look after you. So, tell me about yourself then? What's it like being a food inspector?'

They chatted for a few moments while they waited for their food, Emily trying as hard as she could to have a normal conversation. It wasn't helped by a bunch of young lads pulling faces at her from over William's shoulder. They were annoying at first, but when one of them got to his feet and thrust his hips back and forth and mimed slapping the backside of his imaginary bent over partner, Emily could feel the corners of her mouth starting to twitch.

It turned out that William wasn't a fan of talking and eating at the same time, and they ended up eating their food in silence. The only conversation they had was when Emily dropped a large dollop of ketchup mixed with mayonnaise on the back of her hand.

'Here,' William had said, putting what was left of his burger on the table. 'Let me get that for you.' Reluctantly, Emily let him take her wrist and pull it towards her, but instead of wiping her hand with a tissue, he licked it clean.

'Sorry, just need to nip to the ladies,' Emily said when they had both finished their meal. She got to her feet, grabbed her handbag, and rushed for the toilets to wash her hands and find the fire exit. A few moments later, she was back at the table. If there was ever a fire in the Castle Mall, trying to escape through the toilets wouldn't be an option. 'Gosh, I'm tired,' Emily said, not even sitting back down at the table. She mimed a yawn and started to stretch her arms. When she realised that William was staring at her breasts, she crossed her arms over her chest instead.

'Cool,' William said with a ketchup stained grin. 'Are we going to go back to your flat and have sex now?'

They were walking back to William's car in the underground car park. Emily had tried to insist that she was more than capable of getting a taxi, but he wouldn't have it. He told Emily that his mother would kill him if she knew that he'd let a young lady make her own way home after a date. Emily shuddered at the use of the word 'date', but at least he'd not asked her again about having sex. It was, Emily had said, a lovely offer but not one that she wanted to take him up on. When she'd explained about her strict Catholic upbringing, and about how angry God would be if she didn't wait for her wedding night, he'd seemed to understand. Emily just hoped that God would, come the time.

A few feet from his car, William grabbed Emily's wrist and pulled her round to face him. She looked at him, realising that his grip on her wrist was tighter than it should be.

'How about just a kiss, then?' he asked.

'God's watching, William,' Emily replied, shaking her head.

'I don't believe in God, though.' William tightened his grip on her wrist and started pulling her towards him. Emily was just preparing to deliver a swift but very decisive knee to his bollocks when she heard another male voice from a few feet away.

'Is this bloke bothering you?' She turned to face the

voice, but the fluorescent lights meant that all she could see was a silhouette.

'Who are you?' William asked. The silhouette stepped forward, and Emily almost laughed with relief.

'That's Andy,' she said, pulling her wrists away from William. 'My boyfriend.'

41

C atherine wrapped the bag of ice in a tea towel and pressed it to the back of Andy's hand. He winced as she tried to shape it round the large lump just above the knuckle of his little finger.

'I don't think it's broken,' she said with a sympathetic smile.

'Yeah, but it could be,' Emily replied from her seat on the sofa next to him. 'I still think we should go to the hospital. Do you want a glass of water, Andy? You're looking a bit pale.'

He nodded in reply, and Emily got to her feet and hurried to the kitchen.

'Quite the little hero, aren't you?' Catherine asked. 'Good move though, beating up a policeman.'

'I didn't know he was a policeman,' Andy sighed, 'and I hardly beat him up. I only hit him once, then he sat down on the floor and started crying.'

'Andy,' Catherine shushed him. 'Never let the truth get in the way of a good story, especially one where you turn into a knight in shining armour.'

'I feel a bit bad, though,' he replied. 'I think I'm going to have to go and say sorry. Do you know where he's based?' Emily came back into the lounge, clutching a tumbler of water with ice cubes floating in it.

'Here you go,' she said with a nervous look at Andy's hand. He thanked her, and took a large sip.

'Andy,' Catherine said. 'What do you think will happen if you walk into a police station and ask to speak to the copper you beat to within an inch of his life so you can say sorry?'

'Catherine, I told you what happened. I only hit him once.'

'That's all it takes sometimes.'

'What do you mean?' Emily asked, her eyes wide.

'I saw a programme on telly a few weeks ago. *One Fatal Punch*, it was called. All about people who'd died after being hit once and landing badly, like.' Catherine saw Emily's eyes widen even further, and her jaw drop a couple of centimetres. 'Bleeding on the brain mostly. Comes on slowly. One minute they're fine, next minute they're gasping their last.'

'Oh my God,' Emily gasped. 'Do you think he's dead?'

'I doubt it, babes. Do you want to have a bit of Andy's water? You're looking a bit pale now.'

'I've not killed him, Emily,' Andy said as he passed her the glass. 'It was only his pride that was hurt, that was all. He was fine once he'd stopped crying.' Catherine saw Andy flex his hand and wince again. 'I think it's me that's come off worst, to be honest. I only cut through the car park because it was pissing down. Then I saw you being assaulted by the copper.'

'Oh, okay,' Catherine said. 'And there was me thinking you were a stalker, hiding in the dark waiting to pounce on poor old Emily.'

'Catherine?' Emily asked.

'What?'

'Shut up.' Catherine looked at Emily, who was giving her a hard stare. As she looked at her, she saw Emily's eyes flash towards the front door.

'Yep, got it, babe,' Catherine replied with a grin. 'You want me to bugger off for about thirty seconds so you can have make-up sex.' Emily flashed a very brief smile at Andy which he returned. About bloody time they sorted themselves out, Catherine thought. It was just a shame Andy had got into a fight over Emily. Or almost a fight, at least.

'I think I'd better go,' Andy said, with a reluctant glance at Emily. 'But maybe—'

'I'll call you,' Emily cut him off with a grin. 'Later this evening, okay?'

'Okay,' he replied, getting to his feet. 'Thanks for the ice and all that.'

'Are you sure?' Catherine said, looking up at Andy with a wicked grin. 'I mean, if you do get put away for murder, the only sex you'll be having for a while will be of the back-door variety.'

'Catherine, please,' Emily said with a frown.

'And you'll be on the receiving end, whether you like it or not. There'll probably be a queue.'

'Jesus Christ, would you stop?' Catherine looked at Emily and saw from the look on her face that her next joke about Andy screaming the same words at the top of his voice probably wouldn't go down that well.

Catherine flicked through the channels on the television while she waited for Andy and Emily to say goodbye at the front door. By the length of time it took them, Catherine figured that they were well on their way to making up their differences. Eventually, Emily came back into the lounge and threw herself down on the couch.

'Blimey,' she said, blowing a breath out of her cheeks.

'Quick knee-trembler, was it?' Catherine asked with an impish grin. 'You're looking a bit flushed, babes.'

'Piss off and put *Masterchef* on, would you? It's the semis on tonight.' Catherine flicked through until she found BBC1, and then turned the volume down so she could talk to Emily.

'Talking of semis, you'll never guess what happened to me this evening,' Catherine said. Emily sighed in reply. 'You can tell me all about the two stags rutting over you in more detail in a bit, but I've just got to tell you about Jack before you go all dreamy eyed.'

'Go on then,' Emily said, trying and failing to get the remote control off Catherine. 'But can you just turn it up a notch?'

'No,' Catherine replied, shoving the remote under her arse cheek. She couldn't see Emily trying to get it from under there. 'So, I invited myself over to the farm earlier, and managed to get my tongue down his throat pretty quick.'

'Really?' Emily started laughing. 'You do surprise me.'

'Oh, shut up. Anyway, few minutes of tonsil hockey and there's nothing back from him at all. So, I give it the old *my God, my heart's beating so fast, can you feel it* trick, but nothing!'

'Sorry, what's the heart trick again? I know you've told me before, but I've forgotten that one?'

'Jesus, Emily,' Catherine said. 'I give up on you sometimes. It's an open invitation for a bit of a tit fumble.'

'Is it? I thought you took someone's pulse at their wrist?'

'Yeah, well, that's because you're not a man.'

'Oh,' Emily replied. 'I've just not seen that technique on *Casualty*, that's all I'm saying.'

'Bloody hell. Anyway, I was thinking that it was getting a bit boring, so mentioned that he'd not shown me his bedroom yet, and next thing I know I'm getting the whole wanting to take it slowly speech.' Catherine sat back and looked at Emily, who was starting to giggle. 'What's so funny?'

'Nothing,' Emily replied. 'I can just imagine the look on your face.'

'Piss off. He was being nice. He said he respected me too much to go to bed with me straight away.'

'Respects you my arse,' Emily laughed. 'He either doesn't want to catch anything nasty, or he's gay.'

'Piss off.'

'Not into older women, perhaps?'

Catherine stifled a laugh at Emily's reply. For her, that was actually quite funny.

'Do you know what the weirdest thing was, though?'

'What, apart from the fact that he didn't want to jump into bed with you?'

'No, seriously, Emily. He told me that his dad got murdered, and his mum was in prison.'

'Might explain why he's a bit odd, then,' Emily replied. 'I already told you, there's something about him that I don't like.'

'Anyhow, enough about my complete failure to get laid,' Catherine said, waving her hand dismissively. She didn't want Emily going off on one again about Jack, and how she didn't like him. 'Tell me about the fight. I bet you were loving it.'

'Not really,' Emily replied. 'It was all a bit pathetic.'

'Were you like, leave it Andy, he's not worth it?'

'No. Like I said, it was all a bit sad. Andy went to hit him, but his hand glanced off William's face and straight into a concrete pillar. Next thing I know, William's on the floor sobbing his heart out, and Andy's got his hand between his legs and swearing about how much that hurt.'

'At least Andy had a go,' Catherine replied. She'd never tell Emily this, but the reality was Catherine was the tiniest bit jealous of two men fighting over her, no matter how pathetic it turned out to be. 'I can't believe you just let him leave, though. That's got to be worth at least a quick blowie.'

'Catherine, why don't you shut up and let me watch *Masterchef.*'

42

A ndy stared at the gathered faces around him. He was sitting in the Heartsease pub, his fourth pint in front of him, and was wearing a brand-new plaster cast on his arm. All was good in Andy's world. He'd had a long chat with Emily earlier, and she'd apologised for being such an arse about things. She had, according to what she'd said on the phone, not been sure about his commitment to their relationship in the longer term. Andy wasn't quite sure what that meant, but they were definitely back on good terms. In Martin's opinion, that meant that there was lots of sex in Andy's immediate future which Andy was quite looking forward to.

'So, anyway,' he said as he took a sip of his lager. 'I had this bloke up against the wall of the car park, my hand bunched around his collar.' He took another sip.

'What happened next?' Martin asked, leaning forward. As he did so, several of the other blokes who were listening also leaned forward. Andy realised that there were a fair few faces he didn't recognise, and figured that they were just in it for the story.

'I said to him,' Andy continued, lowering his voice a fraction. The faces leaned a few inches closer. 'I said to him. Mate, last chance before this gets really nasty.' He lowered his voice and paused for effect. 'Then I just said, really slowly. Leave. My. Girlfriend. Alone.'

'What did he say?' a fat lad Andy had seen in the pub a couple of times before asked.

'He didn't say anything at first. He just sneered. That's when I snapped.' There was an audible gasp from the small group, and Andy took the opportunity to have another mouthful of his lukewarm lager. 'So I just pulled my hand back and smacked him right in the kisser.' Another gasp, this time much louder, which Andy cut through as he continued the story. 'He wobbled, looking all confused like, then he went down like a sack of spuds.'

There was a mumble of approval around the small group before Martin silenced them.

'You hit him so hard you broke your own arm?' Andy didn't reply, but just soaked up the atmosphere. 'Even though he was like, huge?'

'Did you put the boot in fella? When he went down?' an anonymous voice asked.

'No need,' Andy replied, sitting back in the chair. 'He knew he was beaten, and that's not my style. When a man's down, he's been bested.' Andy shrugged his shoulders and tried his best to look disinterested. 'Call me old school, but that's just the way I roll.'

'That's not all, boys,' Martin said to the small group, a smile playing across his face. 'The bloke who was about to get rough with Andy's girlfriend?' Andy managed not to smile as Martin built up the suspense.

'What?' the fat lad asked.

'He was Old Bill.'

When the raucous conversation had died down, and the small crowd dispersed with several masculine slaps to Andy's shoulders, he realised that there were several fresh pints of lager on the table in front of him.

'That's a great story, mate,' Martin said to Andy. 'Shame it's absolute bollocks.'

'Yeah, well,' Andy replied. 'You weren't there.'

'Andy, we've known each other since primary school.'

'So?'

'So, the last time you got into a fight was with that witch in the canteen when she was trying to make you eat a Brussel sprout. What was her name?'

'Mrs Nixon,' Andy said. 'What a cow she was. I've never been able to look at a Brussel sprout since. Didn't you try to nob her daughter when you were in sixth form?'

'Oh, my God,' Martin replied. 'Juicy Lucy. I'd forgotten all about her. She was a big old unit, so she was. Like mother, like daughter.'

'Did you nob her, though?' Andy asked with a mischievous smile, knowing full well that the only thing Martin had got from Juicy Lucy was a black eye. Better that than chlamydia, Andy remembered thinking at the time.

'My point is,' Martin continued, 'the last proper scrap you were in was with a dinner lady two decades ago, and you lost.'

'I was seven,' Andy complained, 'and she must have weighed twenty stone in her pants.' They both laughed. 'Jesus, I've not thought about her for years, and now I've got an image of my old dinner lady in her underwear.' Martin scrunched his face up, and the two of them laughed even harder.

'Shall we have a chaser?' Martin asked, glancing across the pints on the table in front of them.

'Bit cheeky, but why not. It's been a good day, apart

from the bit at the hospital. Thanks for coming to pick me up.'

Martin started singing a song by Celine Dione about a hero coming along as Andy got to his feet and made his way to the bar. As he got closer, the people standing around melted away, making a clear path for him to get through. There were several nods in his direction which he deliberately ignored, and the odd 'alright mate?'.

'Can I get a couple of large Jameson's please?' Andy asked the man behind the bar, a large tattooed man who Andy hadn't said more than one sentence to in all the time he'd been coming in here. A couple of seconds later, two glasses arrived with far more than a double in each of them.

'Cheers. How much is that?' Andy asked, fishing in his pocket for his wallet.

'On the house, fella,' the barman said. 'I've heard the story off the boys here, so these are on me. Do you want a sausage roll?'

'Er, oh,' Andy replied, momentarily stuck for something to say. 'No, I'm good thanks.'

'Not because he was Old Bill you understand, but because you didn't put the boot in when he was down.' Andy saw the barman glance down at the plaster cast. 'Hit 'em hard, hit 'em once. If they get back up again,' the barman smiled revealing an impressive set of yellow teeth, 'run like fuck.'

'Yeah, I mean like I told the others,' Andy replied, realising that he was talking like someone out of *Eastenders* but not able to do anything about it. 'Once a man's down, he's down.'

'Could have done with more boys like you back in the day,' the barman said, leaning forward in a conspiratorial pose. 'Now the football's all seats and stuff, the fun's gone from the game. Saturdays always used to be about a fair few pints, a football match, and a damn good scrap.' Andy watched the barman squint at his customers. 'Now it's all chat, chat, chat, and straight to a knife. No honour in that, is there?'

'Er, no,' Andy replied. 'Not at all.' The barman leaned in even closer and started whispering in Andy's ear.

'Thing is mate, I'm thinking about getting a new crew together. Now Norwich City is back in the Champion's league there'll be loads of foreigners coming over here, trying to shag our birds. We need a new bunch of boys to sort them out, and I'm looking for a lieutenant.' He stared at Andy through rheumy eyes. 'Someone new, someone tasty who's not afraid to get stuck in, but who's old school. Know what I mean?'

'Er....'

'Once you get that cast off, you stop by for a chat. Yeah?'

'Okay,' Andy squeaked before lowering his voice. 'Okay. Definitely. I'm right up for that.'

'Good lad,' the barman replied with a theatrical wink. 'Just come in here and if I'm not about, ask for Pete. Don't let me down.'

'Drink up, mate,' Andy said to Martin before he'd even put the two whisky chasers on the table. 'We're going.'

'What?' Martin replied. 'No we're not, look at all this free beer.'

'Yeah we are. I've just had a very odd conversation with the ugly bastard behind the bar, and we need to get going.'

'What sort of conversation?' Martin asked as he picked up his whisky and drained the glass. 'Jesus, that's rancid. Is that whisky or drain cleaner?'

'He's putting a crew back together, and he wants me in it.'

'What, is he a Blues Brother? He doesn't look like a musician.'

'Not a band, a crew. We will fight them on the beaches, we will fight them on the terraces. That sort of crew.' Martin started laughing.

'A Norwich City crew?' he asked, picking up a spare pint of lager. 'I can just see Delia Smith with a pair of knuckledusters, and Stephen Fry behind her whirling a pair of nun-chukkas.'

'I'm serious, mate,' Andy said, draining his own whisky and picking up a pint. 'He went all Herman Hesse on me. Started talking about foreigners coming over here and impregnating our women.'

'He looks even less like an author than he does a musician,' Martin replied, glancing over at the barman. 'Are you sure you don't mean Heinrich Himmler?'

'Martin,' Andy said. 'Just finish your drink. We're going.'

43

J ack could hear Beth shouting from a good fifty feet
away from the abattoir, despite the thickness of the
stone walls. So much for it being soundproof.

'Jesus wept,' he muttered as he opened the door to the
main building. 'Alright, alright,' he shouted as he walked
into the room. 'I'm here.' By the time he had put the
carrier bags — one full of biscuits, one full of well-packed
sealant tubes — the shouting had stopped. He pulled his
phone from his pocket, logged into the wi-fi, and brought
up the camera feed. To his surprise, Beth was sitting on the
commode in the middle of the room, her arms already
clamped to the hand rests, staring expectantly at the door.
Jack reached behind him and tugged the gun from his
waistband, putting it down next to the green piping on the
counter. He wouldn't be needing a weapon to subdue her
from the looks of things.

When he opened the door to the interior bedroom,
Beth was staring at him.

'I thought you'd forgotten about me,' she said, a toothy

grin on her face. 'Have you come to feed me? I'm bloody starving.'

Jack left the door to the bedroom open for the few seconds it took him to go back and get the carrier bag. Beth hadn't moved an inch when he got back to the room, and he passed her the bag with an outstretched hand.

'Here you go,' he said as she grabbed the bag and ripped it open, deciding on a packet of chocolate Hob-Nobs. Jack closed the door behind him and crossed to the counter to prepare the sealant gun. He'd had to buy some more jam earlier that day, but he'd made sure not to get sugar-free. That would defeat the purpose, really.

By the time he'd coated the pipe with jam and re-opened the door, Beth was starting on her second packet of Hob-Nobs. When she saw Jack walking towards her with the jam covered pipe, she dropped the biscuits and ignored them as they rolled across the floor.

'Oh, you star,' she said, eyeing the pipe with anticipation. 'I thought you were kidnapping me for sex. If I'd know you just wanted to feed me, I've have come willingly.' Beth tilted her head back and opened her mouth.

Jack hadn't thought about that particular scenario. The whole premise for getting Beth into this room was that she wanted to lose weight, or so he'd thought. Perhaps for the next one, he'd offer an intensive feeding programme instead of an intensive weight loss one. Either way, Jack thought as he approached Beth, she was almost there. Almost big enough to fit into his mother's dress.

He jumped as she grabbed the pipe from him, shoving it towards her mouth. Beth licked the jam from the end of the pipe, and then crammed it into her throat. Jack watched with wide eyes as her neck muscles worked to get the pipe into her stomach, and by the time she'd managed

to swallow the entire pipe down, he was seriously considering his approach to the next woman he took.

Five tubes of high-calorie food later, Beth was looking
very sleepy. He pulled the tube out of her throat and sat on
her bed to wait for her customary belch which arrived a
few seconds later.

'Bloody hell,' Beth groaned, rubbing her ample stomach. 'That's got it.' Her eyes flashed around and settled on
the half finished packed of biscuits near the drain in the
middle of the floor. Jack was just about to go and get them
for her, figuring that she probably couldn't be bothered to
fetch them for herself, when she continued. 'So what's the
plan, then?'

'What do you mean?'

'What's the plan? Are you going to keep me here until
I'm too big to fit through that door?' She belched again,
and Jack watched, horrified, as a sick bubble appeared on
her lips before being licked away and swallowed.

'No, I'm just going to keep you here until you're big
enough.'

'Big enough for what?'

'Big enough for what I need you to be big enough for.'
Beth squinted at him, and Jack realised that she was trying
to stay awake.

'Very mysterious. How big's that?'

'Little bit bigger than you are now.'

'Then what?'

'Then,' Jack replied, hiding his excitement. 'Then you
get to dress up for me.'

'I like dressing up,' Beth replied, her eyelids drooping.

'You're going to look lovely.'

'Am I?'

'Beautiful,' Jack said.

He sat on the bed until Beth was fast asleep. Her head

lolled to the side, and a faint snore escaped from her mouth. Jack got to his feet, and as he didn't trust her one hundred per cent, kept a close eye on the woman as he picked up the packet of biscuits and laid them gently on her lap. At least she wouldn't be hungry when she woke up. He locked the door to the bedroom carefully as he left, and then looked at his watch to see how much time in the workshop he had before he had to go to bed.

'Excellent,' he said to himself as he realised he'd have a good two hours in there. After all, he had a candlestick to finish, and you couldn't hurry art.

44

Emily unplugged her iPad from its place by the side of her bed and carried it through to the lounge. She wasn't sure what it was, but there was definitely something that she didn't like about Jack, and if Catherine was about to get involved with him, then doing a little bit of background research into the man wouldn't hurt. That was what friends were for, after all.

It wasn't just the fact that Catherine was trying to jump into bed with the bloke. If Emily was concerned about every man that her flat mate exchanged some bodily fluids with, then she would be a nervous wreck. But every once in a while, Catherine would change a bit and start going out less, toning down her behaviour, and generally being a bit more sensible. In Emily's experience, this was normally when Catherine was interested in more than just a one night liaison.

Emily plonked herself down on the sofa and turned the television on before turning the volume down until it was just background noise. While she waited for the apple on her iPad to disappear and her home screen pop up, she thought about where to start looking for information on Jack, and what to look for. The problem was, she didn't even know his surname.

'Right then, sunshine,' she muttered as she brought up the browser on her iPad. 'Let's see what you're hiding.' The first thing she did was google the gym he worked at. Sure enough, under the 'About Us' tab was a list of staff. Jack was about half way down the page, gurning at the camera. 'Jack Kennedy,' Emily said as she looked at his picture. It was a head and shoulders shot, the same as the other staff photos, but Jack had made sure that when his photo was taken, he was pushing his biceps forwards with his hands to make his arms look as big as possible. That pose, and the shit-eating grin on his face, just made Emily like him even less.

There wasn't a great deal in Jack's biography, especially when it was compared to the profiles for the other staff members. All it said was that Jack had joined the gym about six months ago, and had got a string of qualifications in a load of fitness stuff. The profile for one of the other fitness instructors — some buff bloke called Dave — was at least three times as long and detailed to the point Emily knew what Dave's cat was called. But at least she now knew what Jack's surname was.

The only problem with that, as Emily found out a moment later, was that there were a lot of people called Jack Kennedy. She spent a few minutes scrolling through page after page, momentarily distracted by a Jack Kennedy in Suffolk whose local community had decided that he was a wrong 'un. Emily brought up the page with the full story on. It turned out that this Jack Kennedy — who was in his sixties so definitely not the same one — had enraged the

locals by escaping justice for his alleged crimes. A disaster
had narrowly been avoided when the police arrived at his
house, which was surrounded by a mob of locals determined to raze it to the ground with him inside it.
According to the Suffolk Advertiser, this Jack Kennedy was
a paediatrician, not a paedophile. Emily read the follow on
report about the bus stop at the end of his road being
torched, presumably by a mob pique of frustration later
that evening, and moved on.

Twenty minutes later, she was no nearer to finding
anything at all out about the Jack Kennedy that Catherine
was so keen to get involved with. She'd tried an image
search to see if she could recognise him anywhere else on
the internet, but hadn't found anything. Facebook and
Twitter revealed nothing that she didn't know already,
which was that Jack Kennedy was a surprisingly common
name.

'Jesus, Emily,' she mumbled as she wandered into the
kitchen to get a glass of wine. 'You'd make a crap stalker.'
Emily chuckled to herself as she poured herself a generous
measure and wondered where else she could look for some
dirt on the man.

By the time *Eastenders* had come on, she was completely
out of ideas, so put the iPad down and settled back to
watch the soap. Emily hadn't seen the soap opera in ages,
so hadn't really got much of a clue what was going on. It
didn't take long to work it all out, though. Someone had
slept with someone they shouldn't have slept with, someone
else was having some contemporary issues — drug addic-
tion in the current storyline — and someone else was in
court. Emily glanced at the clock. It wouldn't be long until
the drama ended with its traditional 'doof, doof, doof'
musical ending. On the screen, a right old cockney geezer

was just about to hear whether the jury had found him guilty or not guilty of murder. Just before the jury spokesman revealed the ending, the music cut in leaving the entire United Kingdom with something to talk about at work.

The storyline reminded Emily of something that Catherine had told her about Jack, or more specifically, his father. Hadn't she said that he'd been murdered? Emily frowned, thinking hard. There was something about music as well. Not music like the end of the soap opera, but what Jack had played to Catherine.

'Ooh, I wonder,' Emily said as she picked her iPad back up and opened the browser. There couldn't be that many murdered vicars in the country, could there?

'Bloody hell,' she said as she looked at the web page that a search on Google for 'murdered vicars in the united kingdom' had brought up. According to this page at least, being a man of the cloth in the United Kingdom was a pretty dangerous occupation. Emily wasn't sure how many vicars there were, but they seemed to be highly likely to be stabbed, poisoned, or mugged to death. 'So much for The Man upstairs looking after you lot,' she said as she scrolled down the depressingly long list. Even though there were a lot of them, none of them were called Father Kennedy. Or Reverend Kennedy, Padre Kennedy, or even Bishop Kennedy.

Emily was just about to close the iPad down and give up when one of the pictures on the list caught her eye. It wasn't a vicar called Kennedy, but there was something about the picture that piqued her interest. She opened up the link and enlarged the picture. It showed a friendly looking grey-haired vicar, probably mid-sixties, who'd been battered to death in his vicarage. It wasn't the kindly face of the victim that had attracted her attention though. It was the man that the priest had his arm slung around. The priest's companion was a lot thinner than he looked now, but Emily recognised him straight away.

'Hello Jack,' she whispered with a grin. 'There you are.'

45

Andy stood on Emily's doorstep, waiting for her to open the door. He glanced towards the alley to the side of her flat, grateful that he'd had the good sense to go for a pee behind Emily's next-door neighbour's hedge a few minutes ago. The only small snag with that was that he'd got the end of his plaster cast a bit wet, but he didn't think that she'd notice.

'Hello you,' Emily said as she opened the door a couple of inches. Andy rearranged the flowers he'd bought from one of the poshest florists in Norwich and grinned at her.

'Hello.'

'Have you come to fix my washing machine?' Emily opened the door another couple of inches, and Andy could see that she was wearing something silky, pale cream coloured, and unless he was very much mistaken, quite insubstantial.

'Is Catherine out?' he replied. 'I'm guessing she is if you're wearing what I'm hoping you're wearing?'

'Andy,' Emily replied, sighing and flicking her eyes

upwards for a second. 'Let's try again.' She closed the door, and a few seconds later, opened it again.

'Hello,' she said, trying not to laugh. 'Have you come to fix my washing machine.'

'Ya,' Andy replied in his best non-specific foreign accent. 'I come to plumb. I plumb to come.'

Emily opened the door, and just before she hid behind it, Andy could see that she was wearing something very similar to what he had hoped for.

'That's quite funny for you,' she said as he walked past her and into the flat. 'Now put those cheap flowers down and take me to bed, or lose me forever.'

A little while later — not quite as later as Andy had hoped, but it had been a while — they were lying in bed together, both completely spent. He angled his head to look at Emily, snuggled in his armpit, and was grateful that he'd spent a couple of extra quid on some decent Lynx deodorant instead of the normal shite that he bought.

'You okay?' he asked her. She opened her eyes and looked at him sleepily.

'I am now,' Emily replied. 'Short and sweet. Just what I needed.'

'Er, okay. Good.'

'My washing machine's still broken, though.'

'Give me a few minutes, and I'll see what I can do.' Emily traced her fingernail down Andy's chest, and he shivered.

'I've missed you, you know,' Emily whispered. 'Even if you are a complete idiot at times.'

'I've missed you too,' Andy replied with a chuckle. 'But you wouldn't like me so much if I wasn't a bit of an idiot.'

'True, true. Catherine told me all about the visits to the gym.'

'Sneaky cow,' Andy said. 'She wasn't supposed to say anything.'

'Yeah, right. You should know by now that the best way of telling the whole of Norwich something is to tell Catherine. She should get a job in media or something.'

'She's not found anything yet then?'

'No, not yet.' Emily raised her eyes to the ceiling. 'But she's looking, apparently.'

'Is that where she is now?'

'Doubt it very much. She's probably sniffing around that fitness instructor.' Emily's voice changed as she said the words 'fitness instructor', and Andy looked at her. 'What?' she asked. 'What's that look for?'

'I take it you don't like him, then?'

'Not really, no,' Emily replied as she leaned herself up on one elbow and padded the top of the duvet to find her slip. 'I'm going to show you something.' Andy started laughing as she gave up and put his t-shirt on instead. 'What's so funny?'

'Emily, we've just had some, as you call it, personal time. Both with no clothes on, naked as the day we were born, and unless you're a very good actress, I know what you look like when you–'

'Stop it,' Emily said, slapping at him with her hand. 'Don't be crude.'

'I'm not being crude. I'm just wondering why you're getting dressed.' She didn't reply, but just pulled the t-shirt off over her head, got to her feet, and padded her way into the lounge, giggling as she did so. Andy grinned, very much looking forward to the view when she came back in, but when she did, she had one arm across her breasts and the other was holding her iPad over her pelvis.

'It's rude to stare,' Emily laughed as she slid back under the duvet. 'Now, look at what I found.'

Emily brought up a web page on her iPad and leaned over to show it to Andy.

'Look at this,' she said, pointing at the screen. Andy did as instructed, but all he could see was a webpage from a newspaper.

'What am I looking at?'

'There, fool.' Emily pointed at a photograph on the screen. 'That's Jack Kennedy, except it's not.' Andy used the fingers on his non-broken hand to zoom in on the photograph.

'So it is. Is that his dad, the vicar bloke?'

'It was,' she replied. 'Until he got himself murdered. But according to the photograph, Jack's last name isn't Kennedy, it's Green. His real name is Jack Green, and that was his dad, Reverend Green.'

'Blimey,' Andy said, trying to read the article so that he could work out what Emily was going on about. 'He got his head smashed in, it says here. In his vicarage of all places.'

'Keep reading. It gets better.'

'That's a bit harsh, Emily,' Andy said with a smile. 'I can't see how it's going to get much better.'

'Oh, shut up. You know what I mean.'

Andy zoomed in a bit more and read the rest of the article. It was written in the typical style of a local news-paper — not very well — but when Andy got to the bit about Jack's mother being arrested for her husband's murder, he was astonished.

'Shit,' Andy gasped. 'That's desperate, that is.'

'I knew there was something not quite right about Mr Kennedy, or whatever his name is.'

'Does Catherine know?'

'Not yet,' Emily replied. 'I've texted her a couple of

times, but she's not replied. Which probably means she's on her back somewhere.'

'Talking of being on your back,' Andy said, 'why are we looking at this?'

'But he lives in the farm where The Butcher and those weirdos lived?'

'Yeah, I know. That's why I'd rather not get into this now. Not when I have such an attractive — and naked — woman in front of me.' Andy had an idea of how to get her attention away from the iPad.

'Oh, you old charmer. What have you got in mind instead?'

'How about a bit of role play?'

'Er, well, I'm not sure about that.' She wrinkled her face but Andy could see Emily grinning underneath her grimace. 'It's got an animal theme.'

'Right...'

'Well, I've made you bark like a dog.'

'You so have not!'

'And now I'm going to make you squeal like a pig!' Andy angled the iPad screen away from Emily's view as she creased up with laughter, and brought up a web page that he'd been looking at earlier. He navigated to the section that he wanted to show Emily.

'Talking of role play,' Andy said as he angled the screen back round. 'What do you think of this?'

'Oh my Lord,' Emily replied, looking at the screen and gasping. 'How is that possible? Give it here.' Andy smiled as she grabbed the iPad back off him and turned it round. 'Are those her feet?'

'Yep.' He carried on smiling at her until she looked at him. When she did, he arched his eyebrows. 'So, shall we give it a go and see if we can get this little piggy to go "wee wee wee" all the way home?'

Emily grinned and bit her lip. She put the iPad on the bedside table, much to Andy's relief, and slid her hand under the covers. Andy gasped as she grabbed him.

'Christ, you've got cold hands,' he said.

'Stop grumbling, you dirty old hog.'

'Do we need a safe word?'

'How about "get off me you fat bastard"?' Emily said as she wriggled closer.

46

C atherine felt Jack increase the pressure on her hand just a tiny bit. The palm of his hand covered the back of hers, and their fingers were intertwined.

'That's it, you need to be gripping it just enough so that you can feel the friction,' he said quietly in her ear. She could feel his breath on her neck. 'Now just slide your hand up and down.' He moved her hand just as he'd suggested. 'Can you feel that?'

'What am I feeling for?' she asked, confused.

'Friction. Just the slightest bit. If your hand feels as if it's slippery, you're not gripping it hard enough. But if you grip too hard then it'll be painful.'

'How's that?' Catherine asked as she moved her hand as he'd told her to. Jack let go of her hand, and she continued the rhythmic motion.

'Perfect,' Jack replied. She looked at him and realised that he had his eyes closed. 'Maybe just a little twist of your wrist at the end of each stroke?'

'How can you tell, when you've got your eyes closed, what my wrist is doing?'

'I just know,' Jack replied, opening his eyes and grinning at her. She returned his smile and carried on moving her hand up and down, ignoring the fact that her forearm was starting to ache. 'Keep going, it won't take long.'

The next thing Catherine felt was a sharp stabbing sensation in the fleshy part of her thumb.

'Ouch,' she gasped, looking down at her thumb. 'I've got a bloody splinter.'

'That's because you let go of the sandpaper,' Jack laughed. 'I told you, it's all about the grip.' He took her hand and moved it away from the vice on the workbench in front of them. 'Mind you don't get any blood on the wood.'

A few moments later, Catherine's thumb was expertly bandaged. Jack had removed the splinter, which turned out to be a lot smaller than it had felt when it went into her thumb, and was running the sandpaper over the piece of wood that she'd been working on.

'See,' he said, glancing up at her. 'You were almost there. Can you see how the fine sandpaper has brought the grain out?' Catherine looked at the cylindrical piece of wood she'd turned on the lathe under Jack's careful supervision, now firmly secured in the vice on the workbench. Try as she might, she couldn't see what difference the sandpaper had made, other than a hole in her thumb.

'Bloody typical,' she replied, looking over at the lathe. 'I can use a power tool with no problems, and then I hurt myself with a bit of bloody sandpaper.' Jack laughed in response.

'Don't worry about it,' he said as he opened a drawer and pulled out a couple of strange pieces of metal with spikes attached to them. He held one of them up for Catherine to look at, but she wasn't sure what it was. It looked like a small tripod, but with a spike. 'This is the base,' Jack explained. 'The spike just gets hammered into the wood. And this is the top.' He held up the other piece of metal, which looked to her like the lid of a jam jar, but smaller. And spikier.

'Okay,' Catherine said. 'Do you trust me with a hammer?'

By the time Catherine had tapped the metalwork into either end of the piece of wood, it had taken shape and looked like what they had set out to make.

'There you go,' Jack said, standing the wood on the workbench in front of them. 'Your first candlestick.'

'Wow,' Catherine replied, trying to inject some enthusiasm into her voice. 'That's going straight on my mantelpiece, that is.' Even with the metal pieces hammered into either end, the entire thing was only about six inches high.

'If you've not bled for something, then it's not art,' Jack said, beaming at her. 'Do you want to make another one so that you've got a pair?'

'I'm good, thanks,' she said. 'It's only a small mantelpiece.' She was just about to add that there was enough shit above the fireplace in her flat already when she decided not to. Catherine looked instead at the candlestick that Jack had removed from the lathe when he'd offered to show her how to make something. He'd put the candlestick in the corner of the room as if it was made from glass, despite the fact that it was almost three feet tall and looked to Catherine as if it was solid as anything. 'If I put something like that on it, the whole mantelpiece would collapse.'

She saw Jack look over at the large candlestick and glance away quickly, almost as if he'd forgotten he'd put it there.

'Is that one a commission?' Catherine asked. Jack had spent a while earlier on that evening telling her about the various customers who hired him to make bespoke pieces for them. It wasn't, he'd explained, about the money. It was all about the beauty, the art, and the fact that someone wanted something he'd made badly enough to pay quite handsomely for it.

'No, that one isn't. Would you like a drink?' It could have been her imagination, but Jack suddenly seemed nervous.

'Are you making it for yourself, then?'

'Kind of,' he replied, getting to his feet. 'Come on, I'll light the log burner and we can have a glass of wine.' His eyes flicked over again at the candlestick in the corner of the room before he looked back at her. Catherine let Jack pull her to her feet, and she ran her hand over his arm as they walked into the kitchen. His biceps were almost as solid as the wood that they'd been sanding.

'Can I ask you something?' Catherine said an hour or so later, emboldened by the fact she'd had almost an entire bottle of wine. She'd not complained when Jack had kept topping her glass up, but knew he must have known that she was way over the limit for driving home.

'Sure,' he replied. 'Ask away.' Catherine paused for a few seconds before saying anything.

'Do you want to sleep with me?'

'Er,' Jack said. 'Er, well, yes. At some point, yes. Of course.' Catherine looked at him through half closed eyes.

'I sense there's a "but" in there somewhere.'

'Catherine,' he said, looking at her intently. 'There is nothing I would like more, but that's not something that I can do just at the moment. In time, definitely, but just not now.' She opened her mouth before realising that she had no idea what to say to that. This wasn't a situation that had ever happened to her before. She was chasing this man harder than she'd ever chased anyone in her life, and that wasn't something she'd ever done before. Her usual philosophy was to move on if nothing penetrative happened by the second date, and although this wasn't a date as such, it wasn't far off one.

'Okay,' she replied slowly. 'I mean, there's always other things we can do that are quite good fun?'

Jack crossed his legs over each other before grimacing and uncrossing them again. Catherine thought maybe there was something going on in his trousers, after all?

'I'd rather just sit here and chat, to be honest. That way, when we do go to bed, it'll be that bit more memorable.' Jack stared at the flames through the small window in the log burner before turning to look at Catherine. 'Shall I put another log on the fire?'

Jesus wept, Catherine thought to herself as Jack busied himself with opening the log burner and throwing what looked like a deformed candlestick into it. He'd better be worth the wait.

47

E mily closed the door to her flat, not bothering to close it quietly like she did when she knew Catherine was sleeping in. She'd not come back last night, so Emily supposed that she had finally managed to get down and dirty with Jack Kennedy, or Jack Green, or whatever his name was. That was fine by Emily as it had given her and Andy some space to get down and dirty themselves and make up for lost time. Her hips were aching quite badly though, but that was a price worth paying. She grinned to herself as she remembered what they'd got up to, and she was miles away as she walked down the path in front of her flat.

'Morning, babes,' Emily jumped as she heard Catherine's voice in front of her. 'Sorry, didn't mean to make you jump. You off to work, then?'

'Jesus, you frightened the crap out of me,' Emily replied, giggling. She looked at Catherine, well used to seeing her slope back in the morning after a strenuous night. This time though Catherine looked, well, normal. 'Did you have a good night?'

'Not quite as good as I would have liked, but it was entertaining enough.' Emily watched Catherine reach into her handbag and pull out an object that looked like some sort of miniature torture device. 'Look, I made a candlestick.'

'Oh, is that what it is?' Emily said. 'Which way up does it go?'

'Bugger off,' Catherine laughed. 'It was the closest I got to any wood all night, I'll tell you that for nothing. Whereas you,' she prodded Emily in the chest with her finger, 'you've got the look of the recently laid unless I'm very much mistaken.' Emily was just about to reply when their postman walked around the corner and handed her a bunch of leaflets. Emily was just wondering if he'd heard what Catherine had said when she saw his knowing look, and realised that he had. She waited until he'd walked off to deliver a pile of useless leaflets to the next block.

'Thanks, Catherine,' Emily whispered, her cheeks colouring. 'Now the postman knows as well.'

'Oh, hold the front page,' Catherine said as she walked past Emily. 'Woman has sex with boyfriend.' Emily took a few steps towards the pavement when Catherine called after her. 'Babes, you okay?'

'Yeah, all good,' Emily said, stopping and turning to face Catherine. 'Why?'

'You're limping.'

'Just my hips hurting a bit, that's all,' she replied. A slow smile spread across Catherine's face.

'Oh, do they now,' Catherine said. 'You dirty little slut bucket. Why might that be?'

'I'll see you tonight,' Emily said, ignoring Catherine and hoping the postman was out of earshot. 'Can you sort some clothes out for Mr Clayton? He's coming round this evening.'

Twenty minutes later, Emily was stuck fast in a traffic jam. It was the same traffic jam that she sat in every morning, even to the point where she recognised some of the other drivers. As she crawled past the end of one of the only roads out of a new housing estate, she saw a little old lady sitting in a large BMW, hunched over the wheel as she peered at the traffic. She'd been in exactly the same spot the day before, and for a moment Emily wondered if the little old lady and the queue of cars behind her had actually been there all night.

Emily flicked the radio on and changed the channel to the local radio station. It was bang on eight o'clock, and time for what passed as news.

'Good morning Norwich,' the annoyingly chirpy radio presenter said. 'It's time for the news from our fine city at the top of the hour, with me, Bob Rutler.' Emily strummed her fingers on the steering wheel as the jovial presenter continued. 'Police have stepped up their efforts in the search for missing Norwich woman, Beth James, who has been missing for almost a week. Miss James, an internet model on a website for the larger lady, disappeared after telling her parents that she was just popping out for a Chinese takeaway.' Emily tuned him out for a few seconds as he urged anyone who might have seen the missing woman to call the police, or the free helpline set up by Beth James' weight loss group. By the time Bob had finished the news, Emily had made it as far as the traffic lights at the end of her road. Almost three hundred full yards in ten minutes. When Bob played a trail for a feature that promised to highlight the man inside the Captain Canary mascot costume at Norwich City, and his lifelong struggle against alcohol and Class A drugs, she turned off the radio.

'Morning Emily,' Mr Clayton said as Emily breezed into the office. 'Gosh, you're looking well. Have you just won the lottery or something? You're almost glowing.' Emily could feel herself start to blush as she thought back to what Catherine had said earlier on. From what the two of them had said, Emily might as well have had a sign round her neck that said 'I've just had sex'.

'Fine, fine, thank you,' Emily said, walking past him and towards her desk. To her dismay, he followed her over and perched on the edge of it as she sat down and turned her computer on. In the far corner of the room, Emily could see that witch Miss Daniels from Marketing staring over at them.

'Are we still okay for this evening?' Mr Clayton whispered. 'Did you get a chance to speak to your flat mate?'

'Yes, I did,' Emily whispered back. 'I saw Catherine when I was leaving my flat. She's going to sort out some stuff for you to try on, and I can help with some of the other stuff just like we talked about.'

'Fantastic,' he replied. 'I'm so nervous.' Emily looked at his face. Although he was smiling at her, she could see the faint trace of fear behind the smile and reached out her hand, putting it on top of his.

'You don't need to be,' she said. 'You'll be amongst friends. You know Catherine, don't you?'

'Er, I think I met her at the Christmas party. Didn't she get up to something in the stationery cupboard.'

'Yeah,' Emily replied, rolling her eyes to the ceiling. 'That would be Catherine.'

'I did see that video of her in the boardroom that was doing the rounds.'

'You and half the bloody internet saw that video.'

Mr Clayton didn't reply, but got to his feet and looked at Emily, his head cocked to one side.

'You really do look like that cat that got the cream this morning,' he said. 'You're going to teach me how to get that look at some point. It's quite something.' Emily frowned as he turned away and walked off. Perhaps Andy would help Mr Clayton out with that, she thought as she raised a middle finger in the general direction of Miss Daniels from Marketing.

48

'What you doing?' Beth asked Jack as he lifted another plank of wood into place. He paused for a second, wondering what to say, before he lowered the plank onto the brackets he'd put into the thick stone walls of her bedroom.

'I'm trying to make it a bit more homely for you, Beth,' he said, checking that the plank was straight with a spirit level app on his phone. Jack grinned as the digital bubble settled bang in the middle of the two lines. The shelf was absolutely level, just as he'd known it would be. He turned to look at Beth, who was sitting on her bed on the other side of the room, swinging her legs like a child.

'Aw, thank you,' she said with a smile. 'What's it going to be?'

'It's a bookcase,' Jack said. 'Or when it's finished it will be. This is the first shelf, but it needs to be straight so that all the others are as well.'

'You're very good with your hands, aren't you?' Jack didn't reply, but pulled a screwdriver from his utility belt to fasten the shelf into place. Since he'd started working earlier that evening, he'd been concerned about being in the same room as Beth with a whole bunch of sharp objects. She'd not moved from her position on the bed though, and if anything, was actually being friendly. He had, however, promised her an extra tube if she behaved herself, so maybe that was why. 'Can I tell you something?' Beth asked.

Jack finished screwing the shelf to the brackets and turned to face her.

'Sure,' he said, touching the back of his waistband to reassure himself that the pistol was where he'd put it earlier. 'Fire away.'

'I thought you were going to kill me when you brought me here,' Beth said, stopping her legs for a moment and staring at him. 'But you're looking after me.'

'Yeah, I am,' Jack replied.

'Why?'

'Because I want you to look beautiful.'

'When you dress me up?'

'Yeah. When I dress you up.'

'So, what happens after that? Will you let me go?'

'You'll be free, yes,' Jack said. That wasn't quite the same thing as letting her go, but he figured that Beth probably wouldn't work that out.

'What if I don't want to go?' Beth asked, resuming the leg swinging. 'What if I want to stay here?'

'Er…' Jack replied. He'd not thought of that as a plan of action. 'How'd you mean?'

'I could stay. Help with stuff around the place.' The only thing she could help with would be emptying his farmhouse of anything remotely edible, Jack thought, but he didn't say anything. An image of Beth breathlessly pushing a vacuum round before trying to eat the face off his Henry Hoover sprang into his mind, and he had to stop himself laughing.

'We can talk about that, sure,' Jack said, returning his attention to the shelves. 'But I do need to get these shelves up for you. Do you like reading?'

'Not really,' Beth replied. 'But I will if you want me to.'

An hour later, bookcase completed and Beth fed — it was almost getting to the point where Jack could leave her alone with the pipe and the sealant gun and she would sort herself out — Jack made his way back to the farmhouse. He was tired but satisfied, and found his thoughts drifting to Catherine as he walked down the track from the abattoir to the main house. Jack had an appointment the next day at the hospital to have his stitches taken out, and then it would be game on. He allowed himself a daydream where Catherine became his next project, and over the course of weeks, or months perhaps, he could feed her up until she was where Beth was now. The thought made his stitches start to tighten, so he tried to remember the rules of cricket until the sensation went away. By the time he got back to the farmhouse, his main concern was whether a ball that bounced back off a picket fence without hitting the field first scored four or six runs, but at least it had stopped the ache in his testicles.

Jack poured himself a generous helping of whisky, checked his phone to make sure that Beth was asleep, and made his way into his workshop. In the corner was the candlestick that would be his crowning glory — or rather Beth's crowning glory even if she wasn't aware of that yet — and he put his glass down on the workbench and walked over to it. He picked up the candlestick, wrapping his fingers around the main shaft, and held it in front of him. As he swung it slowly from side to side, enjoying the weight distribution that the heavy ends gave it, he started laughing.

'This isn't a candlestick,' he chuckled, raising it above his head. 'It's a mandlestick!' He made a swooshing sound through his teeth as he brought it down in front of him in slow motion, and then swore to himself when he heard the doorbell ringing. 'Oh for fuck's sake, seriously?'

It was too late for Jack to pretend to be out. His van was parked outside the farmhouse for one thing, instead of hidden inside the barn like it normally was, and most of the lights in the farmhouse were blazing. He glanced at his watch, realising that it wasn't as late as he thought it was, and gently put the candlestick onto the workbench. The doorbell rang again, more insistent this time if that was possible, and Jack muttered to himself as he left the workshop and crossed the kitchen to the front door, flinging it open and preparing himself to be annoyed.

'What?' Jack barked at the man standing on his doorstep. His visitor was dressed mostly in black, maybe mid to late twenties, and had a large hat shaped like a navy blue breast tucked under his arm.

'Are you the farmer?' the man said, shuffling his feet. Jack looked out into the courtyard in front of the farmhouse, and saw a small white car parked next to his van. On top of the car was a pathetic looking bubble light. 'My name's William,' the visitor said. 'I'm a policeman. Can I come in?'

49

C atherine sighed as she walked out of the hotel, her high heels clicking on the hard marble floor. The job interview hadn't gone particularly well. In fact, if she had to rate it, she would probably place it fairly near the bottom of interviews that she'd done, even if was only for a waitressing role. It wasn't just that she'd just flunked an interview for a waitressing job, but it was for a waitressing job in Great Yarmouth.

There had been twelve applicants for the role, all female, all of a similar age to Catherine. While she'd been waiting in the hotel foyer to be called through, she'd listened to some of the conversations between the other applicants. There was a lot of talk about 'generous guests' and 'massive tips', which Catherine had listened to with interest, but the closest she'd come to a conversation with any of the other applicants was a brief discussion in the ladies toilets about what colour lipstick to wear during the interview. The other woman — a skinny girl with improbably large breasts — had decided on black, and even offered Catherine some of the make-up on the basis that 'it might help'. Catherine had declined the invitation, deciding instead on a slightly more demure shade of light pink.

Catherine hadn't been to many interviews, having landed her job in the human resources department of her previous firm based mostly on her performance with the brother of the woman who owned the firm. But none of the other job interviews that she had been to had started with the question that this one had.

'Can you dance?' the male interviewer had asked Catherine before she'd even managed to cross her legs after sitting in the hot seat. He was a rotund man in his fifties with a pony tail no doubt designed to compensate for his receding hairline. The other interviewer was female, about the same age, and had a face that must have taken a lot of smoking to achieve.

'Er, well yes. Of course I can dance. But I thought...'

'So, dance then,' the man had replied. Catherine had looked at the woman for help, but none was forthcoming. Catherine got to her feet, and started shuffling from foot to foot, waving her arms about. Try as she might, she couldn't summon up any music inside her head to dance to. 'Come closer,' the man had said. 'Dance just for me, like we're the only two people here.' Catherine had taken a few steps towards the man until she was just in front of him and lifted her hands to her head before gyrating her hips in his general direction. The next thing she knew, he had a hand on her buttock. Although she was tempted to slap the dirty bastard around the chops, she just took a step away from his wandering hand and continued dancing. 'Okay, that'll do,' the man said, sounding disappointed.

Catherine went back to her chair and sat down, frowning as the two interviewers had a whispered conversation. Finally, the female interviewer made a note on the pad that was balanced on her lap and looked at Catherine.

'Right then,' she said to her, waving her pen in Catherine's general direction. 'Let's see what you've got.'

'Sorry?' Catherine replied, genuinely confused.

'Clothes?' the woman said, gesturing again with her pen.

'What about them?'

'Take them off so we can see what you've got.'
Catherine looked at the pair of them before replying. It might have been advertised as a waitressing job, but she was beginning to think that it might not be.

'Er, no. I don't think so,' Catherine replied, crossing her arms and fixing the woman with a hard stare.

The man laughed before turning to his companion. They had another whispered conference before he glanced down at his companion's notepad and turned back to Catherine.

'Yeah, sorry er, Catherine is it?' he said. 'We're not sure that you'd be that suited to work at Fallen Angels. We're looking for people with a bit more about them.' He clenched his fists and shook them in front of him. 'Know what I mean?'

'If you're looking for whores,' Catherine replied as she got to her feet, 'why don't you put that in the fucking advert?'

'We're not looking for whores, young lady,' the female interviewer said. 'Any money paid is for time and companionship only.'

'Whatever,' Catherine replied over her shoulder as she walked out of the hotel room.

Twenty minutes later, Catherine was sitting on a bench

over the road from the Food Standards Agency Headquarters. She was still smarting from the interview, even more so after she had seen the girl with the black lipstick in the lobby of the hotel. The skinny bitch had got the job, but as far as Catherine was concerned, she was welcome to it. The girl with the lipstick had thought that was hysterical, and it had taken a fair bit of self-control for Catherine not to smack her.

Catherine's phone buzzed, and she looked at the incoming text message.

On my way. X.

Catherine got to her feet and crossed the road to meet Emily outside the building.

'Hey babes,' Catherine said with a wan smile as Emily came down the steps of the building.

'Hey you. How's tricks?'

'Won't be turning any soon,' Catherine replied. 'Not in Yarmouth, anyway.'

'Sorry,' Emily frowned. 'You've lost me.' Catherine linked her arm through Emily's and pulled her away from the building.

'Let's go for a drink,' she said. 'I bloody need one.'

'Okay, but we can't be too long,' Emily replied. 'Mr Clayton's coming round, remember?'

'So he is,' Catherine groaned.

'You didn't forget, did you? You said you were going to sort some clothes out for him to try.'

'It won't take long, babes. I've got a drawer full of clothes that have shrunk. There'll be plenty of stuff that'll fit him. What time's he coming round?'

'Seven, I think.'

'Cool,' Catherine replied, glancing at her watch. 'That's a clear hour and a half in the pub. God knows I need it.'

'Why?' Emily asked, concern crossing her face. 'Is everything okay?'

'Come on you,' Catherine replied, tugging at her arm. 'Let's get a glass of Pinot Grigio and I'll tell you all about it.'

50

'Bloody awful, ain't it mate?'

'Sorry?' Andy said, looking up from his phone at the taxi driver.

'Bloody awful.' The elderly cabbie shook his head from side to side, pointing with a bony hand at the radio on his dashboard. 'That missing girl.'

'Oh, yeah. I did hear about that.' Andy thought back to an article he'd read on the Eastern Daily News website earlier that day during one of the extended periods between customers.

'That'll be one of them foreigners what's done her in, don't you think?'

'I don't remember reading that. Is that what the police are saying?' Andy asked.

'Nah,' the cabbie replied. 'I just know. Coming over here, impugnating our women.' Andy thought for a second before replying.

'Impregnating?'

'Yeah, that too.'

Andy returned his attention to his phone, keen to avoid

any more conversation with the taxi driver. Everyone was entitled to their opinion, but he wasn't convinced that the cabbie's was a particularly palatable one. They sat in silence for a few moments until the taxi turned into the end of Emily's road.

'Just at the end, please mate,' Andy said, not looking up from his phone. He'd had a text from Emily twenty minutes earlier, asking him to come round to her flat immediately. He knew it wasn't an emergency as the text ended with a couple of exclamation marks and kisses. If it weren't for the fact that Martin had just got them both a fresh pint in, he'd have been there even quicker.

'You on a promise, are you fella?' the driver asked. Even though he tried to hide it, Andy felt a grin start to creep onto his face.

'Well, it's my girlfriend's flat.'

'Girlfriend, eh? There was me thinking you were one of them gays.'

'Well, I'm not,' Andy replied, frowning into his phone.

'Is she fit, is she? Does she like it when you get to the vinegar strokes, or does she shut her eyes and hope for the best?'

'What?'

'Does she like it, I said. I bet she does. I bet she's a right dirty little cow. They all are down this street. Slapper Alley is what we call this street in the office.' The taxi driver pulled into the kerb just outside Emily's flat. 'Twenty quid, mate.'

'You can fuck off with your twenty quid,' Andy barked. 'It's not even three miles, and I'm not your mate.' He tossed a crumpled five pound note onto the driver's lap. 'Keep the change, and buy yourself a life, you sad old tosser.'

'Very generous of you, fella,' the taxi driver replied with a toothy grin. 'Have a good night. Eh? Eh?'

'Sod off, you twat,' Andy mumbled under his breath as he slammed the taxi door behind him. He could still hear the driver cackling as the taxi pulled away.

'Bloody hell, you took your time,' Emily gasped as she opened the door. Andy grinned at her as she stepped onto the doorstep and gave him a quick kiss, followed by another much longer one.

'What's going on?' Andy asked when she pulled back from him. She looked excited, and from her flushed cheeks, he could tell that she'd had more than one glass of wine.

'Right, whatever happens, behave normal. Can you do that for me?'

'What do you mean?'

'Just be normal. You've just popped round and interrupted a girly night in, right?'

'Does your washing machine need fixing again?'

'No,' Emily giggled. 'But it might do later. Come on inside.'

Curious, Andy followed Emily into her flat. She was definitely acting strangely, but if the evening ended with him fixing her washing machine, then he could put up with a fair bit of strange. Emily walked towards the lounge door with Andy following her.

'Andy's just nipped round for a bit,' Emily announced as she walked into the lounge. Over her shoulder, Andy could see Catherine sitting in one of the armchairs. It wasn't until Andy walked into the room properly that he noticed the man wearing a pink dress and a slightly wonky blonde wig sitting on the sofa.

'Andy,' Catherine said, her voice unusually loud. She

leapt to her feet. 'How fantastic.' Andy stared at her, determined not to break eye contact with Catherine. 'Have you met Roberta?'

'Um,' Andy replied, turning to look at the sofa's occupant. He'd not been mistaken. It was definitely a man in a pink dress. 'No, I don't think I have.'

Roberta readjusted her wig and started to get to her feet. Both Emily and Catherine waved at her, and Andy realised that they were trying to get her not to stand up.

'Hi, er, Roberta. I'm Andy, Emily's boyfriend.' Roberta extended a hand with bright pink fingernails towards Andy. He shook it, ignoring the tufts of dark hair on the backs of her fingers.

'Hi Andy,' Roberta replied in a deep baritone. Out of the corner of his eye, Andy saw Emily move her hand up toward the ceiling a couple of times. 'I've heard a lot about you,' Roberta continued, this time a couple of octaves higher.

'Emily,' Andy said in a firm voice. 'Could I have a drink please?'

'What the fuck?' Andy said in a hushed voice, even though the kitchen door was closed.

'She's my boss,' Emily replied.

'She?'

'Yes, she.' Emily walked to the fridge and put her hand on a can of beer before changing her mind and reaching beyond it for a bottle of gin at the back of the fridge. 'She's on a journey.'

'She's got quite a long way to go.'

'Shh,' Emily replied with a giggle, pouring a generous measure of gin into a glass. 'The longest journey starts with a single step, and this is his. Hers, I mean.'

'Emily,' Andy said. 'Not being funny, but I've come round to your flat hoping for a bit of sexy time. The last thing I was expecting was a large man wearing your underwear and a dress in the lounge, and you quoting Chinese philosophers at me.'

'She's not wearing my underwear,' Emily replied. 'She's wearing Catherine's. Now get that down you, and then we're going to go back into the lounge and you're going to just be nice to Roberta.' She shoved the glass in his direction, and he picked it up with his good arm and took a healthy drink. 'If you're good, I'll show you the web page that I found earlier. It looks, well, challenging.'

'So, Roberta,' Andy said a few moments later as he walked back into the lounge. 'How do you know these two?'

51

J ack looked at the policeman sitting at his kitchen table, sipping from a mug of tea and nibbling on a chocolate Hob-Nob. He looked more like a stripper on his way to a hen night than a copper, and was sporting a very faint black eye.

'So,' Jack said as the policeman took another mouthful of biscuit. 'How can I help you? William, was it?'

'Yes, that's me,' William replied, a crumb falling from his mouth and onto his navy blue uniform. 'These biscuits are lovely, aren't they?' Jack didn't have a clue whether they were or not. He wasn't really a biscuit kind of guy, and only kept the long out of date Hob-Nobs for unexpected and unwanted guests. Like William.

'Good. So?'

'Hang on,' William said. 'Just let me finish my biscuit.' Jack crossed his arms over his chest while he waited. Even though he had his best *I'm really pissed off* look on his face, the policeman seemed completely oblivious to it. Finally, William popped the last piece into his mouth and chewed it slowly before taking a sip of his tea.

'Right then,' he said, reaching into his inside pocket and pulling out a photograph. He placed it on the kitchen table and swivelled it round so that Jack could see it. 'Have you seen this woman?' Jack leaned forward and examined the photograph. He wasn't surprised to see it was a picture of Beth. In the photograph, Beth was a fair bit thinner than she was now, but even so it wasn't the most flattering picture of her.

'Nope,' Jack replied, keeping his face as neutral as he could. 'Why? Who is she?'

At first, William didn't reply but just picked up the photograph and put it back in his pocket. For a second, Jack thought he was going to get up and leave without another word, but he sat back in his chair instead.

'Can I have another biscuit?'

'You help yourself,' Jack replied. 'In fact, why don't you take the whole packet and eat them in the car on your way back to Norwich.' William just stared at him before reaching out and taking another biscuit.

'Her name's Beth James, and she's been missing for a couple of weeks.' William took a small chunk out of the biscuit. 'We're starting to get concerned.'

'What, two weeks later?' Jack laughed. 'I know Norfolk Police's response time isn't the best in the country, but two weeks is a hell of a long time.'

'I know,' William replied, laughing through a mouthful of crumbs. 'It's not like it is on the telly, is it? All blue lights and woo woos on *Police Interceptors*. Not like that in real life, really.'

'Anyway, I've not seen her, so if there's nothing else?' Jack nodded at the front door, but William didn't seem to get the hint.

'My sergeant says she's probably met some bloke and just buggered off with him because she didn't want to tell her parents,' the policeman said. 'But we're supposed to look as if we're doing something, so they sent me to check the farms in case she's hiding out in an outbuilding or something.'

Jack thought quickly. William was a lot closer to the truth than he realised, but Jack thought he'd better come up' with an excuse in case the policeman decided he wanted a look round.

'Well, she's not,' Jack said as firmly as he dared.

'I think she's in Tenerife, personally.'

'Probably.'

'Were you serious about the biscuits?'

'Fill your boots.' Jack watched as William picked up the packet and wound the wrapper tight before putting the biscuits into his pocket. 'What happened to your eye?'

'Bit of a scuffle with a gang of armed robbers,' William replied. 'I managed to nick them though.' He touched his face briefly with his hand. 'All four of them.'

'Really?' Jack asked. 'What, in Norfolk? I didn't see that on the news.'

'No, you wouldn't have done. It's all being kept a bit hush hush.' William got to his feet, looking as if he was suddenly keen to leave. 'Operational security, you know how it is. Right, must be off. Thanks for the biscuits.' Jack showed the policeman to the door, and as he watched William make his way to his sad little car, wondered why the crime rate in Norfolk wasn't a hell of a lot higher than it was.

Twenty minutes later, Jack was humming to himself as he stirred the disgusting looking mixture in a saucepan on his stove. He'd just got off the phone with a nutritionist he'd hired off the internet. The woman had been trying to give him some advice on how to make his special recipe even more fattening than it already was. It had taken a while for her to get the message that he didn't care how foul it tasted, or how much it stank. After a brief argument with the nutritionist, who definitely wasn't getting a tip for her crap advice, Jack had given up and just added an entire jar of peanut butter to the mix. That had made it too thick, so he'd added some ice-cream. Then Jack had realised that when the mixture had cooled, the ice-cream would make it too thick to get down the green piping easily, so he'd added a load of full fat coke to water it back down a bit.

He leaned forwards and sniffed the gloopy liquid. It smelt absolutely disgusting, but seeing as it would be going straight down into Beth's stomach and bypassing her taste buds completely, Jack didn't think that it mattered. It wasn't as if he was going to be eating it any time soon. He turned the gas ring off and reached out for the sealant pipes that had been going through the dishwasher while he'd been talking to the policeman. He had five of them altogether, which seemed to be just about the right amount to keep Beth from getting hungry in-between feeds. According to his nutritionist, each tube contained some-where between two and a half and three thousand calories. No wonder Beth got a bit sleepy after feeding time.

52

Emily looped her arm through Catherine's as they walked through Norwich Market and towards the Forum, a large modern building that housed a variety of different businesses such as the city library, the local television studios, and — most importantly for Emily and Catherine — a pizza restaurant on the top floor.

'Pizza for lunch isn't going to help your waistline, Catherine,' Emily said as they walked past a stall promising to sell anything to do with mobile phones that you could ever want. Including stolen ones according to Andy, Emily thought, although they didn't advertise that fact very widely.

'I don't care,' Catherine replied. 'With a bit of luck, I'll be getting the sort of exercise that you've been getting over the last few days pretty soon.'

'Is that the voice of envy I hear speaking there?' Emily asked with a grin.

'I am getting a bit fed up with all the grunting, to be honest.'

'I've told you, I don't grunt.'

'That's not what Andy says,' Catherine replied. 'He told me that he's been with a fair few screamers, but never a grunter.' Emily stopped in her tracks, jerking Catherine to a halt.

'He said that? Seriously?'

'Er, no,' Catherine laughed. 'I just made that up. Come on, I'm bloody starving.' She tugged at Emily's arm and the two women walked up to the glass fronted building. On opposite sides of the small plaza outside the impressive glass front of the Forum were two groups of women, several with placards with a woman's face on them.

'What's going on?' Emily asked Catherine as they stopped next to a couple of young lads with skateboards propped up next to them, no doubt annoyed at the temporary loss of their normal skateboarding area. One of the skateboarders — a spotty young man with a baggy clothes and a wispy beard — replied.

'They're doing a campaign thing to find that missing fat bird,' he said in a nasal voice. Emily looked at him with a frown. In her opinion, any male who was old enough to grow facial hair, no matter how pathetic it looked, was automatically too old to prat about on a skateboard.

'That's not very nice, mate,' she said to the lad. 'That could be your sister who's missing.'

'His sister's well fit,' the second skateboarder said. 'She's someone I've slept with that he never can. Isn't that right, Tom?'

'Piss off, you melt,' the almost bearded man replied. 'She said she was pissed, it was a pity shag, and that she didn't realise you were a needle dick until it was too late because you'd already finished.'

'That's not what your Mum said,' his friend replied with a cackle. They wandered off, still trading banter, and

Emily figured they were trying to find an empty bit of pavement to annoy people on.

As Emily and Catherine walked towards the two groups of women, Emily realised that the one thing they all had in common was that they were on the larger side. When they got to the edge of the group nearest them, an overweight, sweaty woman approached them with a clutch of leaflets in her hand. She looked at Emily, flicked her eyes up and down at her, and then turned her attention to Catherine.

'Here you go, pet,' the woman said to Catherine. 'Take one of these.' She thrust a leaflet into Catherine's hand. 'Our number's on the back if you're interested.'

By the time Emily and Catherine's pizzas had arrived, the crowd outside the Forum had almost doubled, and a solitary policeman was watching from the edge of the plaza. The two women were sitting on the top floor of the Forum, looking down at the plaza through the floor to ceiling windows. Emily was still chuckling about the fact that Catherine had been handed a leaflet advertising *Weight Wizards*, complete with an emergency phone number on the back.

'Can you stop giggling?' Catherine asked, causing another fit of laughter from Emily. 'It's not bloody funny, you skinny bitch.'

'Sorry,' Emily said, taking a large bite of her pepperoni pizza. 'It was funny though. The look on her face was so, I don't know. Earnest?' She nodded at the leaflet on the table. 'Have you put them on speed dial yet?'

'That's enough, Emily,' Catherine replied. 'I mean it.'

Emily looked at Catherine and realised that she was actually being serious. That was new. They'd always exchanged insults about their weight, but they'd been good natured. Time to change the subject, Emily thought as she chewed a rather dry bit of pepperoni.

'Who's that lot then?' Emily asked, pointing with the crust of her pizza at one of the groups of women. 'If the other lot are the Weight Wizards, who are that bunch?'

'War on Weight, they're called.'

'How'd you know that?' Emily replied. 'Did they give you a leaflet too?' Catherine fixed Emily with a hard stare.

'No. That's what it says on their placards, you thick bitch. Now eat your pizza and get those carbs down you so you can sign up.'

Emily and Catherine watched the two groups for a while. There was a definite division between them, with a no-mans-land extending across the middle of the plaza. Even through the thick glass of the windows, they could hear the two groups trying to out shout each other.

'Was everything okay with your meal?' Emily turned to see a waitress standing next to their table.

'Very nice, thank you,' Emily replied, deciding not to mention the dry pepperoni on top of her lukewarm pizza. It wasn't as if the waitress had cooked it, or cared in the slightest what Emily actually thought. They were interrupted by screaming from the plaza below them.

'Bloody hell,' the waitress said. 'Would you look at that?' Emily turned her attention to the plaza, where two women — presumably from opposite sides of the gathering — were going hammer and tongs at each other. Emily thought at first that it was like the few female fights she'd witnessed in nightclubs. Lots of pushing, shoving, and a bit of hair pulling. When the first few proper punches were thrown, she realised that it wasn't.

'I think we'll have another drink,' Catherine said to the waitress. 'I'm not going out there for a bit.'

'I think I'll join you,' the waitress replied, staring at the plaza. The three of them watched as the two groups surged forwards, backwards, and then finally forwards and into each other. Placards became weapons, the screaming became louder, and the solitary policeman disappeared into the background as a full-scale riot developed.

53

A ndy sat, open mouthed, with a half-finished pint on the table in front of him. On the television mounted to the wall of the pub he was sitting in, there was a live report from outside the Forum.

'What's going on?' Martin asked as he walked up to the table with a couple of fresh pints. He put them on the table and shuffled in next to Andy so that he could see the television. 'Looks like a bloody football match back in the eighties. Why are they fighting?'

'No idea,' Andy replied before turning to the barman. 'Mate? Can you turn it up a bit?'

The barman gave them both a scathing look, but did as Andy asked. It wasn't as if any of the other customers were going to be annoyed. There weren't any.

'So, Amelia,' the bearded journalist on the television said as a small banner scrolled across the bottom of the screen announcing that he was live at the Forum in Norwich where a large disturbance had broken out. 'I'm live at the Forum in Norwich where a large disturbance has broken out.'

'What's going on, Bob Rutler, live at the Forum?' a woman's voice asked off screen.

'Can she not see behind him?' Andy asked with a laugh. 'There's a big fight in the background, Amelia.'

'Well, Amelia,' the reporter replied. 'It started out as a peaceful vigil to raise awareness for the plight of local missing girl, Beth Baker. Two groups of weight loss enthusiasts gathered together, putting aside their differences for a common goal.' Bob flinched as a placard flew over his head, missing him by inches. 'But it all seems to have kicked off.'

'What are their differences, Bob,' Amelia asked.

'I've got absolutely no idea, Amelia,' Bob replied, his voice almost drowned out by the sound of sirens approaching. Behind him, a police van screeched to a halt and its rear doors flew open and discharged a couple of policemen dressed in riot gear. Bob stepped to the side to let the camera get a good view of the policemen.

'Do you think one of them's the copper you beat up the other night?' Martin asked, taking a sip of his pint. 'I can't believe they only sent two policemen to a riot though. They're going to get the shit kicked out of them.'

'Shut up, Martin,' Andy replied. 'Do you want some dry-roasted?'

'Go on then,' Martin said.

By the time Andy had returned with a couple of packets of peanuts another — much smaller — police van had arrived. Over the sound of the screaming and shouting, a deep frenzied barking could be heard.

'Blimey,' Andy said. 'Now the police dogs have turned up as well.' He ripped the top off his packet and grabbed a handful of nuts. 'This is bloody great, this is. What do you think's going to happen?'

'Maybe they'll burn the Forum down for not selling

enough high calorie snacks?' Andy sniggered. On the screen in front of them, they watched the two policemen in riot gear take a few tentative steps towards the mob. 'I think they're going to need a few more Old Bill, though.'

Andy's phone buzzed in his pocket, and he pulled it out and swiped the screen.

Are you in the city? There's a big fight going on. It was Emily. He thumbed a reply.

I know. We're watching it on the telly. Where r u?

In the pizza restaurant in the Forum. Emily's reply came in a few seconds later.

'Bloody hell, Emily's there,' Andy said to Martin.

'I never had her down as a scrapper,' Martin replied, munching on a handful of peanuts.

'No, she's in the pizza place on the first floor.'

'Bet she's got a great view. Look, here go the coppers.'

As Andy watched the riot policemen disappear into the sprawling crowd of fighting women, he couldn't help but feel sympathetic towards them. They tried to grab one of the women who was on the floor, being kicked by another protestor, and drag her to safety. The main problem was one of physics. They couldn't even drag her away from the fight, almost certainly because of her size. Despite their attempt to pull the woman to safety, within a couple of seconds the pair of them had disappeared underneath a pile of screaming women.

On the screen, Bob stepped back into the camera's view. He looked shocked and had a small trickle of blood running down the side of his forehead and into his beard.

'Oh my goodness, Bob. Are you hurt?' Amelia, still off camera, squealed. Behind the reporter, the van with POLICE DOGS written on the side was rocking from side to side, the sound of frenzied barking from inside still loud and clear on the television.

'What do you think happened to him?' Martin asked.

'Probably got hit by a pork pie or something,' Andy replied with a snigger as a large woman charged into the fray over Bob's shoulder. 'Martin, was that who I think it was? Behind the beardy bloke?' He glanced at Martin to see him staring at the television, his jaw slack.

'Bloody hell,' Martin said under his breath. 'That's my Tina. What's she doing there?'

'Battering a policeman from the look of it.' Andy looked again at Martin's girlfriend who was using a broken piece of wood from one of the placards to hit one of the policemen, who was curled on the floor in a foetal position, over the back of the head. As they watched, the doors to the dog van flew open, and a dog leapt out before standing on the pavement, barking at everything and anything.

'Um,' Andy said. 'Is that a police dog?'

'Seeing as it just got out of a van with POLICE DOGS on the side, I think so,' Martin replied. The dog disappeared from sight, and Bob and Amelia continued their pointless conversation on the television. A second later, Bob shrieked and ducked out of the camera's view.

'Bob, what's going on?' Amelia's voice asked. 'Is everything okay?' Bob's head popped back up into view.

'That fucking police dog just bit me on the ankle,' he spluttered. Both Andy and Martin started laughing as, while Amelia apologised for the bad language, the dog could be seen in the background staring at the sprawling mob. They could hear the growling over the top of everything else, and as they watched, the dog launched itself into action. For large women, the protestors starting running away pretty sharpish as the police dog got to work.

'Aren't they normally a bit bigger?' Andy asked Martin, nodding at the police dog on the screen. 'Only unless I'm mistaken, that's a Daschund.'

54

'I'll tell you what I'm going to do, babes,' Catherine said, stretching out on the sofa. 'I'm going to go round there and give him one last chance.'

'Hmm?' Emily replied, looking up from the magazine she was reading. 'Sorry, give who what?'

'Jack,' Catherine said firmly. 'He's got one last chance with me, or I'm moving on. I'm too young to be wasting my time on someone who won't come up with the goods.'

'You'd have been buggered in the old days, you know that?'

'What? Literally?'

'Possibly, I don't know if they had that sort of thing in the old days.' Emily put her magazine down on the coffee table in their lounge with a sigh as Catherine started laughing. 'My point is that in the old days, you wouldn't have been able to have sex with anyone at all until you were married.'

'Bollocks,' Catherine replied. 'They were at it all the time. That's why they all had about twenty children. Talking of being buggered, what time's Andy coming round?' Catherine grinned as Emily's cheeks coloured up and she pointedly ignored the question.

'Nothing to do with the lack of contraception or high infant mortality rate, then?'

'Bloody hell, Emily. What're you reading? The Nun's Weekly or something? Now listen in, babe.' Catherine leaned towards her flat mate, her eyes crinkling as she tried not to laugh. 'Just because you're being speared on a regular basis doesn't mean you can lord it over us celibates.'

'Did you just say speared?' Emily started giggling. 'And celibates? In the same sentence?' Her giggles turned into full on laughter. 'This from a woman who's slept with most of Norwich?'

'I have not slept with most of Norwich.'

'Well, you've certainly done your best to work your way through half of them. Genetically speaking, at least,' Emily replied, picking her magazine back up and nodding at the page she had been reading a moment ago. 'It says in here that if you don't have sex for a full year, then you're officially a virgin again.'

'Bloody hell, if that is The Nun's Weekly, it's changed since I last read it.'

'Is there really a magazine called The Nun's Weekly?'

'There must be. What else are they going to read, apart from the Bible?' Catherine asked, leaning back in the sofa and flicking through the channels on the television before settling on the local news. 'Oh, look! There's that fight we saw earlier.'

On the screen, the intrepid reporter Bob Rutler was being interviewed by an orange female presenter with no dress sense. Either that, Catherine thought, or the woman had seriously pissed off someone in the wardrobe department.

'So, Bob,' the female presenter said. 'Can you tell us what happened?'

'Well, Amelia,' Bob replied, touching a hand to the tiny plaster on his forehead. 'It started out as a peaceful candlelit vigil to raise awareness of the missing local woman, Beth James.'

'But it didn't stay peaceful for long, did it Bob?' Amelia leaned forwards with a concerned expression that highlighted either years of smoking, or far too long on the sun bed. Possibly both, Catherine concluded.

'Jesus wept,' Emily said, before returning her attention to her magazine. 'This isn't scripted at all, is it?' On the screen in front of them, Bob continued.

'It's difficult to say what the exact flashpoint was,' Bob explained. 'But the event was attended by two local weight loss groups with a long history of antagonism. There was an incident a few months ago when the Weight Wizards were distributing leaflets in an area known to be a stronghold of the War on Weight group, and it all turned nasty.' On the screen behind Bob and Amelia, footage showing a burning building flashed up onto the screen.

'That was when the Thorpe St Andrew Community Centre was razed to the ground?' Amelia asked. Catherine was fairly sure that Bob already knew the answer to that question.

'That's right, Amelia. Although the police tried to play it down, my sources tell me that the Weight Wizards were behind it.'

'Really?' the orange presenter replied with a passable expression of fascination on her face.

'Oh, Botox is a bitch, isn't it?' Catherine mumbled under her breath.

'Who's a bitch?' Emily asked, looking up from her magazine. 'The one on the telly?'

'You need to get your hearing tested, you do.'

'Sorry?'

'Very funny.' Catherine got to her feet, bored with the news report. 'Can I borrow your tweezers?'

'Yeah, they're on my shelf in the bathroom cabinet,' Emily replied. 'Just put them back when you're done.'

'Cheers,' Catherine called over her shoulder as she left the lounge. 'I've lost mine somewhere. I need a bit of a trim down below and don't really want razor burn.'

Catherine pulled the door behind her and skipped towards the bathroom with a giggle, ignoring Emily's protestations about the fact that she used those tweezers for her eyebrows. She wasn't really going to use Emily's tweezers for anything other than perhaps a quick tidy up of her own eyebrows — an eye-watering waxing session at a local salon earlier that day had seen to that — but what Emily didn't know wouldn't hurt her. Either way, tonight was the night with Jack, come what may.

Twenty minutes later, Catherine stuck her head back round the door of the lounge.

'Um, Emily,' she said. 'Can I ask a really big favour?'

'What is it?' Emily replied. 'I thought you'd gone to get yourself speared?'

'Oh, I had. But my car won't start.'

'You're not borrowing mine.'

'Come on babe,' Catherine replied, hating herself for pleading. 'You don't need it this evening, not with Andy coming round.'

'But I might,' Emily said. 'Andy said there's a lay-by near Thetford that he wants to show me.'

'Emily,' Catherine replied. 'If he really said that, then

me taking your car would actually be doing you a massive favour.'

'Keys are in the ashtray in the hall,' Emily said with a snigger. 'But if you do take it, then you have to return it with a full tank.'

'Deal,' Catherine shot back, hoping that Emily's Mini wasn't almost empty like it was the time they had made that particular deal. She left before Emily could change her mind.

A few moments later, Catherine cursed Emily from the driver's seat of her Mini. The bloody thing was on fumes.

55

Jack opened the cupboard door, and gingerly took the green dress, which was still wrapped in the plastic from the dry cleaners, out before laying it on the bed. Even though it was in his cupboard, hanging up alongside all his ironed shirts every time he opened the cupboard door, he tried not to look at the thing. Leaving it wrapped up in plastic helped, but he could still see the green of the material showing through. Jack knew that he was being irrational but at the same time he didn't want the dress to be too far away from him. It had too many memories for him to even put it in the cupboard in the guest room.

He closed his eyes and tried to picture Beth wearing the dress. Try as he might, Jack couldn't summon up the image in his head. There was only one thing for it. He was going to have to get her to try it on. Jack reached into his pocket and pulled out his phone, bringing up the camera app so that he could see what she was doing. To his surprise, she was pacing up and down the room, reading one of the books that he'd stocked the shelves with. Jack had got no idea what book it was — he couldn't make out the title on the small screen. Besides, it wasn't as if he'd chosen the books. He'd gone into the charity shop next to Sainsbury's and just given them twenty quid for a large boxful of well-thumbed paperbacks. To him, it didn't matter what the books were. They could have been cook-books for all he cared. Jack laughed at the thought. That would have been particularly ironic. All he wanted them for was for the effect they had on the room.

Jack picked up the dress and walked out of the farm-house to his van. He opened the back door and placed the dress down on top of a large flat box that contained the latest addition to Beth's room. It had been delivered earlier by the same miserable bastard of a delivery driver that had delivered the hoist, along with some rather large cylinders that Jack had bought at the same time. Jack had just got the driver to drop off the deliveries outside the farmhouse — he didn't want to risk the driver hearing anything down at the outbuilding. When Jack closed the van doors and couldn't see the dress any more, he sighed with relief.

'Hi, anyone home?' Jack called out when he opened the door to Beth's room. 'Knock knock.'

'Hey you,' Beth replied. She was sitting on the bed on the opposite side of the room. 'I was wondering when you were coming round.' She smiled at him and crinkled her eyes. Sure you were, Jack thought. Wondering when your next meal was going to turn up. He returned the smile anyway. There was no need to be rude.

'I've brought you a present,' he said.

'For me?' Beth clapped a chubby hand onto her chest and put on a surprised expression. 'Really?'

'Yeah,' Jack replied. 'Something for you to try on.'

'Ooh, I love new clothes.'

'It's not exactly new, but it's in very good condition. It's been hanging up in my cupboard for a while,' Jack said. 'Until I found the perfect person to wear it.'

He turned and walked back into the main area of the abattoir, not bothering to close the door behind him. If Beth made a run for it, he'd hear her thundering across the room in plenty of time to close it before she got anywhere near the door. Jack picked up the dress and returned to Beth's room with it draped over his arm.

'Here you are,' he said, crossing to the bed and placing the dress next to her.

'Wow,' Beth replied, putting a hand on the plastic and stroking it. 'It looks lovely. Do you want me to try it on?'

'Of course I do,' Jack answered, managing to keep his expression neutral. What did the stupid cow think he wanted her to do?

'You'll have to pop outside then,' Beth said. 'I'm very shy.'

'Right,' Jack replied, turning to leave. 'Just call when you're ready. I'll leave the door ajar.' This would be a useful test to see if she had any inclination to escape or not, and Jack made sure that the pistol in his waistband was nice and snug just in case he needed it to persuade her that she wasn't going anywhere. He thought for a moment about bringing the camera app up on his phone, just to keep an eye on her, but decided instead to fetch the box from the back of the van. It was heavier that he remembered, and by the time he'd dragged it into the abattoir, he was sweating so sat down to get his breath. A few moments later, he heard Beth calling from inside the room.

'I'm ready.'

Jack took a deep breath, got to his feet, and walked towards the door. He paused outside it, glancing at his

FitBit to see what his heart rate was doing. No surprise there — it was thumping along at a right old rate of knots.

'In through the nose, out through the mouth,' he whispered to himself as he took a few more deep breaths. He was nervous as hell, but at the same time excited to see what she looked like. 'Okay, coming in now,' Jack said, more for himself than for Beth, as he pushed open the door.

Beth was standing in the middle of the room, her arms clasped behind her back. She was moving slowly from foot to foot. Jack gasped at the sight of her, or more specifically at the sight of her wearing the dress. His heart thudded in his chest, and he felt his mouth go dry.

'What do you think?' Beth asked, doing a clumsy pirouette on the spot. 'Do you like it? I think it's lovely. It's so, I don't know, retro.' Jack opened his mouth to reply and then closed it again. His breath was coming in short gasps, his knees were starting to tremble and he wondered for a few seconds if he was having a panic attack. Jack mumbled something under his breath. 'Sorry?' Beth said. 'I didn't catch that.'

'I said,' Jack replied, licking his lips to try to moisten them. 'I said, just a few more pounds.' He took a few steps backwards towards the door, not wanting to take his eyes off Beth and the green dress for a second. 'Can you change back now, please?'

He walked out of the room and closed the door softly behind him, inching it shut until he heard the latch click. Jack's heart was still thumping in his chest at the sight of Beth wearing the dress, and he sat down on the box he'd dragged in from the van to gather his thoughts. She was almost there in terms of size. Just a few extra inches around the middle and Beth would be perfect. Then it would be time.

Jack got to his feet and walked to the door of the abattoir. Earlier that day, he'd prepared five tubes of food for Beth, but he figured she deserved a treat. It would mean that he would have to pop out to the supermarket for more supplies, but the more he thought about it, the more he thought it would be worth it.

'I wonder if she could handle seven tubes,' he mumbled to himself.

56

'So what's the plan for this evening then?' Andy pressed his mobile to his ear so that he could hear Emily over the noise of the bus that was revving its engine at the traffic lights.

'Dunno,' he heard Emily reply. 'What do you fancy?' Andy paused before saying anything, partly because he wasn't sure that what he fancied was necessarily what Emily fancied, and partly because he didn't want to be overheard.

'Do you want to go out or stay in?' he asked.

'I think I'll have to stay in. Catherine's got my car. Jesus wept, what's that noise?' Andy waited until the Number 24 roared away as the lights changed to green.

'It was a bus,' he said when the racket had died down, 'being driven by Lewis Hamilton.'

'Right,' Emily laughed. 'I was saying, Catherine's got my car.'

'Yeah, I heard that bit. I guess we're staying in then?'

'Unless you want to get Delia out of the garage?' Emily was referring to Andy's pride and joy — a bright yellow

MG Trophy 160 convertible that he took out of his parents' garage once a week without fail. Once he had washed and waxed it, he put it back again.

'Not really,' he said, looking at the clear early evening sky. 'It looks like it might rain.'

'God forbid that your car might get wet,' Emily giggled down the phone. 'Let's just stay in, then. Catherine will be out all evening, maybe even all night if she gets her way.'

'We could Netflix and chill?'

'Oh, er, yeah. Okay.' Emily sounded disappointed.

'What? You don't fancy that?'

'Well, I don't mind. I was thinking we could maybe spend some time in the bedroom as opposed to watching telly.' Andy paused for a second, not sure whether Emily was trying to wind him up or actually being serious. 'What do you think?'

'I think maybe you need to look up Netflix and chill on your iPad.'

'Hang on a second.' Andy waited for a few seconds until he heard Emily laughing down the line.

'So what are you waiting for? Get your skinny arse round here. I've got a great idea for a game we can play.'

'Does it involve a safe word?'

'It might.'

'I'll be there in twenty minutes.'

A couple of hours later, Andy and Emily were sitting in the lounge of her flat, both exhausted. The game that Emily had come up with had involved an egg timer, a freezing cold tub of whipped cream, and some extraordinary stamina on Andy's part. There was a stain on the front of Emily's negligee that could have been whipped cream, or something else entirely. Andy grinned as he realised that either way, he didn't care.

'Bloody hell, Emily,' he said with a sigh. 'Where the hell did you get that idea from?'

'The internet,' Emily replied, snuggling up to him. She moved his arm to rest the plaster cast on a cushion. 'When's this thing coming off, anyway?'

'A couple of weeks, I think. Have you got a knitting needle?'

'Seriously?'

'Yeah. I've got a bastard of an itch on the inside of my arm. It's your fault for making me all sweaty.'

'No, do you seriously think I've got knitting needles?' Emily prodded him in the ribs, making Andy laugh. 'Do I look like that sort of girl?' Andy thought about replying that she did on occasion, but decided against it.

'Has Catherine?'

'Er, no,' Emily replied, jabbing Andy again. 'She's even less likely to have some than I am. Now make yourself useful and fetch the wine.'

'Where's the old trout gone tonight, anyway?' Andy asked, ignoring Emily's request.

'She's gone round to Jack's. It's do or die time for him, apparently. If he doesn't do the business tonight, then he's toast.' Emily shuffled to the edge of the sofa and got to her feet. 'That reminds me, I found something out about him that's pretty weird. Stay there and I'll get my iPad.' As Emily got to the door of the lounge, Andy turned and called out after her.

'Emily?'

'What?' She turned to look at him, and for a second, Andy was speechless. She looked, well, he wasn't sure quite how to describe her. Whether it was the light coming in through the window, whether it was the way she was standing, or whether it was the fact that he'd just had some of best sex in his life, Andy wasn't sure. But she looked absolutely beautiful. 'What is it, you gormless twat?' And as quickly as it had appeared, the moment vanished and she was back to being Emily.

'Seeing as you're up, you might as well get the wine.'

'Oh, you tosser,' Emily giggled as she left the room.

'Look, here,' Emily said, sitting back down next to Andy and pressing her iPad into his hands. 'Read that.'

Andy read in silence as Emily poured them both a glass of Pinot Grigio. The article was about a vicar who'd been battered to death in the study of his own vicarage.

'Jesus, Emily. Not again,' Andy said when he reached the bottom of the page. 'You've told me all this already. But I don't get what the story's got to do with Jack, unless you're turning into his stalker.'

'You distracted me by trying to make me go oink, but look at the picture at the bottom of the page.' Andy looked again but couldn't make the connection. Emily hadn't actually squealed like a pig, but they'd had a great time giving it a go. So much so that Andy had been on the top deck of the Number 24 from Thorpe St Andrew into Norwich earlier, and had experienced an entirely unexpected erection when they'd driven past a pig farm. Not that he was about to tell Emily that, though.

'What about it?'

'That's Jack Kennedy. The bloke that Catherine's trying to do her siren act on.'

'No it's not,' Andy replied, trying to forget the corrugated iron pig sheds full of promise that he'd seen earlier. 'The bloke in the picture's way thinner, and his last name isn't Kennedy. It's Green.'

'Look closer,' Emily said, insistent. She leaned across him, and Andy was momentarily distracted as one of her breasts slid carelessly across his arm. She made a swiping movement with her thumb and index finger to enlarge the image. 'See? It's definitely him.'

'Bloody hell,' Andy said. She was right. The man in the photograph with the dead vicar's arm around him was a much weedier version of Jack. 'He's buffed up a bit since this was taken, hasn't he?'

'Yeah. I don't get the name change though,' Emily said, doing the thing with the breast again as she moved back to her original position. 'If the vicar bloke was his dad, then he's Jack Green, not Jack Kennedy.'

'That is a bit weird, you're right. Maybe he just wanted to get away from what happened to his father?'

'Could be,' Emily replied, taking the iPad off Andy and stabbing at the page. 'There's another article here with a bit more information.' She read in silence for a few moments, Andy contentedly sipping his wine and thinking. Mostly about breasts. 'Oh my God,' Emily continued. 'This is awful. The poor man.'

'You're joking?'

'Nope, look.' She pointed at the screen. 'Reverend Green was murdered in the study with one of his own candlesticks. Right in front of his son, Jack.'

'That is a bit rubbish, isn't it?'

'It is when it's the vicar's wife that's doing the battering.'

57

Catherine was still smarting at the fact that Emily had lent her the car with no fuel in it, so she'd only put a tenner's worth in at the Sainsbury's at the end of the road. Well, she'd tried to put a tenner in, but her fingers had slipped at the last minute and she'd managed to put in ten pounds and six pence worth. That wouldn't have normally been a problem, but she only had a single ten pound note in her pocket, and knew that her bank account was almost empty. After a long argument with the acne riddled young woman behind the counter, Catherine had ended up paying the ten pounds in cash, and putting the six pence on her bankcard. She thought she'd managed to hide the relief when the transaction had gone through.

Catherine sat back in the seat and drummed her fingers on the steering wheel while she waited for the lights to change. There was no way she was going to let Emily bring her mood down. Not tonight. Especially as her flat mate was probably on the shag right now. The thought of it brought a smile to Catherine's face. For years she'd been trying to get Emily to live a bit more like a young woman and a bit less like an elderly extra in a habit on the set of *Call the Midwife*. Finally, it seemed, Emily had seen sense.

When the light changed to green, Catherine put her foot down on the accelerator. At first, nothing happened, but then a couple of seconds later, Emily's Mini coughed and moved off. Catherine drove down Prince of Wales Road, which she knew would be teeming later that evening with young people full of booze, anger, and sexual frustration. There would be violence and blood would be spilt just like every single Saturday night on that particular street, and that was just the women. She made her way to the outskirts of Norwich and, a few moments later, Catherine was deep in the countryside and heading for Hill Top Farm.

'Destination not recognised,' the annoying woman on the sat-nav repeated.

'Oh, for God's sake, come on,' Catherine sighed as she tried again to enter Hill Top Farm into the screen. She'd had to pull over into a lay-by to programme the sodding thing after nearly careering into a tractor that didn't see the need for any lights when she'd tried it while driving. 'What do you mean you don't know where it bloody well is?'

'Destination not recognised,' the sat-nav repeated before returning to the search screen. For a moment, Catherine considered trying to change the voice to a male one to see if he might know where Hill Top Farm was, but she didn't think it would make any difference.

'Bitch,' Catherine snapped at the machine and flicked it with a finger. The suction cup that was holding the sat-nav to the windscreen came loose, and the whole thing tumbled to the floor of the car. From the splintering noise she heard as it hit the gear stick on its way down, the screen had probably broken as it fell. 'Cheap bitch,' she muttered, realising that she was going to have to buy Emily a new sat-nav. She could just reattach it to the windscreen and plead ignorance, but although Emily could be a bit thick at times, she wasn't that thick.

Catherine looked through the windows into the gloom, trying to work out where she was. In the distance, there was the orange glow of a town or city. It could be Norwich. It could be Kings Lynn. Catherine had been driving round in circles for so long that it could even be Ipswich for all she knew. The air didn't smell funny though, so it probably wasn't. She reached into her pocket for her phone. At least Google Maps would know where Hill Top Farm was. Her phone lit up as she pressed it. Or at least, most of it did. The bit in the top corner that told her how strong the signal was didn't light up at all. 'You have got to be kidding me,' Catherine mumbled.

She cracked open the door and got out of the car, walking a few yards away and holding the phone up in the air to try to get a signal. Catherine walked from one end of the lay-by to the other, but there was no signal at all showing on the phone. She thought for a few seconds. The only thing she could do would be to drive around for a bit until she got a phone signal, download the maps to her phone if she could work out how to do it, and take it from there. Catherine walked back to the car and got back in the driver's seat. As she turned the ignition, she kicked the broken sat-nav to the side of the footwell with her shoe.

The engine turned over a couple of times before finally catching. Catherine put it into gear and moved off, but the car only travelled about twenty feet before the engine died. She turned the ignition again, but this time it wouldn't even start. Catherine grabbed the steering wheel with both hands and thought about screaming. This wasn't fair. She was supposed to be bathing in a post-orgasmic glow by now, or at least a pretty passable impression of one. Not sitting in a stupid bloody car that wouldn't work, with a sat-nav that couldn't find its own arse in the dark, and a phone that she couldn't even play Angry Birds on.

She shook the steering wheel, cursing Emily in her head for having such a shit car, when she remembered a discussion that they'd had a few weeks before. Emily had been bumping her gums about the fact that why, when it was supposed to be cheaper to run a diesel car, was the cost of diesel so much more than petrol. Like the petrol that Catherine had put into the car earlier that evening. Instead of the diesel that the bloody thing actually took.

Catherine leaned her head back on the backrest and screamed, for real this time. Just like in space, where no one can hear you scream, she figured that no one could hear you in the arse end of Norfolk either.

58

Emily stared at her iPad, skimming through the rest of the article. It was from one of the more serious newspapers, so she thought that it was probably fairly close to the truth.

'It says here,' she said to Andy, 'that Mrs Green — Jack's mother — went bananas after she found out that Reverend Green had been dipping into their pension fund.'

'Really?' Andy replied. 'Was it gambling?'

'Hang on, I'm still reading.'

'I reckon prostitutes.'

'Andy, shut up,' Emily said, giggling. 'He was a man of the cloth.'

'They're the worst for that sort of thing. If it's not whores, it's choirboys. Hey, that almost rhymes.'

'He put it into the steeple fund, apparently.'

'Bloody hell,' Andy replied. 'My Mum's been trying to get Dad to fix our roof for years. She would have been delighted, pension fund or no pension fund.'

Emily scrolled down the screen until she got to the

bottom of the article. Underneath the advertisements for hearing aids and competitively priced conservatories, there was a series of follow up articles with click bait headlines.

'Andy, could you do me a favour?' Emily said, not taking her eyes off the screen.

'Sure, anything.'

'Could you just leave my tits alone while I'm reading this?'

'Oh, sorry,' Andy replied. 'I was thinking maybe round two?'

'Yeah, in a bit. I just want to look at something.' One of the headlines had caught her eye. 'Police search for murdered vicar's son'. She clicked on the article, and her eyes widened as she read it.

'Jesus,' Emily mumbled. 'Andy, would you listen to this?'

'Can I listen to it after we've had sex?'

'No, listen. This is important.'

'During maybe?'

'Andy, shut the fuck up and listen.' Emily stared at him, and from the change in his expression, he'd realised straight away that she wasn't messing about.

'Sorry,' Andy apologised, picking up a pillow and pressing it on his lap. 'I'm listening.'

'It says here that the police are looking for Jack Green or Kennedy or whatever his bloody name is in connection with the disappearance of a woman.'

'Are you serious?' Andy leaned over Emily to look at the screen of the iPad.

'Yep. Apparently, the day his mother got sentenced to life in prison for murder, our Jack disappeared. The same day as a woman from the area.'

'Oh, shit.'

'You're not kidding,' Emily said. 'According to this article, the woman worked as some sort of web cam model on a ropey web site. When the police looked into her computer, they found that she'd arranged to meet a bloke who she met via the web site.'

'Let me guess, Jack Kennedy?'

'It doesn't actually say that, but apparently he used the same website.' Emily frowned at the screen. 'So they're putting two and two together, and looking for him in connection with her disappearance.'

'He doesn't strike me as a web cam model, really.'

'Not as a model, you melt. As a customer.'

By the time Emily clicked through another couple of articles, she was starting to get really concerned.

'My God, Andy, listen to this,' Emily said before reading from the screen. '"Police today confirmed that the body discovered in a shallow grave in the cemetery next to St Barnabas Church is that of missing local women, Jessica Godfrey." That was Jack's father's church.'

'They found a body in a graveyard?'

'That's what it says here. Talk about hiding something in plain sight.' Emily continued reading from the same article. '"Police are growing increasingly keen to speak to Jack Green, who has not been seen since her disappearance." Then it goes on about head injuries to the poor woman.'

'Do you think she got candlesticked?'

'Oh, be serious Andy. What are we going to do?'

'How'd you mean?'

Emily leaned forwards on the sofa, put the iPad on the coffee table, and took a deep breath.

'Christ, you're thick as mince sometimes, Andy. What are we going to do about Catherine? She's currently trying to get her end away with a man who's wanted for murder.'

She looked at him and could almost hear the gears grinding in his head as he put it all together.

'Shit,' Andy said a few seconds later.

'Yeah, shit,' Emily replied, getting to her feet. 'Right, we need to do something. Phone 999 and get the police, and then phone for a taxi. I'm going to get dressed.'

'A taxi to where?'

'Hill Top Farm. That's where Jack lives.'

'The Butcher's place?'

'Yes, Andy. The Butcher's place. Now come on, chop chop.' Emily turned to leave, but then thought of a better plan. 'Scratch that, get a taxi to yours and we'll get Delia. It's on the way, and it'll be a lot quicker than sodding Canary Cars.'

Emily rushed into her bedroom to throw some clothes on. Her hands were shaking as she got dressed, and she could hear Andy talking on the phone as she picked up her clothes from where they'd been thrown earlier on that evening. Catherine was in trouble, Emily knew that. It wasn't the first time she'd been in trouble — there'd been a long string of incidents over the years they'd lived together — but nothing like this. As she did up her blouse, fingers slipping on the tiny plastic buttons, Emily swore under her breath.

'Jesus, Catherine,' she muttered. 'You'd better be sitting there in bed in the wet spot when we get there.' It was that or she would be lying on the floor with a blood-stained candlestick next to her. Emily ran back into the lounge. 'Have you phoned them?' she barked at Andy.

'Yes, I have,' he replied, a wounded expression on his face. 'The taxi's on its way. They said it'll only by five minutes. The nearest driver's in a pub just round the corner.

'Well bloody well go and get dressed then,' Emily

shrieked. 'You can't rescue her with your pasty acorn flapping about, can you?'

To Emily's relief, Andy finishing getting dressed and the taxi arriving both happened within a few seconds of each other. She had tried Catherine's phone several times, but it was just going straight through to the answer phone. Emily pushed Andy out of the door and towards the waiting cab before slamming the door behind her.

Once she had given Andy's parents' address to the taxi driver, she sat back in the seat and took a deep breath in through her nose, ignoring the smell of stale beer and what she thought might be something faecal in origin.

'Can you put your foot down, mate?' Emily said to the driver. He turned and leered at her over his shoulder.

'Not really, pet,' the driver replied. 'I don't want to get pulled over by the Old Bill. They might not appreciate the fact that I'm still driving a cab when I've lost my license.'

Emily tutted and sat back in her seat. She fished in her pocket for her phone to try Catherine again when Andy leaned forwards to speak to the driver.

'Have you looked for it? I couldn't find mine for ages and it turned up down the side of the sofa.'

59

J ack sat on the box for a few moments, thinking. The sight of Beth in the green dress had really got to him, and although he wanted her slightly larger than she was now, he wasn't sure that he could wait any longer. He tapped his foot on the floor, not sure what to do. A moment later, he decided that he needed to do something with his hands while he thought things through. He always did his best thinking when he was working on something. Jack thought for a moment about going back to the farmhouse and working on the candlestick, but it was as good as finished. His father used an expression — polishing a turd — which he used when Jack was refusing to accept that something was done and kept fiddling. If he went back to the farmhouse, that's exactly what he would be doing.

He got to his feet and picked up a Stanley knife from one of the counters. Flicking the blade open, he returned to the box he had been sitting on and sliced it open. Jack opened the lid and fished inside for the instructions which he set to one side as he upended the box and watched the contents spill out onto the floor.

Two minutes later, Jack was thoroughly confused. The instructions he was holding bore no relationship to the pieces of chipboard in front of him, and the small plastic bag taped to the inside of the lid had completely the wrong number of screws and fixings in it. When Jack leafed through to the end of the instructions and saw a drawing of a child's bed, he swore under his breath. Looking at the number and shape of the chipboard, he was fairly sure that he had the wrong instructions, as opposed to the wrong contents. But why did he need instructions, Jack asked himself. Wasn't he a master carpenter? He crossed back to the counter and picked up a hammer and screwdriver, crumbling up the useless instructions and throwing them into the corner of the room as he did so.

It took Jack a while, but he managed to lay out the chipboard into a logical pattern, and had distributed the screws and fixings against the holes in the wood where he thought they needed to go. When he started putting the piece of furniture together, the noise attracted Beth's attention.

'What are you doing out there, Jack?' he heard her ask, her voice muffled through the closed door. Jack paused, hammer mid swing, and replied.

'I'm making something.' He lowered the hammer and wiped his brow with the back of his hand.

'What are you making?'

'Something for your room.'

'Is it another present?' Beth asked.

'Yeah, kind of.'

'Can I watch you make it?'

Jack thought for a second before deciding that there was no reason why she shouldn't. It wasn't as if she was going to rush out, disarm him and take the hammer before sprinting across the fields to safety. She wouldn't even get as far as the external door before she would need to stop for a bit of a sit down. Seeing as that was partly his fault, he opened the door.

'You'll need to sit on the commode in the middle of the room where I can see you,' he told Beth as she tried to peer past him to see what he was making. 'Over there, okay?'

'Okay,' Beth replied with a sly smile. Jack watched her as she made her way slowly to the commode and sat on it. He realised that she could only just fit into the chair, whereas when she'd arrived she'd been able to get in and out of it easily.

'So, what is it?' Beth asked, nodding at the few pieces of chipboard that Jack had managed to fit together.

'Wait and see, cheeky,' Jack replied as he returned to work.

It took Jack another fifteen minutes or so, but finally he stepped back and admired his work. While he'd been working, Beth had kept making inane comments like 'gosh, aren't your arms muscular' and 'blimey, your shoulders are amazing'. She was right of course. That was exactly why Jack spent so much time in the gym.

'What do you think?' he asked Beth.

'I still don't know what it is,' she replied. Jack frowned for a second, about to come up with a sarcastic reply, when he realised that from the angle she was looking at it from she wouldn't be able to see it properly. He grunted as he turned the piece of furniture round so that it was facing her.

'Oh, it's a desk,' she smiled and clapped her hands. 'That's fantastic, Jack. Now I've got somewhere to read my books.'

Jack fetched the sack trolley from the other side of the room, keeping half an eye on Beth as he did so. He managed to get the desk onto it, and manhandled the trolley into the inner room before placing the desk in front of the bookcase. It wasn't much of a desk to be honest, and it looked nothing like the original desk that Jack wanted it to symbolise. It wasn't heavy because it was made of mahogany like the old one, but because it was made of low quality chipboard that was more compressed paper than wood. Instead of ornate brass handles it had thin aluminium ones that had been sprayed with gold paint. But, and this was the most important thing as far as Jack was concerned, it was a desk in front of a bookcase.

'Wow,' Beth said, clapping her hands again like an excited child. 'It looks like a library.'

At the sound of the word 'library', Jack froze. Had Beth just said that? He turned his head slowly to look at her, and remembered her earlier in the green dress. In that instant, he made his decision. Beth was big enough. Tonight was going to be the night. It was, he realised with an involuntary shiver, time.

'I just need to nip back to the farmhouse for a few more bits,' he told her as he walked to the door.

'Okay,' Beth replied with a smile. 'Are they more presents?'

'Yeah, they are,' Jack said over his shoulder.

By the time Jack got back to the farmhouse, he was starting to get properly excited about the evening ahead. Everything that he'd been planning for well over a year was finally going to happen. When Beth had said the word 'library' earlier, it had been like a thunder clap going off in his head. It was then that he knew this was all meant to be, and that it was meant to be that evening. It was a sign.

He rushed into the workshop and picked up the candlestick. On the base of it, in carefully carved letters, was the name 'Beth'. He'd done that the other night. Even though the original candlestick didn't have a name carved onto the bottom, it had felt right to him. As he looked at it now, he thought that was a fantastic idea. It was, after all, Beth's candlestick. Or at least it would be by the time the evening was over.

The next thing that Jack fetched was a picture frame that he kept, face down, in the same cupboard as the dress. Making sure that he kept the frame face down, he picked it up and took it with him as he made his way back to the abattoir.

'What have you got?' Beth asked as he unlocked the door to her room and walked in. 'Is that a picture?' Jack knew that she wouldn't be able to see the candlestick from where he'd put if just outside the door. He also had the green dress hanging over his other arm which he laid on the bed.

'Yes,' he replied. 'It's a picture.' He walked over to the desk and placed it carefully on the top of the desk before looking away quickly so that he wouldn't have to look at the photograph in the frame. Jack moved back towards the door as Beth started walking over to the desk to look at the photograph. 'Can you put the green dress back on for me? I need to nip out to the supermarket, but I won't be long.'

'Who's that in the picture?' Beth asked as she picked up the frame. 'She's got the green dress on.'

Jack took a deep breath before replying.

'That's my mother.'

60

A ndy eased the gearstick back down into second gear as he slowed down for a red light up ahead. At least they were making progress now, which they weren't in the bloody taxi, but they seemed to be catching every red light in Norwich. In the passenger seat next to him, Emily was fretting with her phone.

'Why are we slowing down?' she said, irritated as Andy eased his foot onto the brake pedal and touched it like he was walking over very thin ice. From the way the car pulled ever so slightly to the left as he did so, he thought he might need to check the passenger side brake pads at some point. He wasn't sure why one brake pad would be wearing more quickly than the other one, and he always changed the pads at the same time to make sure everything was symmetrical. 'Andy?'

'Sorry, what?'

'I said, why are we slowing down?'

'Red light.'

'Christ, another one?'

'Yeah.' Maybe it was because Emily was in the

passenger seat? That must be it, Andy surmised. It was the extra weight that was pulling the car to the side.

'Andy?'

'Hmm?'

'It's green.'

Andy put his foot down and felt the car leap forwards. He glanced at the tachometer, waiting until it just touched the number seven before he shifted up into second gear. That was the optimum power to fuel ratio for the MG Trophy and would tease every inch of acceleration out of every single one of the one hundred and sixty brake horsepower in the engine.

'Andy?' Emily asked again. He frowned slightly before answering. Couldn't Emily just enjoy the drive? That was the problem with women. They just wanted to talk all the time, instead of appreciating the finer things in life like the sadly almost defunct engineering of Morris Garages.

'There you go, Delia,' he whispered as he slipped into third gear at precisely the right moment before returning his attention to Emily. 'Sorry, what?'

'I'm just not getting the impression that you're taking this whole situation very seriously.'

'I am too,' he replied, glancing over at Emily who was staring at him with an earnest expression on her face. 'Why'd you say that?'

'You're talking to the car.'

'I am not.'

'There you go, Delia,' Emily snapped back. 'We're supposed to be saving Catherine from an axe murderer, and you're talking to your bloody car.'

'I thought it was a candlestick?' Andy asked.

'What?'

'He's not an axe murderer,' Andy said, squinting at the approaching corner. He eased Delia a couple of feet to the right as he lined up for the best trajectory for the curve ahead. 'He's a candlestick murderer.'

'Oh, for fuck's sake, I don't believe it.'

'Neither do I,' Andy said as he saw the light a couple of hundred yards in front of them turn to orange.

'I wasn't talking about the traffic lights.'

Andy downshifted through the gears, knowing it would maximise fuel economy, reduce the wear on the brake pads, and prolong the life of the tyres. And at a hundred and fifty quid a pop, the tyres needed all the prolonging he could give them.

As they sat at the red light, Emily turned to Andy. He looked at her, realising that she had her really serious face on. That was never a good sign in his experience.

'Andy, listen to me,' she said, and he had to struggle to hear her over the purring of the engine. He did his best to ignore the nagging thoughts at the back of his mind about tweaking the fuel injector to improve the idling speed and listen to her. A serious face and a lowered voice were pretty important combat indicators. If Emily started using the index finger of doom, he was in trouble. 'Are you listening?'

'Yes,' he replied, turning to give her his full attention. Bollocks to the fuel injector. 'I'm listening.'

'Now,' she replied. 'This is a sports car, right?'

'Oh, yes.'

'So, you...' There was the index finger, right in his face. 'You need to drive it like one. Catherine is in mortal danger, and you driving like the bloke in Miss Daisy instead of Ayrton Senna isn't helping.'

'Do you want me to put the roof down before the lights change?'

'No, Andy. I don't want you to put the sodding roof

down. If you don't drive this bloody thing like you stole it, I am never having sex with you ever again.'

Andy jammed his foot onto the accelerator even though the light was still red. Emily squealed as the car leapt forward like it had been hit from behind. Andy didn't need telling twice, especially with the threat of a total loss of privileges on the table. He waited until the needle was on nine and the engine was screaming before he slammed the car into second, and a few hundred yards later, into third. When Delia hit seventy, he eased up on the accelerator and shifted into fourth, knowing that this would help them round the slow left hander coming up.

'Bloody hell,' he heard Emily shout over the noise of the roaring engine and the wind rushing over the canvas soft top of the car. 'That's more like it.'

It didn't take them long to get beyond the suburbs of Norwich and into the countryside. The main dual carriageway that led all the way to London stretched in front of them, but to Andy's disappointment, they didn't stay on it for long.

'It's this one,' Emily barked, pointing at a slip road to their left. 'Last exit at the top.' Andy jammed the steering wheel over, and they shot up the narrow slip road at almost a hundred miles an hour. He pressed the brakes hard, not caring any more if they pulled to one side or the other, and shifted down into third to take the roundabout at the top. The engine screamed in pain as he leaned into the roundabout, which was a fair bit smaller than he remembered. The back end of the car started sliding, and he had to correct it pretty sharply with the steering wheel and a jab on the brakes.

When they cleared the roundabout, an open stretch of

road lay ahead of them. Andy flicked his full beams on and accelerated down the tree covered narrow road. He was beginning to enjoy this.

'Jesus Christ, look out!' Emily screamed. Andy peered through the windscreen and, a few seconds before he hit her, saw a woman standing half in the road with her thumb held up. He jarred the wheel over, missing her by inches, and she disappeared into the inky blackness behind them. 'Did you hit her?'

'No, almost did. Stupid bloody cow.' Andy could feel his heart thumping in his chest. It had been close, and he eased up on the accelerator a notch.

'That's not a good place to hitch hike, really,' Emily replied. 'Middle of bloody nowhere.' Andy saw her peering through the windscreen. 'There's a tree up here somewhere. The turning to the farm's just before it.' Andy couldn't see anything but trees.

'Not very helpful, Emily,' he muttered.

'It's shaped like a swastika, you can't miss it.' They drove on in silence for a couple of minutes before Andy jumped as Emily shouted at him. 'There it is!'

He touched his foot to the brake to prepare to swing into the track, but when he took his foot back off the pedal, the brakes were still fully engaged.

'Shit,' he said as the back end of the car started to swing round. 'That's not good.'

61

'You absolute fucking tosspot,' Catherine shouted from her position in the ditch at the side of the road. She was half sitting, half lying in a knee-deep hole that was full of stagnant water and God knew what. She'd had no choice though. When the twat in the little yellow car had come screaming down the road, if she hadn't leapt into the ditch then she would have been in a right old mess. So much for Norfolk being a friendly county.

Catherine tried to pull one of her feet out of the mud at the bottom of the ditch, and with a squelching sound, she managed to remove it. Minus her shoe. At least she'd managed to hang onto her phone when she'd jumped into the ditch to avoid certain death, even if the bloody thing was next to useless.

'Oh, come on,' she said. 'Seriously?' It turned out that the ditch was a lot more attached to her shoes than she was, as the other one chose to stay at the bottom of the ditch as well. Catherine was faced with a decision of getting her hands and arms into the sludge underneath the water in the ditch, or going without shoes. It didn't take her long to decide to go barefoot. If they'd been real Jimmy Choo's, as opposed to knock offs that cost her a tenner at Snetterton Market, she would have thought differently.

Brushing herself down as best she could, Catherine decided to head off in the same direction as the car had been going. The muppet must have been going somewhere, she figured, so she might as well follow him. She went back to the car to retrieve her handbag, and set off down the road, wincing at the sharp stones that dug into her feet. Catherine was only twenty yards away from Emily's Mini when a bird scarer fired in the distance, making her jump. It sounded like a gun shot, and Catherine wondered why a farmer was leaving it on all night. She was no expert on farming, but she was fairly sure that birds didn't need scaring when it was pitch black outside.

As she picked her way down the road, trying and failing to avoid the sharp stones that dug into her bare feet, she thought about how crap this evening had turned out to be. It wasn't just this evening though, she reflected as she stepped on what felt like a bit of broken glass. It was her whole bloody life at the moment. No job, no real prospects of getting one, and a reputation around Norwich as a bit of a slapper, not helped by the fact that YouTube still hadn't taken that bloody video down. At least her name had stopped trending as a hashtag on Twitter.

Every few yards, she looked down at her phone to see if it had managed to pick up a signal, but there was nothing at all. She was using it as a torch to avoid the worst of the stones, but when she realised her battery was a lot lower than she thought it was, Catherine had to turn it off. Within a couple of steps in the pitch black, she trod on a really sharp stone.

'Oh, for fuck's sake,' she shouted into the dark,

hopping on her other foot and trying to reach whatever was stuck in the sole of her foot with her hand.

What happened next almost seemed to happen in slow motion. Catherine hopped her way into a large pothole in the road which was not only full of water, but also bloody deep. Her ankle rolled over, she felt a crack followed by a sickening pain in the bottom of her leg, and she lost her balance completely. When she landed on the hard tarmac, it was the palms of her hands and her knees that took the worst of the impact. Her phone, which skittered away into the darkness, didn't fare much better.

Tears rolling down her face, Catherine got to her feet and tested her ankle. It was bloody painful, but she could put some weight on it. That was something, at least. Wincing at the pain, she tried to brush the stones out of her palms. They were soaking wet, but she wasn't sure if it was blood or water from the pothole. Either way, the pain was excruciating.

Catherine blinked, but apart from brushing the tears away from her eyes, it didn't make a blind bit of difference to what she could see. Which was next to nothing. There wasn't even a bit of moonlight to help her find her phone. Crawling around on her hands and knees wasn't going to be an option, so she spent a few minutes shuffling around and trying to find it with her feet. She was just about to give up when she felt her big toe nudge against something.

'Thank God for that,' Catherine gasped with delight as her hands closed over the familiar hard plastic. She ran her fingers over it to find the 'Home' button and pressed it. The fact that the screen wasn't broken was probably the only bit of good luck that she'd had that whole sodding evening. She turned the torch back on and used it to inspect the damage. The wetness on her palms was blood, not water. There wasn't much of it, but her palms were scraped red raw. Her knees were in even worse condition, with pink patches of whatever the stuff underneath her skin was called. Little dots of blood peppered the tattered skin. That was going to hurt like a bitch when she cleaned it up properly.

Catherine fought back a sob as she turned the torch back off. What should she do? She looked in the direction that the twat in the yellow car had gone, but she couldn't see anything apart from what looked like a faint white glow in the distance. A house, maybe? In the other direction was Emily's car, and way beyond it, the glow of the town that she'd seen earlier. Neither of the lights looked reachable with a knackered ankle, so it would have to be Emily's car.

She was hungry, tired, in pain, and starting to get cold. The idea of a night in a broken-down car wasn't particularly appealing, but Catherine didn't see what other options she had.

62

J ack whistled to himself as he walked down the cold meat aisle, swinging the supermarket basket which only had a packet of ginger nut biscuits in it so far. He smiled at an old woman who was trying to reach a packet of pork chops on the top shelf. A few years ago, she probably would have been able to reach the shelf without any problems, but the way that her spine was bent over, that wasn't going to happen any time soon.

'Can I get that for you?' Jack said, widening his smile as he approached the woman. She looked at him with hostility, squinting up through hooded eyes. 'It's no trouble.'

'Well, I suppose you could,' she grumbled. 'If you wouldn't mind.'

He reached out and picked up the pork chops, handing them to her. She turned her squint to the packet.

'Fuck me sideways, they're expensive, aren't they?' the little old lady said.

'Er, yeah,' Jack replied, his smile faltering for a second as he briefly considered the logistical and moral difficulties of actually fucking her sideways. 'I guess they are. Do you need anything else?'

'I used to go to that nice butcher in the village until he got closed down.' The woman put the chops into her basket next to a single potato. 'He was lovely. Frank Pinch, his name was. He could pinch me any time he wanted,' she cackled, showing Jack a set of teeth that made him wince. At least they were hers, he supposed, even if they were almost green. As Jack walked off, he heard the woman muttering something about Frank Pinch and the things that she could do with his sausage.

As he wandered around the almost empty supermarket, he planned out the evening ahead. Once he'd got all the stuff for another couple of tubes for Beth, he would head back to the farm and mix them up. Jack still wasn't sure that she would be able to handle seven tubes, but she deserved a treat before, well, before the end of the evening. Two jars of peanut butter — smooth this time, not crunchy — went into his basket. The crunchy one just got stuck in the pipe, and he wanted to be able to re-use it on the next one. Then ice cream and some more full fat coke. Finally, a bottle of Prosecco. That wasn't for Beth though, that was for him. For afterwards.

Jack wandered towards the only open till where a bored looking woman was doing something complicated with her nails and a bright pink emery board. As he approached, she looked up and flashed him a very brief smile. She was perhaps mid-thirties, a slight purple tinge to her hair, and when she spoke Jack knew she was very local.

'Hi, did you find everything you needed this evening?' she said in a sing-song voice.

'I think so,' he replied as he put the basket down and started emptying his purchases onto the conveyor belt.

'Cool,' the cashier replied, picking up the peanut butter

and waving it across the scanner. 'I normally try to guess what people are having for tea based on what they're buying, but maybe not with you. Peanut butter, ice cream, booze and a large packet of antibacterial wipes.' Jack stared at the woman, not sure where she was going. 'Interesting evening ahead, is it?'

'Sorry, not with you?' he replied. What could she possibly know about the evening he had planned? 'I've got a quiet night in on my own planned.' She leaned forward and spoke to him in a conspiratorial whisper.

'Looks to me like you're into sploshing?'

'What's sploshing?'

'I guess it's okay on your own, but it's much more fun if there's two of you.'

'I'm sorry,' Jack glanced at her name badge. 'I'm sorry, Karen. But I haven't got a clue what you're talking about.'

'I get off at eight.'

'Oh, that's nice. How much is that, please?'

'I'm very flexible.'

'Do you want my reward card?' Jack pushed his loyalty card in her direction. 'It's just I'm in a bit of a hurry.' Karen paused, staring at him as he waved the small purple card. With a sigh, she turned to the till.

'Twelve pounds fifty.'

Jack paid the cashier, who decided that her nails needed some more work before he'd even put his change into his trouser pocket. He made his way to the supermarket exit, stopping just before it to check his receipt. His eyes ran down the thin piece of paper, and at first everything seemed to be just how it should be. Then he turned the receipt over.

'Excuse me, sir,' Jack heard a male voice say. He looked up to see a burly man dressed in a security guard's uniform. Jack ran a practised eye over the man. The security guard was big, that much was for certain, but he wasn't fit. Not by a long shot.

'What?' Jack replied.

'Could you move away from the door? It's an automatic one, and you're standing in the beam.' Jack took a large step backwards, and the doors hissed to a close.

'Happy?' he asked the guard before returning his attention to the receipt. The silly cow behind the till hadn't put his reward card through. 'Bitch,' Jack said, turning on his heel and walking back towards the checkouts to have it out with the woman.

It wasn't really the loss that annoyed Jack, it was the principle. He saved up his reward points every year without fail, and then used them to buy himself a Christmas dinner. Just like his mother had taught him. A good few years ago, when Jack was probably twelve or thirteen, he'd used the points to buy himself a new computer game one October. When the festive period came around, he'd sat there on Christmas day looking at a Pot Noodle instead of the turkey with all the trimmings that his parents were tucking into. It wasn't even a chicken and mushroom one, but a beef and tomato instead. His father had tried to defend him, but Jack's mother was having none of it. Jack had to eat the entire thing, even the bits of dehydrated tomato. He hated tomato, dehydrated or otherwise.

Later that night so many years ago, Jack was lying in bed on his side to keep the weight off his buttocks — a Pot Noodle wasn't punishment enough for his mother — when his dad crept into his room and left a congealed cocktail sausage wrapped in a thin slice of fatty bacon on his bedside table.

'I saved you a pig in blanket,' his father whispered as he ruffled Jack's hair. 'I don't think she saw me, but not a word.'

63

E mily blinked a couple of times, wondering what on earth was going on. For example, why was her face buried in a pillow? Why did she have such a bastard of a headache? Why could she hear Andy sobbing?

She shifted her position, shaking her head and wincing at the pain that this simple action caused. The last thing she remembered was sitting in Andy's car, hurtling down a country road. Then it all went blank. It took her a few seconds, but she realised that she was still sitting in Andy's car, but now with an airbag in her face.

'Bloody hell,' Emily said as she pressed at the airbag, trying to persuade it to deflate. She wiggled her toes — all good — but there wasn't anywhere near as much legroom in the car as she remembered. When the airbag had finally deflated, she looked around. Through the windscreen, she could see the thick trunk of a tree that had a crumpled yellow bonnet wrapped around it. Emily saw jets of steam hissing out of the unnatural gaps between the bonnet and the rest of the car before the moon disappeared back behind a thin cloud.

'I've killed her,' Emily heard Andy sob. She turned to the driver's seat, but Andy wasn't there. He'd managed to get out of the car and was crouched on his haunches on the side of the road. 'I've fucking killed her.' Emily's heart went out to Andy. Even from here, she could see the tears streaming down his face in the faint moonlight, and hear the harsh sobs racking his entire body.

'Andy,' Emily called out. To her surprise, her voice came out as a croak. 'Andy?' she called again, putting as much effort into shouting at him as she could. 'I'm not dead, Andy. I'm still here.' He turned to look at her, and Emily waited for the relief on his face when he realised that she was still alive.

'Not you,' he said with a hiccup before he looked at the car and started crying again. 'Delia. I've killed Delia.'

'Is that the farm, then?' Emily heard Andy ask as they both hobbled up a track towards a silhouette on the horizon. 'It doesn't look like I remember it.' She didn't reply at first, still pissed off that he was more concerned about his stupid car than her. He'd tried to explain that he knew she was okay because she wasn't all floppy like dead people are on the telly, but she still wasn't happy. To be fair to the man though, when he realised that she was trapped he'd made a manful effort to free her.

'Yeah,' she replied. 'That blob there is the farmhouse, and over there where that light is, that's the abattoir.' She pointed with her hand, but seeing as she couldn't see anything, Emily figured neither could he. 'Come on, we need to get Catherine.' They walked in silence for a few moments before Emily continued. 'Don't you remember it from before?'

'Not really,' Andy replied. 'That butcher thing, it's all a bit blurry. My therapist said I'd got a shiva.'

Emily stopped walking and turned to Andy. She couldn't really see him, but she needed a rest.

'A shiva?'

'Yeah, that's what she said.' Emily thought for a second. Emily hadn't met Andy's therapist, and she'd declined the services that he offered, but what a Hindu god had to do with what had happened here before was beyond her. After thinking for a few seconds, Emily groaned.

'Do you mean amnesia?'

'I don't know,' Andy replied. 'I can't remember.' Even though she couldn't see his expression, Emily could tell that he wasn't joking. It was a shame really. If he had, it would have been quite funny.

They limped past the farmhouse, which was shrouded in darkness, after a brief argument about whether or not Catherine was in there. Emily had persuaded Andy that they should carry on to the abattoir, as there was a light on in the doorway. When they got close to the outbuildings, Emily pulled at Andy's arm.

'Hang on a second, we need to work out what we're going to do,' she whispered to him. 'I think he's in there, holding Catherine hostage. If he's not murdered her already, that is.'

'Okay,' he whispered back. 'What's the plan?'

'Maybe we should wait for the police?'

'Police?' he replied. 'Oh, cool.'

'Andy?'

'Yep?' Emily took a deep breath before replying.

'You did phone the police, didn't you?'

'Um…'

'I fucking told you to phone the police,' Emily hissed.

'You told me to phone for a taxi,' Andy whined. 'Which I did.'

'Jesus wept,' she sighed. 'Well call them now, for fuck's sake. Have you got a signal?'

'Probably.'

'You've not got your phone, have you?'

'In the car, I have. Somewhere. I think it got knocked out of my hand when Delia died.'

'Would you stop going on about your bloody car? Now shut up, I need to think.'

'You've got a phone, though. Why don't you use it to call the Old Bill?'

Emily thought for a second. The last time she remembered having her phone was just before they crashed. She certainly didn't have it now.

'Er, think it might be in the car.'

'You could nip back and get it?' Andy offered.

'You could piss off,' Emily retorted. 'Right. Here's the plan. We can't hang about. Let's just charge the place, grab whatever weapons we can on the way, and overpower him.'

'He is quite a big bloke,' Andy replied. 'And I have got a broken arm.'

'Yeah, but there's two of us. Three if you include Catherine.'

'That's if she's not been candlesticked.'

'Not helpful, Andy,' Emily hissed. 'Now come on, grow a pair.' She moved off towards the abattoir, and then reached back to grab Andy's arm. 'Come on, you melt.'

Emily and Andy inched their way into the outbuilding which, to her relief, was empty. She blinked against the bright fluorescent lights and looked around for anything that could be used as a weapon, but apart from a wooden candlestick by the door to the inner room, there wasn't much at all. She nodded at the closed door in front of them. Hopefully, Catherine was in there and they could just rescue her and get the hell out of the place.

'In there,' she whispered. 'You need to go in there.'

'What if Jack's in there?' Andy replied, his voice quiet.

'Make friends with him. Just bond.'

'With a murderer? What are you going to do?'

'Andy,' Emily replied with what she hoped was a steely voice. 'Just get in there and see if Catherine's okay. I'm going to stay out here and think of something. Now go.'

As Andy tip-toed towards the door, Emily looked again around the room. It was pretty much just how she remembered it from the last time she was here, and an involuntary shiver ran down her spine.

'Hello?' Andy called through the door. Emily wasn't sure what to expect, but one thing she wasn't expecting was Andy being smashed in the face by what looked suspiciously like a metal bedpan.

64

Jack was still whistling as he walked towards the outbuildings at the end of the track. All in all, it had been a good trip. He'd got his loyalty points, discovered what 'sploshing' was, and had what could be a very interesting meeting with Karen from the supermarket planned for the weekend. He would need to pop back for some more supplies from the supermarket before they got together, but he had a voucher for double points on peanut butter, so it was all good. According to Karen, using crunchy peanut butter was much more tactile, and he was more than happy to defer to her experience.

As he approached the outer door of the abattoir, he realised that something wasn't quite right. He could hear voices. Jack shouldn't be able to hear any voices at all. For one thing, Beth was secured inside her bedroom. For another thing, he'd never heard her talking to herself before. The final thing, and the one that concerned Jack the most, was that one of the voices sounded like a man crying.

Jack put the carrier bag with the freshly prepared tubes

for Beth down outside the building and slipped the pistol out of his waistband. He'd almost not bothered bringing it with him, but he'd grabbed it from the farmhouse at the last minute. Just in case. Maybe his father was looking out for him from up on high? He leaned around the door to the abattoir, but couldn't see anyone inside. The inner door was ajar though, and that was where the voices were coming from.

He tip-toed into the building, holding the gun out in front of him like they did on the telly, and inched his way towards the inner door until he could hear the voices properly. The first thing he heard was Beth, apologising.

'I'm so sorry,' she said, and Jack realised that she was sobbing. 'I thought you were him.' He didn't quite catch the next phrase, spoken by another female voice, but he did hear Beth answer. 'He's going to kill me. I know it.' The next voice he heard was a man's, muffled and nasal. He didn't sound happy. 'I said I was sorry,' Beth said.

'Man up, Andy.' This was a woman's voice. Definitely not Beth. Jack raised the gun and stepped into the doorway.

Inside Beth's bedroom were three people. Beth, and another woman who was crouched on the floor. They were fussing over a man sitting on the floor with a bunch of tissue paper sticking out of both nostrils. It took Jack a few seconds, but he recognised the woman from the gym. She was Catherine's friend.

'Don't move,' he shouted, pointing the gun at each of them in turn. 'Stay where you are.' He stared at three sets of eyes looking back at him, all with looks of horror on their faces. Beth was the first to react, raising her arms in the air.

'Don't shoot,' she whispered. 'Please don't shoot.' Jack turned his attention to the other two. The woman — Emily, he thought her name was — was just glaring at him with undisguised anger. The man on the floor with the tissues didn't look like he knew what was going on.

'Where's Catherine?' the woman said.

'Emily, isn't it?' Jack replied.

'If you weren't pointing a gun at us,' she said, 'I'd be flattered that you remembered my name. Where's Catherine?'

'I don't know. She's not here, is she?'

'So where is she?' Emily asked. Jack just shrugged his shoulders in response.

'Dunno,' he replied. 'But she's not here.' The man with the tissues streaming out of his nose struggled to get to his feet. 'Stay there,' Jack barked, but the man ignored him. 'I said, stay there!' Jack shouted, taking a step towards the other man and gesturing with the gun.

He looked at him, realising that he knew him from somewhere. It must be the gym, Jack figured. It wasn't as if he knew that many people in this godforsaken place anyway.

'Who are you?' Jack asked.

'I'm Andy,' the man replied, pulling the tissue paper from his nose and examining the bloodstained ends that had been up his nostrils. 'And you're Jack. Jack Green.'

Jack felt a fluttering sensation in his chest. They knew who he was. Who he really was.

'No I'm not,' he said, trying to keep his voice even. 'I'm Jack Kennedy.'

'No, you're not,' Emily said. 'You're Jack Green, and you're wanted for murder up north. We know all about you, and that woman you killed.'

'I never killed her,' Jack replied. 'But no-one would believe me.'

'Neither do we,' Emily said. She glanced across at Andy. 'But we can leave that up to the police. They'll be here soon. Isn't that right, Andy?'

'Er…yeah. I guess so.' Emily's eyes widened for a split second. The movement was tiny, but he caught it anyway. Jack caught the look in Andy's eyes, and figured that he was supposed to have called the police but probably hadn't.

'Sorry, excuse me,' Beth said. They all turned to look at her. 'But what the fuck is going on?'

'We've come to rescue Catherine,' Andy replied, nodding in Jack's direction. 'From him. He's a murderer. I suppose we could rescue you as well, seeing as we're here.'

'No-one's rescuing anyone,' Jack said, pointing the gun at each of them in turn. 'Now all of you, sit on the bed and shut the fuck up while I think.' Beth made her way to the bed, but the other two just stayed where they were. 'Move!' Jack shouted.

Andy flinched, but neither of them moved their feet.

'I'm not going anywhere,' Emily replied, crossing her arms and frowning at him. 'There's not much you can do with three of us here.'

'I don't know if you've noticed, but I have got a gun. Now shift your skinny arse onto the bed before I shoot you.'

'You couldn't shoot anyone,' she said. 'You've not got the bottle.'

'Emily,' Andy said, touching her elbow with his hand. 'Maybe we should go and sit on the bed?'

'I'm not going anywhere,' she replied, taking a step towards Jack. 'Just give me the gun and we can sort all this out.'

Jack took a step backwards to keep Emily at a distance, his finger tightening on the gun.

'I said give me the gun,' she said, raising her voice and taking another step forwards. Andy moved forwards as well and stood next to Emily.

'I warned you,' Jack replied, as he lined up the sights of the pistol with Emily's face and pulled the trigger.

65

When Andy saw Jack's finger tightening on the trigger, he knew he had to do something. He couldn't just stand there and just let Emily get shot in the face. Putting all his weight on the ball of his left foot, he launched himself at Emily to shove her out of the way. It worked, but the only problem with his plan was that by pushing Emily, the pistol was pointing directly at him when Jack pulled the trigger.

The next thing Andy felt was a stinging sensation in the middle of his forehead as the small plastic pellet bounced off his skin.

'Ouch, you bastard!' Andy shouted at Jack, who was standing open-mouthed, staring at him. 'That really bloody hurt, that did.' Jack didn't reply, but skipped back-wards and slammed the door behind him.

'Jesus wept,' Beth said with a gasp. 'I thought it was a real gun.'

'No, it's one of those Airsoft things,' Emily replied. 'You okay, Andy?'

'Er, yeah. I think so.' He rubbed his forehead, but

didn't think that the pellet had broken the skin. It still bloody hurt though. 'What's an Airsoft thing?' Emily didn't say anything, but just stared at him.

'What?'

'You didn't know?' she asked.

'Didn't know what?'

'That it was a pellet gun?'

'Nope. Looked pretty bloody real to me. How can you tell the difference?'

'The barrel's much smaller. My brother used to have one when we were smaller. He shot me in the arse with it once, and it stung like a bitch. But seriously, I can't believe you didn't know. You thought you were taking a bullet for me?'

Andy paused before replying, remembering Martin's advice about never letting the truth get in the way of a good story.

'Yeah, I did.' In fact, he wasn't lying. He didn't have a clue about guns, and didn't know when Emily had suddenly become a firearms expert. When he'd shoved Emily, it hadn't been so that he could take a bullet meant for her. He only meant to get her out of the way.

'Blimey,' Beth said to Emily, nodding at Andy. 'You've hit the jackpot there with that one.' Emily didn't say anything, but pulled some more tissues from her sleeve and walked towards Andy. She licked the tissue paper and started to raise her hand towards Andy's face when he slapped it away.

'Get off me with that,' he said, grimacing. 'That's disgusting.'

'I was just going to dab your forehead. You've got a spot of blood there, that's all.'

'It's only a scratch,' Andy replied and despite the situation, laughed. 'It's not like I've just been shot in the head or anything, is it?' He took the tissue from Emily and turned it round to find a dry spot before pressing it to his forehead. 'So, what do we do now?'

'We need to escape.' Emily looked around the room, and Andy could see that she had her thinking face on.

'There's no point,' Beth replied. 'I've been in here for over a week. If there was a way to get out, I'd have found it by now.'

Andy looked at her. He wasn't going to say anything, but she was hardly the most athletic of women. It was possible that between them, he and Emily might be able to find a way out that Beth hadn't. Plus, there were now three of them instead of just one.

'What about up here?' Emily asked. Andy looked over at her standing in the corner of the room, looking up at a vent on the wall. 'Maybe we could get that grille off and squeeze through?'

Andy and Emily dragged the desk over to where the grille was, and Andy stood on it. He could barely reach the bottom of the grille, but he was close enough to see that it was attached to the wall with industrial size screws.

'That's not going to work, Emily,' he said. 'Not unless we can find a large Philips head screwdriver. Even if we do manage to get the front bit off, all I can see behind it is a big pipe. Not even you would be able to fit through it.' Let alone Beth, Andy thought, but he didn't say anything.

'There must be something we can try,' Emily said, looking as if she was on the verge of tears. Andy watched as she crossed to the door and hammered on it.

'Jack, come on,' she shouted. 'Let us out. We'll all just go home and not say anything.'

'I don't think that's going to work,' Beth whispered to Andy. 'I think he's going to kill us all.'

'That's not going to happen without a fight,' he replied, trying and failing to sound convincing.

'I am sorry for hitting you with the bedpan,' Beth said. 'I thought you were him. I was going to knock him out and make a run for it.' Andy managed to keep his face solemn as he imagined Beth running anywhere.

Emily walked over to where Andy and Beth were sitting on the bed and sat down next to them.

'What do you think he's going to do to us?' she asked them both.

'Well, he's kept me here for over a week without killing me,' Beth replied. 'So maybe nothing?'

'Are you from a really rich family or something?' Andy asked. 'Is that why he's holding you hostage?'

'Nope,' Beth replied. 'They wouldn't pay anyway, even if they did have money. My Dad's tighter than a gnat's arse at the best of times. Always complaining about how much it costs to feed me.'

'So why is Jack keeping you here?'

'I think he's trying to turn me into her.' Beth nodded at the photograph which Andy had taken off the top of the desk before they'd moved it. 'That's his mother.'

'Oh my God,' Emily said, picking up the photo. 'That's who killed his father.' She examined the picture carefully. 'Blimey, she's a big girl.'

'Emily,' Andy replied. 'That's not very nice.' Emily's cheeks reddened and she turned to Beth.

'Sorry, I didn't mean it that way,' she said to her. 'I just mean she must have big bones, that's all.'

'Look, she's got your dress on,' Andy said, pointing at the woman in the photo.

'He's been feeding me until I fit into it properly.'

'Why would he want to do that, though?' Andy asked. Beth just shrugged.

'Maybe he's trying to turn you into his mother,' Emily said, frowning.

'But why would he want to do that to me?'

Emily paused for a few seconds before replying.

'So he can kill you.'

66

J ack sat on the counter in the outer room and put his head in his hands. What on earth was he going to do? They knew who he was. All the careful planning for the last year was going to come to nothing, and he would be on the run again. Not only would he be on the run, but he would be on the run with nothing. All the money that his father had left him was wrapped up in the farmhouse. He wouldn't have a place to live. Without a place to live, he wouldn't be able to get a job. Without a job, he wouldn't have any money. But he couldn't get a place to live without any money.

He needed to think, so he went back to the farmhouse after making sure that the door to Beth's room was secure. While he was checking it, he could hear one of them banging on the inside. It was Emily, the pretty little blonde one. She was shouting through the door, something about staying calm and having a cup of tea. Like that was going to happen any time soon.

In the farmhouse kitchen, he poured himself a generous measure of whisky and sat at the table to go over his options. Jack could just let them go, but he couldn't see them going back to their homes and not saying anything, no matter how much they promised. He could keep Beth and just let go of Emily and Andy. He'd not actually done much to either of them apart from shooting the stupid looking one in the face. He'd meant to hit the girl, but it didn't matter. The only reason he'd pulled the trigger was to create a distraction so that he could get to the door, and that's what had happened. But if he let them go, then he still had the same problem. One of them would say some-thing about the fact that he'd got a woman locked up in one of his outbuildings.

He could keep them for a while, just to see what happened. One missing person in a city the size of Norwich wasn't that much of an issue, but three missing people would probably bring more than one gormless policeman to his door. He mulled it over for a while, thinking it through, but no matter which perspective he looked at it from, it wouldn't work. His mood got darker and darker as he thought about the only real option left available to him. He was going to have to deal with them all and, seeing as there were three of them, he was going to have to deal with all of them at the same time. It would be a gamble, and it would only work if no-one knew where Emily and Andy were, but that was a chance he was going to have to take.

Jack poured himself another two fingers of whisky and walked towards the door with the glass in one hand and the bottle in the other. Before he left the farmhouse, he made sure that the lights were off. No point wasting elec-tricity, after all.

By the time he got back to the abattoir, he wasn't drunk,

but he'd had enough of the whisky on the walk down the track to give him a warm glow, and a bit of Dutch courage. He'd dispensed with the glass when it was empty, and just nipped from the bottle instead. When he got to the outer room, he brought up the camera app on his phone to see what his guests were up to. Inside Beth's room, she was fast asleep on the bed and Emily and Andy were pacing the room. They were deep in conversation, no doubt planning how to try to escape or overpower him.

He looked down at the candlestick by the door to the bedroom, and suddenly felt a tinge of sadness when he saw the name carved into the base. Jack had spent so long making it, and had put so much love into it, that to not use it at all would be almost criminal. He put his whisky on the floor and picked up the candlestick, grabbing it with both hands around the stem. Jack frowned, thinking for a few seconds as he looked back at the screen. Beth was fast asleep. Jack didn't think that she would be much of a threat, in any case, even though he wasn't going to be able to threaten her with the gun any more. That left only two of them to deal with. If he timed it right, he could rush through the door and take Andy out before any of them realised what was going on. That would then only leave Emily to deal with, and a quick smack in the face with the blunt end of the candlestick would sort her out. There wasn't much to her.

Jack hefted the candlestick in his hands a couple of times before putting it back on the floor. If he used the candlestick on Andy and Emily, then it would be ruined. He could always make another one for Beth, but that wasn't the point. It wasn't just the candlestick that would be ruined, but then there'd be blood and stringy bits all over his library. He'd only built the room for Beth, and killing other people in it with her candlestick would be like swearing in church. It just wouldn't be right.

Jack angrily kicked at the candlestick, and watched it skitter through the open door of the abattoir. Not the most sensible thing to do, as now his foot hurt like a bastard, but he picked up the whisky for a medicinal swig to numb the sharp pain in his big toe. He was going to have to continue with Plan A and start again if no-one came looking for Andy and Emily. That meant he would have to dig a larger hole down at the end of the field by the treeline, but that wouldn't take long, and it would be good exercise anyway.

In the corner of the room, there were three large cylinders standing almost five foot tall and painted black apart from a grey shoulder on the top of the cylinder. On top of the cylinders were a series of pipes linking them together before joining into a single pipe. He walked over to the corner and tapped the dull side of one of the cylinders, his eyes following the single pipe all the way to the top corner of the room where they fed into a grille in the wall. With a sigh, he started turning the dials on top of the cylinders, spinning them round until they were all fully open.

67

As much as she wanted to sit down and rest, Emily couldn't stop pacing in the room. Her chest was starting to ache, and she wasn't sure if it was from the car accident or from panic.

'There must be something,' she muttered under her breath. 'There must be bloody something.' The problem was, there wasn't. Emily had been watching the television a few nights ago, and there was a sit-com on where one of the characters had made a joke about being invited to a party in an escape room but managing to get out of it. It didn't seem so funny now. She would have given anything to have been sitting in front of her television now, Andy's arm around her and a glass of wine in her hand.

'You got any ideas, Emily?' Andy said. He was also walking up and down, as opposed to Beth who was snoring her head off.

'Not a thing,' Emily replied. She looked over at Beth. 'How can she sleep at a time like this?'

'Weird, isn't it.' He cocked his head to one side. 'Can you hear that?'

'What?' Emily couldn't hear anything other than the thumping of her own heart.

'That hissing noise?'

Emily concentrated for a few seconds. Andy was right. There was a faint hissing sound that definitely hadn't been there before. She tried to work out where it was coming from, but couldn't. Andy took a few steps, stopped, and then moved another couple of feet before stopping again.

'It's coming from over here,' he said when he got to the corner of the room.

'Bloody hell, you've got good hearing. I can only just hear it, let alone work out where it's coming from.' She walked over to where he was standing next to the desk.

'It's coming from the grille.'

Fear gripped Emily. She knew what the room was originally used for, but deliberately hadn't said anything to Andy or Beth because she didn't want to scare them.

'He wouldn't,' she said as she climbed onto the desk and put her hand up towards the grille. Even though she couldn't reach it, she could feel the breeze coming from it. A few seconds later, there was a sharp stinging sensation in her nostrils. 'No, no, no!' Emily shouted as she climbed down from the desk and ran to the door.

'What is it?' Andy asked as Emily started battering the door with her fists. 'What's going on?'

'He's gassing us!' Emily screamed as she hammered the door. 'He's bloody gassing us.'

On the bed, Beth opened one eye and stared at Emily for a few seconds before rolling over and going back to sleep.

'Jack!' Emily shouted at the top of her voice. 'Jack, don't do this. Please!' She stopped hammering on the door to see if there was any response, but all she heard was silence. And a hissing noise in the corner of the room.

Tears were streaming down her face as she slapped at the door.

'He is, isn't he,' Andy said, 'I can smell it. It's like vinegar.'

'You're not supposed to be able to smell it,' Emily sobbed. She could feel her face flushing, and she knew it wasn't from crying. 'You can only smell it when there's lots of it.'

'Stand back, Emily,' Andy said. 'I'm going to break the door down.' Emily took a step away from the door, knowing full well that Andy was just going to bounce off it. She screamed at Jack again as Andy took a run up, launched himself at the door and, as she'd predicted, bounced straight back again.

'Bloody hell,' Andy said with a grimace as he rubbed his shoulder. 'That sodding well hurt, that did.'

'I don't want to die, Andy,' Emily sobbed. 'I'm too young to die.'

'I wasn't planning on it either,' Andy replied. 'Can't we stuff up the grille with something?'

'It's too high up,' she said. 'I don't want to die. I've never even been to Swindon.'

'I have,' Andy said. 'It was shit.'

It was only five or six minutes later that Emily realised it was all over. She and Andy were sitting in the furthest corner from the grille, slumped against the wall and staring at the door. Andy had his arms wrapped around Emily and was holding her tightly against him. She looked up at him. His face was cherry red, his eyes were half shut, and he was breathing heavily. She knew that she must look the same.

'Andy?' He opened his eyes and looked down at her, a faint smile on his face.

'Yeah?'

'I'm cold.'

'Come here,' he tightened his grip on her. 'I'll warm you up.'

'Do you think it'll hurt?'

'What?'

'Dying?'

'I hope not.'

'So do I.'

'I'll tell you something though,' Andy whispered.

'What?' Emily asked, her voice just as faint. They didn't have long. She could feel the life slipping away from her with every breath.

'If I have got to die, I wouldn't want to be with anyone else when I do.'

'If it's all the same,' Emily gasped, 'I would have preferred to be somewhere else.'

They sat in silence for a few seconds until Andy spoke again, his voice even fainter.

'At least we'll always have Milton Keynes.'

Emily frowned. They'd never been to Milton Keynes. She closed her eyes, feeling her eyelids fluttering. She would have kept them open, but she didn't like the way that the edges of her vision were going darker and darker. She thought there was supposed to be a bright light when you died, but it hadn't turned up yet.

'We've never been there,' she gasped.

'I know,' Andy replied, his voice just as shaky. 'Safe word.'

'Mmm?'

'That was your safe word that night we…that night we…' She looked up at him, and her heart lurched as she saw his head lolling forwards. A tear ran down her cheek. He was dying in front of her, and there was nothing she could do except die with him. 'You should say it now,' Andy whispered so faintly she could barely hear him. 'See if it works.'

Emily leaned her head back and closed her eyes again.

'Milton Keynes,' she muttered under her breath. Then she heard the door to the room click open.

'**B**loody hell, babe,' Catherine said. 'You look like shit. What are you doing over there?' She threw the bloodstained candlestick onto the floor, and ran over to where Emily and Andy were slumped in the corner of the room. She thought they were both unconscious, but as she reached Emily, she could see that her lips were still moving. 'Come on you,' she said, leaning forwards and grabbing her under her armpits. 'Let's get you out of here.' Emily kept mumbling something. Catherine wasn't sure what she was saying, but it seemed to be something about Milton Keynes.

Catherine dragged Emily across the floor and out of the bedroom. She carried on, pulling her past Jack's prone body, and out into the night air.

'There you go,' Catherine said, rolling her onto her side. 'I'll be back in a minute. I'm just going back for Andy.' She ran back into the bedroom, and dragged Andy all the way outside, depositing him next to Emily. There was a third person in the room, a rather large woman on a bed, and Catherine wasn't sure if she would be able to drag her anywhere. She at least had to try, though.

The woman on the bed was even larger than Catherine had realised. She tried as hard as she could to move her, but there was no way that was going to happen. The most she would be able to do would be to roll her onto the floor, but Catherine didn't know whether the gas that was in the room was one that went up to the ceiling or down to the floor. Seeing as the woman was still breathing, Catherine decided to leave her where she was. The gas was turned off, and the doors wide open. There wasn't anything else she could do.

Back in the outer room, Jack was also still breathing. In Catherine's opinion, that was a bit of a shame. When she'd crept up behind him, she'd hit him as hard as she could over the back of the head with a huge candlestick that she'd found on the ground outside the outbuilding. He went down like a sack of potatoes, out for the count before he even reached the floor, and Catherine had seriously considered giving him one or two for luck with the candle- stick. Instead, she rooted through a cupboard until she found some thick, black duct tape. A moment later, the entire roll was wrapped around his wrists and ankles.

It had been the thought of spending the entire night in the car that had made Catherine decide to head for the farm. She had looked again at the dim light on the horizon and decided that it probably wasn't as far away as she had originally thought, especially when compared to the brighter light of the town even further away. Even if it took her a couple of hours to get to wherever the idiot in the yellow car had been heading for, whatever was there would have to be better than freezing her arse off in a car.

It took Catherine maybe half an hour to limp her way to the spot where she found the smashed up yellow car. As she had hobbled down the road, the clouds had cleared a bit, and the weak moonlight that peeked through at least meant she could avoid the larger stones. When she saw the car wrapped around the trunk of a tree shaped like a swastika and realised that it was Andy's, she had broken into a run, terrified that he was still inside it.

To her relief, the car was empty. But both airbags had deployed, which meant that there must have been someone in the passenger seat as well. That could only be Emily, Catherine reasoned as she started limping up the track that led towards the lights. A couple of hundred yards up the track, her phone had sprung into life, and buzzed insistently with a whole bunch of missed calls and text messages.

'Oh my God,' Catherine had whispered as she read a string of texts from Emily. Just as she got to the one that explained he was wanted for murder up north, her phone flashed up a warning message to tell her that she had 1% of her battery left. It had been just enough juice to call the police.

Outside the farm building, Emily and Andy were beginning to recover. Andy had rolled over and thrown up, and Emily had come round enough to sit up.

'My God, my head,' Emily said, running her hands through her hair. 'I thought hangovers were bad, but this is way worse.'

'Oh, babes,' Catherine replied, rubbing her back with the flat of her hand. 'I thought you were a goner there.'

'So did I,' Emily murmured. 'Is Andy okay?' Catherine turned to look at him.

'Yeah, he's fine,' she replied. 'He's busy looking at a pile of his own sick at the moment. Aren't you, lover boy?'

'He's my hero,' Emily said with a wan smile.

'Oh, you ungrateful bitch,' Catherine replied with a

brisk laugh. 'I was the one who bloody well rescued you. If your car wasn't as shit, then I'd have been here a lot sooner.'

'You'd better not have done anything to my car.'

'I've not done anything to it, as such,' Catherine said. 'But I can confirm that it doesn't run very well on petrol.'

'It's a diesel.'

'I know that now. Were you in Andy's when he crashed it?'

'Yeah,' Emily said. 'I think we both might have a few bruises in the morning.' They both turned as a noise came from inside the building. Catherine started to get to her feet.

'I should go and see what that was.'

'What if it's Jack?'

'I don't think it will be,' Catherine replied. 'He's wrapped up with the world's largest roll of duct tape. Anyway,' she sat back down and nodded at the procession of blue lights making their way up the track towards the farmhouse, 'here comes the cavalry.'

69

Andy sat on the sofa in the interview room, looking at the stony-faced policewoman opposite the coffee table. Next to him was Emily, and Catherine was sitting in another armchair in the corner of the room.

'My name's Detective Superintendent Jojo Antonio,' the policewoman said, her face breaking into a smile. 'Do you remember me? I interviewed you both after that thing with the butcher.'

'Yes,' Emily replied. 'We remember you.' Andy looked at her. She looked exhausted. The paramedics had checked them both over at the farmhouse and tried to persuade them to go to the hospital. Emily was having none of it though. All she wanted, she'd told the paramedic, was to go back to her flat and have a hot bath and a glass of wine. Unless they were going to offer her that at the hospital, she wasn't going anywhere near it.

'Do you mind if I record this? It's not a formal interview, but it might help us with our enquiries?' She put a small tape recorder on the table, making it clear that it wasn't really a question.

'We told that other copper everything,' Andy replied. 'Can't we just go home?'

'You'll be able to go home soon, I promise,' Jojo said. Andy looked at her. Although she was smiling, the woman had steel behind her eyes. He wouldn't want to get on the wrong side of her, that much was for certain.

'Where's Beth?' Emily asked. 'How come she's not here as well?

'She's still up at the farm,' Jojo said. 'We're just waiting for a, erm, a special ambulance to take her to the hospital. One that's designed more for people her size.' The police-woman leaned forwards and pressed a button on the recorder. She reeled off the date, time, and the names of all the people in the room. What she said next surprised the hell out of Andy. 'I'm conducting the investigation into the death of Mr Jack Kennedy, also known as Green, at Hill Top—'

'What the fuck?' They all jumped as Catherine shrieked in the corner of the room. Andy looked at her. The shocked expression on her face wasn't one he was going to forget for a while. 'I never fucking killed him. I only hit him with a candlestick!'

'Catherine, Catherine,' Jojo said, putting her hands out in a placatory gesture. 'We know you didn't. It's fine.'

'Once! I hit him once!'

'Catherine,' Jojo repeated, her voice firmer this time. 'It's fine. Did the other policeman not go over this with you?'

'Not that bit, he didn't,' Catherine shot back. Jojo muttered something under her breath. Andy wasn't one hundred per cent sure what she said, but it sounded very like 'gormless twat'.

'Okay, let me explain,' Jojo continued. 'When we arrived in the farm outbuilding, we found Mr Jack

Kennedy with Miss Beth James who was apparently unconscious.'

'She was unconscious when I left her,' Catherine said. 'I couldn't move her out of the room. I did try, but she's quite a big girl. I did try, though.'

'Okay,' Jojo said. 'So when you left Miss James — Beth — she was still in the inner room?'

'Yes,' Catherine said.

'Can either of you two corroborate this?' Jojo turned her attention to Andy and Emily.

'Er, no,' Andy replied. 'We were kind of not very well at the time.'

'Where was Beth when you found her then?' Emily asked. 'I take it she wasn't still in the bedroom bit?'

'No, she wasn't,' Jojo replied. 'She's saying that she managed to get off the bed and was making her way to the door when she was overcome with the fumes again, and fainted.'

'But how did Jack die?' Andy asked, not sure what on earth was going on.

'She fainted on top of him,' Jojo said. 'He suffocated to death. When we got to the room, she was sitting on his face, slumped over and apparently unconscious.'

There was a shocked silence in the room. Andy felt Emily reach over and grab his hand.

'My God,' he whispered. 'What a way to go.'

'He was still a murderer, though,' Emily said. 'I'm not saying he deserved it, but he was still a murderer. He killed that woman up north.'

'Actually, he wasn't,' Jojo replied. 'He was looked into very carefully by my colleagues up there, but he had a cast iron alibi. We don't know who killed that poor lass up north, but it wasn't Jack Kennedy.'

'But it said in the papers he was wanted by the police?' Emily asked, her face creased into a frown.

'It says a lot of things in the papers,' Jojo replied with a faint smile. 'But a lot of them aren't true.'

'So what'll happen to Beth?' Andy asked. 'Is she in trouble?'

'It's a bit early to say, but at the end of the day she had been kidnapped by Jack Kennedy and force fed for a week. We're fairly sure that he was trying to turn Beth into his mother, so that he could kill her and avenge his father's death.'

'Bloody hell,' Emily said. 'What a nut job.' She turned to Catherine and grinned. 'Good job you didn't shag him, isn't it?'

'Bloody right there, babes. You're bloody right there.'

70

S he stared at the glow of the laptop screen, the green light reflecting back off her face. On the table in front of her was a selection of confectionary — everything from a small tub full of peanut M&Ms through to her higher end merchandise. The only problem with the higher end stuff was that it was gradually melting in the heat. Frozen chocolate profiteroles took a lot less than twenty minutes to defrost, but as long as they were all gone by the end of the evening, she didn't care.

There was a loud 'ping' in the confines of her bedroom that made her jump. On the screen was a new message.

Hi.

She looked at the message for a few seconds before replying.

Hey. How are you? There was a long pause before the punter on the other end replied.

Good. How much for an M&M?

Jesus, she thought. How much for a single sodding M&M?

What colour?

Red, please.

She thought for a moment before typing out a reply.

Twenty quid. If you don't ask, you don't get, she figured. Not so much as a sniff all evening, and if she could make twenty quid from a single M&M, then so much the better,

Okay, but make it last. Or there'll be trouble.

An hour later, she was well over two hundred quid up, and absolutely stuffed. In the pit of her stomach was an entire pack of Sainsbury's Basics profiteroles, although as far as her punter was concerned, they were from Marks and Spencer and so was the cream topping. If he was happy to pay a fiver a pop, she couldn't admit that a packet of twenty only cost a couple of quid, and that was before the discount for being almost but not quite out of date. The next message that popped up on the screen made her eyebrows pop.

We should meet up. I'd like to watch you eating in person.

She sighed. Since she'd started this job, she'd put on almost an entire stone but had managed to keep the punters at bay on the other end of an internet connection.

I don't think so, she typed out a careful reply. *That would be against the rules.*

Five hundred quid? For a carvery with whatever extras you want?

She strummed her fingers on the desktop, thinking hard for a moment. That was a fair old chunk of change, and there was a free meal on top.

Okay, where and when?

When the arrangements had been made to meet up, along

with a promise of absolute secrecy, Catherine shut her laptop down with a satisfied sigh. Maybe this job wasn't that bad after all?

Made in United States
Orlando, FL
15 October 2022

23441325R00211